Jam
"I am at your service, my lady.

Lady Marianne clasped her hands at her waist and laughed softly, but without mirth. "Such a cold tone to match a cold day. Where is the warmth that once graced your every word to me?"

For several moments Jamie stared at the ground, his lips set in a grim line. He seemed to compose himself, for at last he lifted his gaze to meet hers.

"My lady, I beg your forgiveness for my inappropriate conversations with you last summer."

"But—"

He raised his hand in a silencing gesture. "I will not betray the trust of Lord Bennington by arrogantly presuming an equality that would permit us. . .permit me. . .to pursue a lady so far above me." For an instant a sweet vulnerability crossed his eyes, but then all light disappeared from his face. "You must not ask me to do that which would dishonor you, your family and my faith...."

Books by Louise M. Gouge

Love Inspired Historical

Love Thine Enemy
The Captain's Lady

LOUISE M. GOUGE

has been married to her husband, David, for more than forty years. They have four children and six grand-children. Louise always had an active imagination, thinking up stories for her friends, classmates and family, but seldom writing them down. At a friend's insistence, in 1984 she finally began to type up her latest idea. Before trying to find a publisher, Louise returned to college, earning a BA in English/creative writing and a master's degree in liberal studies. She reworked the novel based on what she had learned and sold it to a major Christian publisher. Louise then worked in television marketing for a short time before becoming a college English/humanities instructor. She has had seven novels published, five of which have earned multiple awards, including the 2006 Inspirational Reader's Choice Award. Please visit her Web site at www.louisemgouge.com.

LOUISE M. GOUGE

The Captain's Lady

Steeple
Hill®

Published by Steeple Hill Books™

STEEPLE HILL BOOKS

Steeple
Hill®

Recycling programs
for this product may
not exist in your area.

ISBN-13: 978-0-373-82832-6

THE CAPTAIN'S LADY

Copyright © 2010 by Louise M. Gouge

www.SteepleHill.com

Printed in U.S.A.

I am my beloved's, and my beloved is mine.
—*The Song of Solomon* 6:3

To my beloved husband, David, who encouraged me to keep writing these books even as he was enduring radiation and chemotherapy treatments. May our God grant us another forty-five years together.

And to my insightful editor Melissa Endlich…thanks!

Chapter One

March 1776
London, England

Lady Marianne peered down through the peephole into the drawing room while her heart raced. Against her back, the heavy woolen tapestry extolling one of her ancestors' mighty deeds pushed her into the wall of her father's bedchamber, nearly choking her with its ancient dust. Yet she would endure anything to observe the entrance of Papa's guest.

Often in her childhood she and her closest brother had evaded the notice of Greyson, Papa's valet, and crept in here to spy on their parents' guests, even catching a glimpse of the prime minister once when he called upon Papa, his trusted friend, the earl of Bennington. But no exalted politician captured Marianne's interest this day.

Her breath caught. Captain James Templeton—*Jamie*—entered the room with Papa, and warmth filled her heart and flushed her cheeks.

The two men spoke with the enthusiasm of friends

reunited after many months of separation and eager to share their news. Unable to hear their words, Marianne forced herself to breathe. Jamie, the Loyalist American captain of a merchant ship. How handsome he was, taller than Papa by several inches. His bronzed complexion and light brown hair—now sun-kissed with golden streaks and pulled back in a queue—gave evidence of long exposure to the sun on his voyages across the Atlantic Ocean. In contrast to Papa's blue silk jacket and white satin breeches, Jamie wore a plain brown jacket and black breeches. Yet to Marianne, he appeared as elegant and noble as Papa.

Hidden high above the drawing room, she could not clearly see the blue eyes whose intense gaze had pierced her soul and claimed her heart less than a year ago. Jamie, always honest, always forthright. No wonder Papa took an interest in him, even to the extent of calling him his protégé, despite his utter lack of social position *and* being an American.

Marianne suspected part of Papa's interest stemmed from wanting to secure the captain's loyalty now that thirteen of England's American colonies had rebelled against the Crown. But last year she had seen that the old dear truly liked Jamie, perhaps even more than his own four sons, a fact that stung both her and Mama's hearts. Yet, despite that affection, the earl's patronage might not extend to accepting a merchant for a son-in-law.

How she and Jamie would overcome this prejudice, Marianne did not know. At this moment, all she knew was that her own affection for him was unchanged. Last summer, against the better judgment of both of them, their friendship had intensified through shared interests, from reading Shakespeare and Aristotle to spending hours sailing on the Thames. On a short excursion with Papa aboard Jamie's large sloop, the *Fair Winds,* Marianne and Jamie had whispered their confessions of undying love. Then he had placed the sweetest, purest kiss on her lips, sealing her heart to his forever. Now her pulse pounded at the sight of him, and her heart felt a settled assurance that no other man could ever win her love.

Wriggling out of her hiding place between tapestry and wall, Marianne brushed dust from her pink day dress and hastened to the door. She escaped the bedchamber undetected and hurried down the hallway to her own quarters.

"Lady Marianne." Emma emerged from her closet, her hands clasped at her waist. "Why, my lady, your dress." She took hold of Marianne's skirt and shook dust from it, then glanced up. "Oh, my, your hair." Her youthful, cherubic face creased with concern.

"Yes, Emma, I am a fright." With a giddy laugh, Marianne brushed past her lady's maid to sit at her dressing table. "Make haste and mend the damage. Oh, dear, look at this." She removed a silvery cobweb from her hair, pulling several long black strands from the upswept coiffure Emma had created earlier. "Please redo this. And I shall need another of my pink gowns." More than one dandy had told her pink brought a pretty blush to her cheeks, so she wore the color often.

Her appearance repaired and Emma's approving smile received, Marianne clutched her prayer book and hurried from her room. With a deep breath to compose herself, she held her head high and glided down the steps to the front entry hall. A quick glance revealed Jamie and Papa seated before the blazing hearth, deep in genial conversation.

Marianne opened the book and mouthed the words of the morning prayer as she entered the room, not looking their way. Last year, Jamie's parting words had encouraged her to greater faith, and she must let him know she had followed his advice.

The rustle of movement caught her attention. She cast a sidelong glance toward the men, who now stood to greet her.

"Why, Papa, I didn't realize—" She stopped before completing the lie, while heat rushed to her cheeks. "Forgive me. I see you have a guest. Will you excuse me?" She could not look at Jamie for fear that her face would reveal her heart.

"Come, daughter, permit me to present my guest." Papa beckoned her with a gentle wave of his bony, wrinkled hand. "You may recall him from last summer. Lady Marianne, Captain James Templeton of the East Florida Colony." His presentation was accompanied by a shallow cough, and he held a lacy linen handkerchief to his lips.

Gripping her emotions, Marianne permitted herself to look at Jamie. His furrowed brow and the firm clenching of his square jaw sent a pang of worry through her. Was he not pleased to see her? Worse still, his gaze did not meet hers. Rather, he seemed to stare just over her head. Surely this was a ploy to divert any suspicion from the mutual affection they had spoken of only in whispers during his last visit.

"Good morning, Lady Marianne." His rigid bow bespoke his lower status, but his rich, deep voice sent a pleasant shiver down her spine. "I hope you are well."

Offering no smile, Marianne lifted her chin. "Quite well, thank you." She closed her book and turned to Papa, her face a mask. "Will you be busy all day, sir?"

The fond gaze he returned brought forth a wave of guilt. "I fear that I must go to Whitehall for most of the afternoon. Is there something you require, my dear? You have but to ask." His blue eyes, though pale from age, twinkled with his usual eagerness to please her.

Marianne's feigned hauteur melted into warm affection.

Truly, Papa did spoil her. Yet she lived in dread that he would never give her the one thing she desired above all else: the tall *should*-be knight who stood beside him. "No, dear. I am content." She sent a quick look toward Jamie, who continued to stare beyond her. "I will leave you to your business affairs."

Before she could turn, Papa coughed again, and she stepped closer, frowning with concern. He waved her off. "Never mind. I am well. But I have need of your assistance." He clapped a pale hand on Jamie's shoulder. "Captain Templeton has just arrived, and I have offered him lodging. Your mother is occupied with one of her charities, and your worthless brother has not put in an appearance for several days. Would you be so kind as to make certain the good captain is taken care of?"

A laugh of delight almost escaped Marianne, but she managed to release a sigh intended to convey boredom. "Very well, Papa. I shall see that he has accommodations." She graced Jamie with a glance. "Do you have a manservant, or shall we procure one for you?"

A hint of a smile softened his expression. "My man awaits out front in our hired carriage, Lady Marianne."

"Very well, then. I shall instruct our butler, Blevins, to receive him." She reached up to kiss Papa's wrinkled cheek, breathing in the pleasant citrus fragrance of his shaving balm. "Do not let His Majesty weary you, darling."

"Humph." Papa straightened his shoulders and pushed out his chest. "I am not yet in my dotage, despite what you and your mother think." Another cough accompanied his chuckle. "You have to watch these women, Templeton. They like to coddle a man."

"Yes, sir." Jamie's tone held no emotion.

Marianne resisted the urge to offer a playful argument

back to Papa. The sooner he left, the sooner she would have Jamie to herself. Yet how could she accomplish that and maintain propriety? She lifted the silver bell from the nearby table and rang it. A footman stepped into the room. "Tell Blevins we have need of him."

"Yes, Lady Marianne." The footman bowed and left the room.

"Blevins will attend you, Captain Templeton." Marianne kissed Papa's cheek again. "Enjoy your afternoon, Papa." She shot a meaningful look at Jamie. "I am going to the garden to read."

Gliding from the room with a well-practiced grace, she met Blevins in the entry hall and gave him instructions regarding Captain Templeton. "I believe the bedchamber at the end of the third floor is best. Do you agree?" With the room's clear view of the garden, Jamie would have no trouble knowing when she was there.

"Yes, Lady Marianne. I shall see to it." Blevins, of medium height but seeming taller due to his exceptionally straight posture, marched on sticklike legs toward the drawing room, his gait metered like a black-clad soldier who heard an invisible drummer.

Seated on the marble bench beneath one of the barren chestnut trees, Marianne drew her woolen shawl about her shoulders and tried to concentrate on the words in her prayer book. But at the end of each Scripture verse, she found herself beseeching the Lord to send Jamie to her. As a guest in their home, he could visit her here in the garden without impropriety. Anyone looking out any of the town house's back windows could see their actions were blameless.

After a half hour passed, Marianne shivered in the early spring breeze, closed her book and stared up at Jamie's window, willing him to look out so that she might beckon him down. Perhaps he did not know they could meet here without censure. Yet had Papa not requested her assistance in making him feel welcomed? Tapping her foot on the flagstone paving in front of the bench, she huffed out an impatient sigh. She had told him she would be in the garden. Why did he not come?

A rear door opened, and Marianne's heart leaped. But it was John, one of the family's red-and-gold-liveried footmen, who emerged and approached her with a silver tray bearing a tea service and biscuits. "Begging your pardon, Lady Marianne, but Blevins thought you might like some refreshment." John set the tray on the marble table beside her. "May I serve you, Lady Marianne?"

"Thank you, John. I can pour." Perfect. An answer to prayer. "I should like for you to inform my father's guest that he has missed his appointment with me. Please send Captain Templeton down straightaway."

"Yes, Lady Marianne." The ideal footman, John bowed away, his face revealing no emotion.

In a short time, Jamie emerged from the house. But instead of striding toward her with all eagerness, he walked as if facing the gallows, looking beyond her toward the stables, the hothouse, the treetops, anywhere but at her. By the time he came near, Marianne had almost succumbed to tears. Instead, she stood and reached out both hands to greet him.

"Jamie." His name rushed out on a breath squeezed by joy and misery.

"You summoned me, Lady Marianne?" He stopped far beyond her reach and bowed. "I am at your service."

She clasped her hands at her waist and laughed softly, but without mirth. "Such a cold tone to match a cold day. Where is the warmth that once graced your every word to me?"

For several moments, he stared at the ground, his lips set in a grim line and his jaw working. He seemed to compose himself, for at last he lifted his gaze to meet hers.

"My lady, I beg your forgiveness for my inappropriate conversations with you last summer."

"But—"

"Please." He raised his hand in a silencing gesture. "I will not betray the trust of Lord Bennington by arrogantly presuming an equality that would permit us…permit me…to pursue a lady so far above me." For an instant, a sweet vulnerability crossed his eyes, but then all light disappeared from his face, replaced by the same blank expression John or any of the household servants might employ, a facade that bespoke their understanding of status and position. "You must not ask me to do that which would dishonor you, your family and my faith." He gave her a stiff bow. "Now, if you will excuse me, my lady." Jamie spun around and strode back toward the house with what seemed like eagerness, something clearly lacking when he had come to meet her.

Chapter Two

The last time Jamie had felt such grief was beside his mother's grave in Nantucket some sixteen years ago, when he was a lad of nine, struggling then not to cry. Now his jaw ached from clenching, and his chest throbbed as it had when a young whale had slammed him with its tail, trying to escape his harpoon. No, this was unlike any pain he had ever endured aboard his uncle's whaling ship. He could not seem to pull in enough breath, could barely manage to climb the wide front staircase without clutching the oak railing.

In the third floor hallway, a footman cast a glance at him, and one eyebrow rose. Jamie stiffened. He was no faint-hearted maiden who swooned over life's injuries. He'd seen the harm he'd just inflicted upon Marianne…*Lady* Marianne. Yet despite the pain pinching her fair face, she had not swooned. Or had she? Perhaps after he tore himself from her presence, she'd succumbed to her distress.

With some effort, Jamie drew air into his lungs and strode down the hallway, bursting into the elegant bedchamber assigned to him. He ignored his friend Aaron's shocked expression and dashed to the window to peer down into the garden where he'd left her. There she sat beneath the leafless tree, staring straight ahead, her shawl carelessly draped over the stone bench.

Pain swept through him again, but this time for her. How brave she was. No tears. Even at this distance he could see her composure. Was this not one of the reasons he loved her? As he had prayed, her unfailing good sense prevailed. She knew their romance was hopeless, and would not protest his declaration that it must end. *See how she clutches her prayer book. Perhaps even now she is seeking God's consolation.* His parting admonition last year had influenced her as he hoped. Surely now she would cling to the Lord, as he did, to ease the agony they both must endure. No doubt she would manage better than he.

She lifted her gaze toward his window, and he jumped back, chiding himself for lingering there. She would survive the dissolution of their love, but only if he stayed true to his course. If she sensed he might waver, she might pursue him, which would lead to their undoing. No, far more than their undoing. Nothing less than the failure of his mission for the American Revolution.

"You'd best sit down, Jamie." Aaron tilted his head toward an arrangement of green brocade chairs near the roaring fireplace. "You're looking a mite pale." Worry clouded his expression.

"Aye, I'll sit." He staggered to a chair and fell into it, clutching his aching head in both hands as warmth from the crackling logs reached him. The itchy collar of his brown woolen jacket pressed against his neck and generated sweat clear up to his forehead, while a cold, contradictory shudder coursed down his back.

Aaron sat in an adjacent chair and clasped Jamie's shoulder. "You've got it bad, lad, no mistake. But you'd best gird up your mind straightaway, or General Washington will have to send someone else to spy on Lord Bennington and his East Florida interests. And by then it'll be too late for any useful information to reach home." His bushy brown eyebrows met in a frown. "I thought you'd worked this all out before we sailed."

Jamie swiped his linen handkerchief across his forehead. "Aye. I thought it, too. Then I saw her."

"Well, you'd best deal with it." Aaron sat back and crossed his arms. "I didn't sail over here to get hanged. My younger brothers aren't yet old enough to manage my lands, you know."

His words sank deep into Jamie's mind, and the unsaid words sank deeper. In truth, now that he'd broken with her, a certain peace began to fill his chest. He lifted a silent prayer of thanks for God's mercy. Determined to shake off personal concerns, he gave Aaron a sidelong glance and snorted. "If you aren't keen on hanging, then you'd best quit pestering me and start playing your own part." He punched his friend's arm. "Up with you, man. When does a valet sit beside his master? And no more 'Jamie.' It's Captain Templeton to you, and don't you forget it."

"That's the way, Cap'n." Aaron jumped to his feet. "And I'm Quince to ye, sir. So watch what ye say, too." He spoke with the affected accent that augmented his guise as Jamie's valet.

The good humor lighting Aaron's face improved Jamie's spirits. Together they could complete their mission and be gone in just over a fortnight. Surely he could evade Lady Marianne for that short time.

Shivering in the brisk breeze, Marianne clutched her prayer book to her chest and stared unseeing toward the back entrance of the house. Over and over, Jamie's words repeated in her mind: *You must not ask me to do that which would dishonor you, your family and my faith.*

Dishonor? Did he truly believe loving her would cause such dishonor? Had all his ardent declarations of last summer meant nothing to him? Where was his honor if he broke his promise to love her forever? She could not think. Could not feel. His words hammered against her heart, numbing her to all, even tears, even to the biting March wind.

The memory of his cold facade burned into her like a fire, reigniting her senses. She tightened her grip on the prayer book. How could he cause her such pain? In answer, his face appeared in her mind's eye. For the briefest moment, she had seen misery there. What his lips would deny, his eyes revealed. He did love her. Of that she was certain. Serenity filled her heart, and she dared to cast a gaze upward toward his window. She gasped. There he stood, looking directly at her. Then he was gone.

Marianne's heart soared like the song of a nightingale, and warmth swept over her despite the wind. Oh, yes, indeed. Jamie Templeton loved her. And if he thought she would let him slip away because of some misplaced sense of honor, then the good captain had an important lesson to learn. She would begin teaching him this very evening.

Marianne's father always insisted on supper in the formal dining room with all his family and followers gathered around the table. No one could escape. Even her brother Robert usually managed to appear and stay sober for the meal, after which he would go off with his friends for a night of activities about which Marianne tried not to think…or worry.

That evening as usual, Papa sat at one end of the long oak table, and Mama at the other. In her seat at Papa's right hand, Marianne was delighted to see he had placed Jamie on his left, a singular honor that she prayed would not grate on her brother, who really should sit beside Papa. While it would be unacceptable for her to speak across the table and address Jamie, perhaps she might comment on his conversation with Papa.

According to his custom, Robert arrived several minutes late, but no hostility clouded his dark, handsome features. Instead, seated beside Jamie, he greeted him as a long-lost friend and insisted nothing would do but that Jamie must accompany him on his nightly exploits.

At Robert's outlandish proposal, Marianne almost spewed her soup across the table, but managed to swallow and force her gaze down toward her plate. *Please do not permit Jamie to go.* Her silent prayer was directed to both her earthly and heavenly fathers. Before she could fully compose herself and observe Papa's reaction to Robert's plan, the gentleman seated to her right cleared his throat.

"Lady Marianne," Tobias Pincer said, "how exquisite you look this evening." As he leaned closer to her, his oily smile and the odors of camphor and wig powder nearly sent Marianne reeling off the other side of her chair. "Do tell me you plan to attend the rout this evening. I shall be nothing short of devastated if you do not."

With the tightest smile she could muster, she muttered her appreciation of his nightly compliments. "You must forgive me, Mr. Pincer, but my mother and I have prior plans." Did this man actually think she would consort with his crowd, even if Robert was a part of it?

"Of course." His smile turned to a simper, but before he could say more, Grace Kendall claimed his attention from the other side.

"Why, Mr. Pincer, you are neglecting this delicious soup." Her pleasant alto tones dropped to a murmur as she shared a bit of harmless gossip. Mr. Pincer bowed to propriety and turned his full attention to her.

Marianne wanted to hug Grace. For the past three years, Mama's companion had frequently sacrificed herself to deflect unwanted attention Marianne received from suitors. Although more than pretty herself, Grace had no fortune and no prospects. At six and twenty, she would likely remain an old maid, but her selfless companionship always proved a blessing to both Mama and Marianne.

Freed from polite necessity, Marianne looked back across the table just in time to see Papa's approving nod in Jamie's direction.

"We shall see to it tomorrow," Papa said.

What had she missed? Would Jamie go out with Robert this evening? From the defeated look on her brother's face, she guessed he would not. Even as her heart ached over the way Papa often crushed Robert's spirits, she could not help but rejoice that Jamie would not be dragged into the gutters of London.

"Papa," she ventured in a playful tone, "what plans are you making? Have you and His Majesty already subdued those dreadful rebels in America?" She saw Jamie's eyebrows arch, and she puckered away a laugh.

Papa chuckled in his deep, throaty way. "You see, Templeton, these women have no sense about such things." He leaned toward her. "Would that it could be done so easily, my dear. No, I have another project in mind, one in which Captain Templeton has agreed to participate. Our good Reverend Bentley—" he nodded toward the curate, who sat at Mama's right hand "—has agreed to school the captain in some of our more tedious social graces."

Marianne turned her gasp into a hum of interest. "Indeed?"

The color in Jamie's tanned cheeks deepened, and charming bewilderment rolled across his face.

"Yes, indeed." Papa straightened and puffed out his chest. "If this partnership goes as planned, I shall be introducing Captain Templeton to other peers and gentlemen. Through our mutual business efforts, we will make East Florida the standard of how to prevent a rebellion, shall we not, Templeton?"

"That is my hope, sir." Jamie's attention remained on Papa.

"Furthermore, daughter," Papa said, "I am enlisting your assistance, as well. Your mother can spare you for a while. I want you to take the captain to see the sights about the city." He glanced down the table. "I suppose Robert should go along for propriety's sake."

She could hardly believe her ears and could not call forth any words to respond. Jamie blinked and avoided her gaze, perhaps as stunned as she was.

Robert stopped balancing his spoon on the edge of his soup plate and stared at Papa, his mouth agape. He shook his head slightly, as if to clear his vision, and a silly grin lifted one corner of his lips. Marianne would have laughed if her brother's reaction did not seem almost pathetic. Papa never entrusted him with anything.

"Humph." Now a wily look crossed Robert's face, and he studied Jamie up and down, then sniffed. "Well, for gracious sakes, Father, before I am seen in public with this fellow, do let me see about his clothes. Look at him. Not a length of ribbon nor an inch of lace. And this awful black. And not even a brass buckle to catch anyone's attention. Gracious, Templeton, are you a Quaker? Who makes your clothes? No, never mind. I shall see that you meet my tailor."

Jamie's narrowed eyes and set lips, if visible only for an instant, steadied Marianne's rioting emotions. How she would love to thump her dear brother right on the nose for his rude words, spoken so shortly after his own invitation to take Jamie out for the evening. But Marianne could see the resolution in Jamie's face. Her beloved could take care of himself. And although he was at least five years Robert's junior, she had no doubt Jamie would have the greater and better influence on her brother. She would make that a matter of most earnest prayer.

"I thank you, Mr. Moberly," Jamie said to Robert with all good humor. "I shall look forward to any improvements you might suggest."

What graciousness he exhibited. Was that not the epitome of good breeding and good manners? Marianne blushed for the rudeness of her father and brother for suggesting that he needed anything more.

As for the favor Father was heaping on Jamie, she felt her heart swell with joy. If he considered Jamie a partner and an ally in saving the colonies for the Crown, this could be regarded as nothing less than complete approval of the man, perhaps even to the point of accepting him into the family, despite his being a merchant. Her parents had never insisted she marry. Was that not very much like permission to marry whomever she might choose? Hadn't they themselves married for love, despite Mama's lower status as a baron's daughter and no title other than Miss Winston? But in the event she was mistaken, Marianne must take great care to hide her love for Jamie, at least for now.

Chapter Three

For the first time since he had set out on this mission, Jamie began to wonder if General Washington had chosen the wrong man. As a whaler and merchant captain, Jamie had learned how to employ patience and strategy to accomplish whatever goal was at hand. But the gale brewing around him in Lord Bennington's grand London home just might sink him.

He had no difficulty maintaining his composure when the earl offered to introduce him to some important people. After all, that was why Jamie had come. But this scheme for improving his manners almost set him back in his chair, especially when the earl instructed Lady Marianne to help. Now he would be forced into her company and that of her foppish brother, a dark-haired fellow not exactly corpulent, but on his way to it. Jamie had only just met the curate, a slender, compliant fellow, but he preferred the clergyman as a tutor, for every minute in Lady Marianne's company would be torture.

Bent over his roast beef, he wondered if he was doing anything amiss. Not that he cared whether someone pointed out a blunder, for he would welcome a chance to learn better manners for future use in such company as this. But he also would like for Lady Marianne to think well of him. *Belay that, man.* He must not think that way. Yet, without meaning to, he lifted his gaze to see how she wielded her cutlery. Her lovely blue eyes, bright as the southern sky, were focused on him, and he could not look away.

She glanced at the earl. "Papa, have you asked Captain Templeton about Frederick?"

Lord Bennington cast a look down the table at his wife. "Later, my dear. Your mother will want to hear the news of your brother, too."

"Oh, yes, of course." Lady Marianne resumed eating, stopping from time to time to speak with the man beside her. From the prim set of her lips and the way she seemed unconsciously to lean away from the fellow, Jamie could see her distaste, especially when the man tilted toward her. If some dolt behaved thus toward a lady aboard Jamie's ship, he would make quick work of the knave, dispatching him to eat with the deckhands. But civility had its place, and this was it. Jamie watched Lady Marianne's delicate hands move with the grace of a swan, and he tried to copy the way she cut her roast beef and ate in small bites. When he swallowed, however, the meat seemed to stick in his throat, and he was forced to wash it down with water in a loud gulp. Anyone who may have noticed was polite enough not to look his way.

Beside him, Moberly chose a chaser of wine, several glasses of it. As the meal progressed, his demeanor mellowed. "I say, Templeton, do you ride?"

Moberly's tone was genial, not at all like his insulting reference to Jamie's clothes, a matter of some injury. Jamie's beloved cousin Rachel had spent many hours sewing his travel wardrobe, and her expertise could not be matched.

"I have never truly mastered the skill, sir."

Moberly snorted. "Ah, of course not." A wily grin not lacking in friendliness creased his face. "Then you must permit me to teach you. 'Tis a skill every gentleman must have."

If Jamie could have groaned in a well-mannered tone, he would have. Having grown up at sea, he could ride a whale with ease, but not a horse—something Moberly clearly did not believe. *Lord, what other trials will You put before me? Will this truly serve the Glorious Cause in some way?* He lifted one shoulder in a slight shrug and cocked his head to accept the challenge. "Then if I am to be a gentleman, by all means, let us ride." The more time he spent with Moberly, the less he would be in Lady Marianne's alluring company. The less he would be tempted to break his vow not to use her to gain information from her father.

Jamie managed the rest of the meal without difficulty and afterward joined the family in Lord Bennington's study, where the earl held court from behind his ornately carved white desk. Lady Marianne's brother and his slimy friend had excused themselves, no doubt for a night of carousing, for both Lady Marianne and Lady Bennington seemed disappointed as they watched Moberly leave.

"Now," the earl said, "we shall see how my youngest son excuses his mismanagement of my money in East Florida." He opened the satchel Jamie had brought and pulled out several sealed documents.

Jamie flinched inwardly. His good friend Frederick Moberly had made a great success of Bennington Plantation, as proved by the large shipment of indigo, rice, oranges and cotton Jamie had just delivered to Bennington's warehouses. Not only that, but Frederick served well as the popular magistrate of the growing settlement of St. Johns

Towne. Jamie had already apprised Lord Bennington of both of these matters in no uncertain words. Yet the earl referred to all of his sons in singularly unflattering ways. Had Jamie been brought up thus, he doubted he could have made anything of himself. As he had many times before, he thanked the Lord for the firm but loving hand of his uncle, who had guided him to adulthood, first in Nantucket and then on his whaling ship.

Jamie's widowed mother had died when he was nine and his sister, Dinah, three. Uncle Lamech, his mother's brother, had secured a home for Dinah with kindhearted friends, then took Jamie along as his cabin boy on his next whaling voyage. Uncle taught him how to work hard, with courage, perseverance, and faith in God, all the while demonstrating confidence that Jamie would succeed at whatever he put his hand to. Would that the four Moberly sons could have received such assurance from their father.

The earl broke open the seal of the letter addressed to him, and once again Jamie cringed. In his spoken report to Lord Bennington, he had omitted one very important fact about the earl's youngest son.

"Married!"

Marianne and Mama jumped to their feet as one and hurried to Papa's side, as if each must see the words for herself. Mama practically snatched the letter from Papa, who stood at his desk trembling, his face a study in rage. Eyes wide and staring at the offending missive, cheeks red and pinched, mouth working as if no words were sufficient to express his outrage.

Mama did not mirror his anger, but her sweet face clouded as it did when she was disappointed. "Oh, my. And to think I have found no less than six eligible young ladies of consequence who would gladly receive Frederick now that he has done so well for himself."

"Papa, do sit down." Marianne took his arm and tried gently to push him back into his chair. He stood stubbornly rigid and waved her away.

Reading the letter, Mama gasped, and her puckered brow arched and her lips curved upward in a glorious smile. "Why, they are expecting…" She blinked and glanced toward Jamie. "I shall be a grandmamma by July," she whispered to Marianne and Papa. "How exquisitely delightful." Her merry laughter brought a frown of confusion to Papa's face.

"Do not tell me that you approve of this match." Papa's cheeks faded to pink, but his trembling continued.

"But, my darling, approve or not, the deed is done." Mama touched his arm and gave him a winsome smile. "Do be reconciled to it. A sensitive young man can endure rejection from the ladies of his own class for only so long. His every word indicates that this Rachel is above average in wit and temper. Did he mention her family?" She lifted the letter to read more. "Ah, yes. 'Her father owns…'" Her eyes widened. "Oh, my. He owns a mercantile. Tsk. Not even a landowner."

"What?" Papa's voice reverberated throughout the room. Marianne jumped once more.

Mama scowled. "Now, Bennington, please do not shout."

Marianne noticed that Jamie had moved across the room and was staring at a painting. Once again, his flawless manners manifested themselves through this tactful removal from the unfolding drama.

"I will shout in my own home." Papa's trembling increased, and he raised one hand, a finger pointed toward the ceiling. "I will shout in the streets. From the halls of Parliament I will proclaim it. For all the world can clearly see that I have spawned nothing but fools for sons." He slammed his fist on the desk. Documents bounced. A bisque figurine of an elegant lady fell to the floor and shattered. "The daughter of a merchant. Not even an Englishman. An American. The next thing he will be telling me is that he approves of that infernal colonial rebellion."

Mama quickly perused the letter. "No, dear. He speaks only of his little wife—"

Papa snatched the letter from her. "I was not in earnest. Should that day come, I would sail to East Florida and execute him myself."

"Oh, look, Mama." Marianne's voice came out in a much higher pitch than she intended. "Frederick wrote to you and me, too." She picked up the letter bearing her name. "You do not mind, do you, Papa? I shall tell you if he has written anything you must hear."

Papa's shoulders slumped, and his reddened eyes focused on her. "You see, Maria," he said to Mama. "The Almighty saved the best for last." He set a quivering hand on Marianne's shoulder and bent to kiss her forehead. "Our wise, beautiful daughter gives us only joy." He pulled her closer in a gentle embrace. "Would that I could leave all to you, Marianne, for never once in your life have you grieved me."

Marianne's eyes stung mightily. At that moment, she was very near to vowing to God that she would surrender Jamie forever, that she would never hurt her parents as Frederick and Robert and Thomas and William had done. But she gulped back the promise. To vow and to break it would be a sin. To vow and to keep it would mean a lifetime of bitter loneliness.

She stared across the room toward the man she loved,

willing him to turn her way, to give her some direction, some wisdom to bear this situation.

But when he did turn, Jamie's wounded frown seemed to shout across the distance that separated them. *You see? I was right. We have no future together.*

Jamie struggled to secure his turbulent emotions to their proper moorings. As captain of his ship, he often managed numerous life-threatening situations concurrently and with haste and acuity. But never had his heart and wits been so at odds in the midst of a tempest. Never had so many threats loomed over all he held dear.

Lord Bennington's rage over Frederick's marriage might extend to Jamie, especially when he discovered the bride was Jamie's beloved cousin, Rachel. Even if the earl did not cast blame on him, Jamie still felt a bitter ache at not being able to comfort Lady Marianne in her distress. Or to declare his love for her. Or to seize her hand and dash from the room, the house, the country, and to make a future with her in the far reaches of America.

Parallel to these agonizing thoughts streamed the keen awareness that this very room might hold documents outlining Lord Bennington's involvement in British defenses of East Florida. Yet this little meeting could scuttle the mission for which Jamie had been sent to England.

He inhaled a calming breath, relaxed his stance and unclenched his hands. Then, just as Lord Bennington looked his way, he directed a sympathetic frown across the room to the earl. If the man had caught him staring at Lady Marianne—

"Templeton, I will see you in private." The glower Lord Bennington directed toward Jamie softened as he gave his countess a slight bow. "My dear, you will excuse us." He turned to Lady Marianne with the same gentleness. "And you, my child."

"But, Papa—"

"Come along, Merry." Lady Bennington used the fond address Jamie had heard Lady Marianne's parents and brother using. Indeed, her sky-blue eyes and merry disposition—subdued now in her unhappiness—warranted such a nickname. Jamie dismissed a fleeting wish that he had the right to address her with such affection. That right would never be his.

As mother and daughter walked toward the door, Lady Marianne cast a quick glance at him. He forced all emotion from his face and gave them a formal bow, then turned to the earl as if the two ladies had never been there.

"What do you know of this?" Lord Bennington lifted Frederick's letter from the desk.

This was trouble Jamie could manage. Man to man. The earl had commended him for his forthrightness, and now he would receive a goodly portion of it. Jamie crossed the room and held the man's gaze.

"They make a handsome couple, milord. Mrs. Moberly is a lady of spotless reputation, pleasant disposition and considerable courage."

Lord Bennington inhaled as if to speak, so Jamie hastened to continue. "You may have heard the account of how she rescued Lady Brigham from being dragged from a flatboat by an alligator."

The earl's wiry white eyebrows arched. "Indeed?" Puzzlement rolled across his face. "When Lady Brigham speaks of her near demise in the jaws of a dragon, she says her husband saved her. She makes no mention of another woman being involved." He studied the letter as if it would set the story straight.

"An oversight, I'm sure, milord. Frederick recounted the incident to me himself." Jamie pushed on with the more important issue. "Mrs. Moberly is the perfect wife for a man who is carving a settlement out of the East Florida wilderness." His own words struck him. Would Lady Marianne be able to survive in that same wilderness after her life of ease? Not likely. Breaking with her was best for her, if not for him, for far too many reasons to count.

"You seem to have some affection for this young woman." Suspicion emanated from the earl's narrowed eyes.

Jamie gave him a measured grin. "I have great affection for her." The earl's eyes widened with shock, so Jamie kept talking. "She is my cousin, reared with me like a sister."

Lord Bennington's face reddened. He placed his fists on the desk and leaned across it toward Jamie. "Are you responsible for this ill-advised union?"

Jamie still stared into his eyes. "No, milord. I was here in England when they formed their attachment. However, I will confess that when Frederick asked for my help, I complied. They were married aboard my ship by an English clergyman."

Lord Bennington straightened, but his eyes remained narrowed. "You could have omitted that information, and I never would have known it."

"That is true. But our shared business interests will prosper only if we are honest with one another, do you not think?" Honor and duty clashed in a heated battle within Jamie's chest, as they always did when he considered his plans to spy on this man. He quickly doused the conflict. "As I told you earlier, your youngest son is performing his duties admirably as magistrate in St. Johns Towne. Bennington Plantation is prospering prodigiously, as you can see from the oranges we were served at supper tonight. Your warehouse is bursting with the indigo, cotton and rice harvests from East Florida, all grown under Frederick's oversight." Jamie paused to let his words reach the earl's business sense.

Lord Bennington's brow furrowed and his jaw clenched. Again he stared at Frederick's letter, but said nothing.

Jamie decided to press on. "Milord, he has found in Rachel the perfect helpmate for who he is and what he is doing for you." Again, Jamie permitted a cautious grin to grace his lips. "Their mutual devotion proves the truth of the proverb, 'Whoso findeth a wife findeth a good *thing,* and obtained favor of the Lord.'" He wondered if it would be going too far to mention the similar devotion he had noticed between the earl and his countess. But Lord Bennington stiffened, and his white eyebrows bent into an accusing frown.

"And you, Templeton, where will you find *your* wife?"

"Ha!" Surprise and shock forced a too-loud laugh to burst forth, and heat rushed to Jamie's face. He grasped his wayward emotions once again. "I am a seaman, milord. 'Twould be cruel to marry, only to leave my wife alone during my voyages. And of course the sea is no place for a woman." Speaking that truth solidified his decision. He would pry from his heart every fond feeling for Lady Marianne, and marry Lady Liberty and her Glorious Cause.

Lord Bennington studied him with a hardened stare. But gradually, the old man seemed to wilt before Jamie's eyes, and soon he slumped down into his chair as if defeated. "I'll not doubt you again, my boy. Your honesty has proved your worthiness." He waved his hand in a dismissive gesture. "You may go. And if you decide to accompany my reprobate son on his nightly jaunts, do remember that Robert is not Frederick."

Several responses formed in Jamie's mind, not the least of which was that the earl's comment seemed to imply a measure of approval of Frederick and perhaps even Rachel. But the man appeared spent from his emotional evening, so Jamie withheld his remarks. "Very good, milord. Good evening."

As he climbed the stairs to his third-floor suite, a grim sense of satisfaction filled him. He had gained Lord Bennington's trust and could begin his search for information regarding Britain's planned defenses of East Florida. And memories of his tender but short romance with Lady Marianne had been safely tucked away in a remote corner of his mind, to be fondly recalled when he was an old man.

Yet a dull ache thumped against his heart with each ascending step.

Chapter Four

"Your hair is so easy to work with, Lady Marianne." Emma's sweet, round face beamed as she set the silver-handled comb on the dressing table.

"My, Emma." Marianne drew over her shoulder the long braid her maid had just plaited. As always, the work was flawless. "What makes you so happy this evening? Could it be Captain Templeton's handsome young valet, whom I saw you talking with earlier?"

Even in the candlelight, she could see Emma's cheeks turning pink. "Why, no, my lady. I mean—" Her smile vanished, and she chewed her lip. "We spoke for only a few moments. No more than a half hour."

Marianne gave her a reassuring smile. "Do not fear. Mr. Quince seems a pleasant fellow. And being in the good captain's employ, he is no doubt a man of character." A tendril of inspiration grew in her thoughts. "You have my permission to chat with Quince as long as you both have your work completed *and* you meet only in the appropriate common areas of the house where anyone passing can see you. I will tell Mama you have my permission."

Happiness once again glowed on Emma's face. "Oh, thank you, my lady." She curtsied and then hastened to turn down the covers on Marianne's four-poster bed and move the coal-filled bed warmer back and forth between the sheets. Once finished, she returned the brass implement to the hearthside. "Your bed is ready, my lady. Will that be all?" She started to douse the candles beside Marianne's reading chair.

"Leave them." Marianne retrieved her brother's letter from her desk drawer. "I wish to sit and read awhile."

Emma seemed to blink away disappointment. "Shall I wait, my lady?"

"No. You may go." Marianne pulled her woolen dressing gown around her, shivering a little against the cold night air. "I can warm the bed again if I need to. Thank you, Emma."

Her little maid fairly danced from the room with a happiness Marianne envied. How wonderful to find a suitable man to love, one of equal rank, whom Papa and Mama would approve of without reservation. But the heart was an unruly, untamable thing, as evidenced by Frederick's marriage and her own love for Jamie Templeton.

After she and Mama left Papa and Jamie, it had been all she could do to keep from pleading for her mother's support for that love, especially since Mama seemed reconciled to Frederick's marriage. But Mama had excused herself to attend to household matters, leaving Marianne to languish outside Papa's study in hopes of seeing Jamie again. That is, until her brother's missive began to burn in her hand. Here was her ally in the family. Frederick would support her love for Jamie, of that she was certain.

Seated now in her bedchamber in her favorite place to read, Marianne broke the seal on Frederick's letter and unfolded the vellum page. A small, folded piece fell out, so she quickly perused the first one, which repeated the information he'd written to Papa. The details about his dear wife assured Marianne that she would love Rachel and call her "sister" the moment they met.

Wishing that meeting might happen soon, she opened the smaller page—and gasped at the first words. "You must not think to do as I have done, dear sister. For reasons I cannot now explain, other than to say it is for your own happiness and written because I am devoted to you, you must release our mutual friend from the premature vows you traded with him on his last visit to London. To continue this ill-advised alliance will bring only heartache to you both. While he is a man of blameless character, he will not make a suitable husband for the daughter of a peer of the realm. I cannot say more except that you must, you *must* heed my advice, my beloved sister."

Scalding tears raced down Marianne's cheeks. Never had she expected such a betrayal from Frederick. Had they not been the closest of friends all their lives? Had she not frequently stood beside him against their three older brothers, the sons of Papa's first wife, when they sought to bully him? Why did he not wish for her the same happiness he had claimed for himself?

Trembling with anger and disappointment, she resisted the urge to crumple the entire letter. Frederick had signed the first page as if it were the only one, no doubt knowing she would share its contents with Mama. But she reread the second one just to be certain she had not mistaken his cruel intentions. No, she had not. So Marianne ripped the page to shreds and fed the pieces to the hearth flames, then watched as the fire's ravenous tongues eagerly devoured them.

Childhood memories of Frederick's devotion sprang to

mind. His comfort when she fell and scraped her chin. Their forays into Papa's chambers to spy on guests. His gentle teasing, edged with pride, when she emerged from the schoolroom and entered society. Why would he abandon her now? She knelt beside her cold bed and offered up a tearful prayer that she might understand why God would let her fall in love with Jamie and then deny them their happiness.

The response came as surely as if the Lord had spoken to her aloud. *Be at peace. This is the man you will marry.*

"Lord, if this is Your voice, then guide my every step."

Joy flooded her heart—and kept her awake into the early morning hours, planning how she would bring God's will to pass.

Following an afternoon visit to an elderly pensioner who had served the Moberly family for many years, Marianne sat at supper wondering at the different opinions people held about Papa. The old servant had extolled Papa's generosity and kindness, calling him a saint. Yet across the table from Marianne, Robert practically reclined in his chair, his usual protest against Papa's nightly berating. Beside him sat Jamie, in the place where the ranking son should sit, his admiration of Papa obvious in his genial nods and agreeable words to everything Papa said. Doubtless Jamie had no idea that Robert should be sitting to Papa's left. Of course Mama, as always, gazed down the length of the table at Papa with the purest devotion, a sentiment Marianne felt as deeply as a daughter could while still seeing his flaws.

Tonight the topic was the Americans and their foolish rebellion against His Majesty. Some anonymous colonist had written a pamphlet entitled "Common Sense," which was causing considerable stir in London, and Papa seemed unable to contain his outrage.

"Common *non*sense," he huffed as he stabbed a forkful of fish and devoured it. "What do these colonists understand about the responsibilities of government?"

While he fussed between bites about His Majesty's God-given duties to rule, and the Americans as recalcitrant children, Marianne glanced directly across the table at Jamie, whose thoughtful frown conveyed his sympathies for Papa's remarks. Eager to turn the conversation to more pleasant topics, Marianne patted her father's arm.

"But, dearest, if these colonies are so much trouble, why does His Majesty not simply break with them?"

From the corner of her eye, Marianne could see Jamie's own eyes widen for an instant, but she turned her full attention to Papa. He returned a touch to her arm, along with a paternal smile.

"Ah, my dear, such innocence. You had best leave governing to the Crown and Parliament."

Any other time, this response might have soothed Marianne. But for some odd reason, irritation scratched at her mind. She was not a child who should have no opinions, nor should she fail to seek information to enlighten her judgments. She knew of some ladies who expressed their political opinions without censure, including Mama's acquaintance, the duchess of Devonshire.

"I agree with Marianne." Robert's voice lacked its usual indolence, a sign that he had not yet succumbed to his wine. "Let the colonies fend for themselves for a while without the Crown's protection. Then when they're attacked and plundered by every greedy country on the Continent, they'll come crawling back under His Majesty's rule."

Marianne sensed the bitterness in his wily wording. His break with Papa had lasted less than three weeks before he came "crawling back."

Papa regarded Robert for an instant, then dismissed his words with a snort and a wave of his hand. "Templeton, what do you think of this rebellion?"

While her heart ached for her brother, Marianne could now study Jamie's well-formed face without fear of who might notice her staring at him. A sun-kissed curl had escaped from his queue and draped near his high, well-tanned left cheekbone. His straight nose bore a pale, jagged scar down one side that added character rather than disfigurement. She wondered what adventure had marked him thus, and would ask him at the first opportunity.

"I find it a great annoyance, milord." Jamie's brown eyes burned with indignation. "East Florida is prospering and should soon prove to be the most profitable of England's American colonies. But shipping goods back and forth from London has become difficult since King George declared the wayward thirteen colonies to be in open rebellion. I cannot sail five hundred leagues without one of His Majesty's men-of-war stopping me to be sure I have no contraband."

"Hmm." Papa leaned back in his chair and rubbed his chin. "Have my flag and my letter of passage been helpful?"

"Yes, sir. They have saved me more times than I can count. But every time I am forced to heave to—no less than four times on this last voyage—especially when I'm ordered to change my course for whatever reason the captain might have, it delays shipments. This isn't a problem when I carry nonperishable goods. But our orange and lemon cargos can spoil if not delivered in a timely fashion." Jamie bent his head toward the fragrant bowl of fruit gracing the table. "We barely managed to reach London with these still edible."

As he spoke, Papa's smile broadened. "That's what I like about you, Templeton. No interest in politics. Just business.

If those thirteen guilty colonies were of the same mind, there would be no rebellion."

Marianne enjoyed the modest smile Jamie returned to Papa, but Jamie did not look at her. While the two men continued to talk, she cast about for some way to gain his attention. When the perfect scheme came to mind, she knew the Lord was continuing to lead her.

"Papa, may we discuss something other than business and the war?"

His wiry white eyebrows arched in surprise. "Forgive me, my dear. I believe your mother is of the same mind." He bowed his head toward Mama, who had sent more than one disapproving frown his way during the meal. "What would you like to discuss?"

"Why, I wonder if you recall that Mama and I plan to visit St. Ann's Orphan Asylum for Girls tomorrow." She could not keep her gaze from straying to Jamie, who seemed to be particularly interested in the aromatic roast beef the footman had just set before him. "Would you like to make a small contribution to our efforts?"

"Of course, my dear. I shall see to it before I leave for Parliament tomorrow." He cut into the meat before him, but paused with a bite halfway to his lips. "Why do you not take Templeton with you? I'm certain he would enjoy seeing more of London, and I would feel more at ease if you had the protection of his presence."

Jamie coughed and grabbed his water goblet, swallowing with a gulp. Marianne did not know whether to laugh or offer sympathy. But as long as her plan worked...

"I say, Merry." Robert sat up and leaned across his plate, his cravat nearly touching the sauce on his meat. "My tailor is coming tomorrow to fit Templeton's new wardrobe. You know how petulant these Dutch tailors can be if one misses an appointment, which, I might add, I had a deuce of a time arranging so quickly. Can you not take Blevins or a footman or someone else on your little excursion?"

"It is not an excursion, brother dear. It is ministry." Marianne knew she must continue talking before Papa began to berate Robert, for she could hear Papa's warning growl that always preceded such scolding. "In fact, I do believe you would enjoy it, too. Why not join us? I am certain Mama will not mind waiting until Captain Templeton has been measured. All of us could go." For the life of her—and even to save Robert's dignity—she could not think of another thing to say.

"Just the thing, Moberly." Jamie appeared to be taking up the cause, and Marianne's heart lilted over his kindness. "Let's accompany the ladies. I still don't have my land legs, so the walking'll do me good."

Robert's eyes shifted in confusion, and he blinked several times before his gaze steadied. "*Rather,* my good man. A splendid plan." His grin convinced Marianne he knew they had saved him. But now mischief played across his face in a lopsided smirk. "Shall we not ride, then? You did agree to riding, you know."

Marianne saw the dread in Jamie's faint grimace. One day she herself would see to his riding lessons, for her brother would be merciless in the task. "But, Robert," she said, "you know Mama and I must take our carriage, for we have many items to carry."

"No doubt too many items to leave room for Templeton and me." Robert nudged Jamie. "Do you not agree?"

Jamie's jaw clenched briefly. "I thank you, Lady Marianne, but tomorrow is none too soon to begin my acquaintance with a saddle."

She could not stop a soft gasp. Would he deliberately

avoid her? Somehow she managed a careless smile. "Of course, Captain Templeton. Whatever you prefer."

The footman behind her removed her half-eaten meat course and replaced it with a bowl of fruit. Marianne glanced at Papa, who was absorbed in his own bowl. Once again she had deflected his anger and thus defended one of her brothers.

But who would work in her defense? Who would see that her dreams were accomplished? Despite the verse in her morning reading, "Be still and know that I am God," her heart and her faith dipped low with disappointment.

Jamie had thought his heart was settled in the matter of Lady Marianne, especially after his first session with Reverend Bentley, who'd expounded on the nature of British social structures and everyone's place in it. As he'd left the good curate, Jamie had felt certain he'd conquered his emotions. But this supper turned everything upside down. The impossible choice set before him demanded an instant decision, and he could see how his words had wounded her. Ah, to be able to comfort her. Yet there could be no compromise, even though by choosing Moberly's invitation, he was now forced to risk his neck to keep his distance from her. Jamie could not bear the closeness that a carriage would afford, even with her mother present.

He'd never had cause to trust or not trust Moberly. But youthful experiences had taught him that privileged gentlemen found great amusement in putting other men through the worst possible trials to test their mettle. In truth, he'd suffered the same treatment as a cabin boy, and inflicted the same on youths under his command. How else did one become a man?

But did his latest trial have to be on horseback?

Chapter Five

Jamie had always dressed himself, and Quince employed his own manservant, who had remained on his farm in Massachusetts. So it was a challenge for both men to go through the motions of acting as master and valet. But they each put on their best performance for Jamie's fitting with Moberly's tailor.

Soon, however, the tall, finicky man irritated Jamie to the extreme as he roughly measured him, tossed about colorful fabrics and barked orders at his harassed assistant, a dark-skinned boy of no more than thirteen. Other than his helper, the man spoke only to Moberly and only in his native tongue—French—clearly regarding Jamie as less than worthy of being addressed. Just as clearly, the tailor had no idea Jamie was fluent in his language and was having difficulty not responding to his insults.

When he turned at the wrong moment, the slender thread of a man lifted his hand as if to cuff him, but Jamie warned him off with a dark scowl.

"I thought you said he's Dutch," he said to Moberly through clenched teeth.

Sprawled out on the chaise longue in Jamie's suite, Moberly gave the remark a dismissive wave. "If Bennington knew I used a French tailor, the old boy would have apoplexy. All that unpleasantness with the Frogs, you know."

At his words, Jamie's crossness softened. Moberly had a deep need in his life, yet how could Jamie speak to him of God's grace while spying on his father? He lifted a silent prayer that somehow Lady Marianne might deliver the message of God's love her brother needed to hear.

Jamie ducked to avoid the long pin the tailor wielded like a rapier to emphasize his ranting. Used to homespun woolen and linen, Jamie chafed at the idea of wearing silk, satin and lace, but he'd decided to tolerate Moberly's choice of fabrics and styles. That is, until the tailor unrolled some oddly colored satin and draped it across Jamie's shoulder. What a ghastly green, like the color of the sea before a lightning storm. He would not wear it, no matter what anyone said.

As if reading his mind, Moberly rested a finger along his jawline in a thoughtful pose. "No, no, not that, François. It reminds me of a dead toad. Use the periwinkle. It will drive the ladies mad."

"*Mais non,* Monsieur Moberly." François sniffed. "That glorious *couleur* I save for you, not this…this *rustique.*" He snapped his fingers to punctuate the insult.

"That's it." Jamie snatched off the fabric and flung it away, ignoring the derisive snort from Quince, who observed the whole thing from across the room. "My own clothes will do."

Moberly exhaled a long sigh. "Now, François, look what you've done. I shall have to find another tailor."

The middle-aged tailor gasped. "But, Monsieur—"

"No, no." Moberly stood and walked toward the door. "I

shall not have you insult Lord Bennington's business partner and my good friend."

The man paled. "Lord Bennington's business partner?" Now his face flushed with color. "But, Monsieur Moberly, why did you not say so?" He turned to Jamie, his eyes ablaze with an odd fervor. "Ah, Monsieur, eh, Capitaine Templeton, for such a well-favored gentleman, *oui,* we must have the periwinkle." He snapped his fingers at his assistant. *"L'apportes à moi, tout de suite."*

The boy brought forth the muted blue fabric, a dandy's color if ever Jamie saw one. When François draped it over his shoulder, Quince moved up beside Jamie and stared into the long mirror with him.

"Aye, sir, that'll grab the ladies' attention, no mistake." The smirk on his face almost earned him Jamie's fist.

"Bad news about your ship, Templeton." Moberly's comment surprised Jamie. "What's all this about repairs?" Perhaps he'd noticed Jamie's difficulty in restraining himself throughout this ordeal. Indeed, Jamie knew the report about the *Fair Winds* had set him back, for it meant he and Quince would be in London for an unknown length of time instead of just a month.

"The hull requires scraping and recaulking." Jamie stuck out his arm so François could fit a sleeve pattern. "And the storm damage to the mast was worse than I thought. 'Twill take some time to fix it all."

"Ah, well." Moberly's grin held a bit of mischief. "Once we finish the charity bits with Marianne and Lady Bennington, we'll find ways to fill your time."

In the mirror, Jamie traded a look with Quince. When his first mate, Saunders, arrived early that morning with disappointing news about the sloop, Quince reminded him of their prayers for this mission. God wasn't hiding when the

Fair Winds received storm damage, and He'd brought them safely to port. The Almighty still had this venture safely in His hands. All the more time to secure important information, Jamie and Quince agreed, but too much time for Jamie to be in Lady Marianne's beguiling presence.

Once the torturous fitting session ended, the now-fawning tailor withdrew, and Jamie gripped his emotions for the coming events. After their midday repast, he and Moberly joined Lady Bennington and Lady Marianne for their visit to the orphan asylum. Yet, other than the brief quickening of his pulse at seeing Lady Marianne—dressed modestly in brown, as was her mother—he had only to deal with riding.

To his surprise, Moberly chose for him a large but gentle mare that followed Lady Bennington's landau like an obedient pup. Jamie began to feel comfortable in the saddle. Moberly also furnished him with a pistol and sword to keep at hand lest unsavory elements be roaming the streets.

The trip across town, however, passed with unexpected ease and some pleasant sightseeing under a bright spring sky. Although the cool March breeze carried the rancid odors of the city waste and horseflesh, making Jamie long for a fresh ocean wind, he did notice some of London's finer points. Upon catching a glimpse of the dome of St. Paul's Cathedral, he decided he must visit its fabled interior. Then some shops along the way caught his eye as possible sources of gifts for loved ones back home or, at the least, ideas for items to export to East Florida.

The carriage and riders entered the wide front courtyard of the asylum as though passing through a palace's gates…or a prison's. The wrought-iron fence's seven-foot pickets were set no more than four inches apart, giving the three-story gray brick building a foreboding appearance, a sad place for children to grow up, in Jamie's way of thinking. Not a scrap of trash littered the grassy yard, which still wore its winter brown, and not a single pebble lay on the paved front walkway. No doubt the denizens of St. Ann's had swept the path with care for the expected visitors. Dismounting with only a little trouble, he saw with gratitude a stone mounting block near the building's entrance. He would have no trouble remounting. Perhaps this horse riding would not be so bad, after all.

Robert assisted his stepmother's descent from the carriage and looped his arm in hers. Jamie had no choice but to offer the same assistance to Lady Marianne. Taking his arm, she gave him a warm smile that tightened when her mother glanced over her shoulder. But the lady's attention was on John the footman, who balanced several large boxes in his arms as he followed them. She gave the man a nod and turned back toward the door. Lady Marianne squeezed Jamie's arm, and a pleasant shiver shot up to his neck. He tried to shake it off, to no avail. Wafting up from her hair came the faint scent of roses, compounding his battle to distance his feelings from her.

"Mama takes such delight in these visits," Lady Marianne whispered as she leaned against his arm. "She loves the children dearly."

He permitted himself to gaze at her for an instant, and his heart paid for it with a painful tug. "It seems you do, too, my lady." Indeed, her eyes shone with an affection far different from the loving glances she'd sent his way. How he longed to learn of all her charitable interests. But that could not be.

"Oh, yes." Her strong tone affirmed her conviction. "They do such fine work here, rearing these girls and teaching them useful skills. My own Emma came from this school."

"Ah, I see." Jamie was glad they reached the massive double front doors before he was required to comment further. He had yet to discover just how deeply Quince cared for Lady Marianne's little maid, but he knew his friend would not play her false. Still, both men would likely end up sailing home with broken hearts.

As the group moved through the doors and into the large entrance hall, which smelled freshly scrubbed with lye soap, the soft thunder of running feet met them. Some hundred and fifty girls of all sizes hastened to assemble into lines, the taller ones in the back ranks, with descending heights down to the twenty or so tiny moppets in front. Each girl wore a gray serge uniform and a plain white pinafore bearing a number.

Jamie swallowed away a wave of sentiment. An orphan himself, he, too, might have been a nameless child raised with a number on his chest, had his uncle not taken him in.

A middle-aged matron in a matching uniform inspected the lines, her plain thin face betraying no emotion as she turned and offered a deep curtsy to their guests. As one, the girls followed suit.

"Welcome, Lady Bennington, Lady Marianne." Another matron, gray-haired and in a black dress, stepped forward. Authority emanated from her such as Jamie had witnessed in the sternest of sea captains, but he also noted a hint of warmth as she addressed the countess.

"Mrs. Martin." Lady Bennington's countenance glowed as she grasped the woman's hands. "How good to see you." Her gaze swept over the assembly. "Good afternoon, my dear, dear girls."

Mrs. Martin lifted one hand to direct the children in a chorus of "Good afternoon, Lady Bennington, Lady Marianne." One and all, their faces beamed with affection for their patronesses.

While the countess made some remarks, Jamie noticed Lady Marianne leaning toward the little ones as if she wished to go to them. The countess then gestured to John the footman, who brought forth one of the boxes. Jamie followed Moberly's lead and moved back against the wall while the two ladies disbursed knitted mittens, scarves and caps they and their friends had made. The children's joy and gratitude punctured Jamie's self-containment, and he tried to grip his emotions. Still, breathing became more difficult as the scene progressed.

When Lady Marianne knelt on the well-scrubbed wooden floor among the smallest orphans, gathering in her arms a wee brown-haired tot to show her how to don her mittens, Jamie's last defenses fell away, and a shattering ache filled his chest.

Lord, forgive me. I love this good lady beyond all sense, beyond all wisdom. Only through Your guidance can I walk away from her. Yet if, in Your great goodness, You could grant us happiness—

Jamie could not permit himself to complete the prayer. He would neither request nor expect the only answer that would give him personal joy. Not when there was a revolution to be fought and a fourteenth colony to draw into the mighty fray. If he must lose at love, so be it.

But he must not lose at war, for in that there was so much more at stake—nothing less than the destiny of a newborn nation.

Chapter Six

"Captain Templeton looks quite presentable in his new riding clothes, do you not think, Grace?" Marianne sat in the open carriage beside Mama's companion, whom she had borrowed for today's outing to Hyde Park. "Robert approves, or he would not have agreed to bring the American with us." She herself had been stunned when Jamie walked into the drawing room just an hour ago, for the cut of his brown wool coat over his broad shoulders and the close lines of his tan breeches over his strong legs emphasized his superior masculine form. Why, if not for his colonial speech, he could pass for a peer of the realm.

Grace looked toward the two men, who rode their horses slightly ahead of the open black landau. "Yes, my lady. The captain has the appearance of a true gentleman." She pursed her lips, and her eyes took on a merry glint. "And I do believe with a little practice, his horsemanship will improve."

Marianne responded with a knowing smile as she searched Grace's face. But the lady's countenance bore no hint of feeling for Jamie other than her usual kindheartedness. A modicum of shame warmed Marianne's cheeks, despite the brisk March breeze that fanned over them. She need never be jealous of dear Grace.

"I agree. But I am not altogether certain my brother can be trusted to see to Captain Templeton's riding lessons."

A shadow flitted over Grace's face. "Surely you do not think Mr. Moberly would permit the American to be harmed." She gazed at Robert, her eyes glowing with a softness that Marianne had never before noticed.

Withholding a gasp of realization, she forced her own gaze to settle on Robert. This morning she had observed the usual shadows beneath his eyes and his languid posture, which bespoke his many nights of intemperance and little sleep. Could pious Grace care for such a reprobate? Marianne hated to think of her brother in terms their father would use, but Robert truly met that description.

Before she could respond to Grace's concern, Robert hailed another open carriage passing from the other direction. "Ho there, Highbury. Do stop for a chat." He waved to Wiggins to stop Marianne's conveyance.

The young man called to his driver, who reined his horses to a stop. Beside Mr. Highbury sat his sister, Lady Eugenia, and Marianne felt a rush of pleasure at seeing these friends. Due to Lord Highbury's Whig politics, Papa no longer associated with him, and out of loyalty, both families deferred to their patriarchs.

Robert presented Jamie to the Highburys, and pleasantries flew about the little group.

"I see you and Lady Marianne have taken advantage of this rare sunny day, too, Mr. Moberly." Lady Eugenia gave Robert a warm smile, and her eyelashes fluttered.

Marianne heard Grace's soft sigh beside her. It was clear Eugenia was flirting with Robert. But Lord Highbury would never permit her to marry a second son.

Robert, all charm and energy now, bowed in his saddle. "My lady, it must be Fate that brought us together."

"I absolutely concur." Mr. Highbury's gaze settled on Grace, and he nodded to her. "Even the ground is dry. We simply *must* take a turn around the park."

With all in agreement, the ladies were assisted from their carriages. While Eugenia maneuvered her way toward Robert, Marianne managed to edge close to Jamie. Mr. Highbury seemed more than agreeable to pairing with Grace, bowing and offering his arm to her.

"Your riding has improved, Captain Templeton." Marianne gave his arm an expectant look.

"Thank you, my lady." He offered it without meeting her gaze. "I would not call myself a horseman, but at least I've remained astride."

A light laugh escaped her, as light as her heart felt over walking beside him on this fine day. "Your modesty is as refreshing as today's weather." Indeed, the invigorating air in Hyde Park carried no hint of the unpleasant city odors.

"It is a good day." He lengthened his stride, as if eager to catch the other two couples walking several yards ahead of them on the brown grass.

After several seconds of trying to keep up with him, Marianne tugged at his arm. "Perhaps when your ship is repaired, we can enjoy a short voyage on the Thames, as we did last year."

Jamie stopped, but his gaze remained on the others as the distance between them widened. "I am sure Lord Bennington will be too busy for such an excursion."

Again, Marianne laughed, a strained sound she hoped Jamie would not notice. "Of course Papa will be too busy. But Robert—"

"Ah, yes. Robert." Jamie looked at her, and his eyes filled

with concern. "My lady, I would not wish to presume…anything. However, Moberly seems to regard me as a friend. It may be that I can have some good influence on his, um, habits." He glanced away. "Please continue to walk with me."

"Yes, of course." Her heart dipped in disappointment.

They resumed their stroll across the almost empty park. She did not wish to discuss Robert, but he was very dear to her. Jamie's Christian charity toward her brother moved her.

"I have often spoken to my brother about his lack of spiritual interest. Our brother Frederick is also concerned about him. But Robert assures us he will take care of that matter when he grows older."

"An error too many people make, if I may be so bold, my lady."

A hint of dread touched Marianne's heart. "I hope you will be bold enough to speak to him of Christ's redemption."

Jamie's expression grew thoughtful, but he did not seem inclined to say more. Her heart heavy for more than one reason, Marianne gazed around the landscape, where trees had begun to bud and tiny shoots of green appeared in the brown grass.

"Moberly would benefit from our prayers." Jamie's deep, rich voice resounded with concern. "In truth, though I would not judge the man, I fear that his immortal soul is in danger."

Gratitude for his observation filled Marianne. "I have the same fear. Oh, Jamie—"

Wincing, he stopped again, but avoided her gaze. "Please, my lady."

The pain and censure in his voice cut into her. "I—I mean, Captain Templeton." She resumed her stroll, and he followed suit. "What can we do for him?"

"I would not wish for Lady Bennington to think ill of me, since I am a guest in her house, but I have considered going to one of these routs with Moberly. They're all he speaks of, and seem to consume his life." Jamie paused. "What does a rout involve?"

The tightness of his tone almost made Marianne laugh. "Why, a rout is just a gathering at someone's home. The hostess invites a huge number of people who want to be seen and to see others." She sobered. "But Robert only says he's going to a rout to avoid stating his true plans. Oh, he may indeed attend one, but he then goes gambling and—"

"You need not continue, my lady." Jamie cast a quick glance her way and patted her hand, sending a pleasant shiver up her arm. "I understand your meaning." He studied the ground before them. "Nevertheless, I feel compelled to go with him."

They walked in silence for a few moments. Jamie's large form blocked much of the breeze that fluttered the edges of her cape and carried the scent of his woody shaving balm in her direction. She could not resist the temptation to lean against his arm, as if she could absorb some of his strength. But he seemed to sway away from her to a degree so small she might have been mistaken.

"You would put yourself in temptation's way…for Robert?" Marianne felt tears forming. Jamie's godly goodness and selflessness were just two of the reasons she loved him.

"By God's grace, I have so far resisted such temptations. The Book of Proverbs fully addresses the subject, and it is my guide."

"But there are other dangers." Marianne shuddered to think of the vicious packs of wellborn miscreants who wandered the night streets of London filled with evil intentions. Thievery, beatings, even murder were their games, and if they chose their victims carefully, they never had to pay.

Jamie nodded. "I'm sure there are. But our Lord dined with the worst of sinners that He might demonstrate God's love to them."

"Oh, Jamie…Captain…" She again tugged him to a stop. "Our Lord knew when and how He would die. He was in full control of everything. You are not. Why would you risk your life this way?" She argued against her own heart, for she did love Robert and longed for his salvation.

Jamie drew himself up to his full height, yet his gaze into her eyes was gentle and full of conviction. "Lady Marianne, there are causes worth giving one's life for. Christ died to free us from sin and give us eternal life. Should I not willingly give *my* life for another man…and for freedom?" He clamped his lips closed and shook his head. "We should join the others."

Confusion filled her. Jamie seemed to think he had spoken amiss, yet she found no fault in his words. "I am deeply grateful for your willingness to befriend Robert. I will pray God will bless your efforts." *And that He will protect you both, my love.*

Jamie was surprised so little time had passed during his torturous walk at Lady Marianne's side. A few more minutes alone with her would be his undoing. He could see she understood his concern for Moberly and that she truly loved her brother. This, along with her earnest words of faith— and the heady scent of her rose perfume—created in him a powerful yearning to confess his love that he was scarce able to deny. His weak, silent prayer for strength brought no relief, and the journey across the park left his emotions ravaged by the time they reached the others.

Not one of the four seemed to have missed Lady Marianne, and certainly not him. With great effort, he forced his mind to address this fortuitous meeting with young Highbury, a lad of perhaps twenty-one. Jamie had learned Lord Highbury was a prominent Whig who, with others of his party, opposed King George's vile treatment of the colonists. In fact, their opposition extended to refusing to take their seats in the current session of Parliament. Jamie's orders from General Washington included uncovering any allies among the Whigs who might help the Revolution, but Bennington's social circle excluded those very men.

"Captain Templeton." Lady Eugenia gazed at him, her eyelashes fluttering. "You must tell us all about the conflict in the colonies."

A pretty girl somewhat younger than her brother, she had a merry disposition, and her flirting was harmless. Yet Jamie would remember his station, at least the way these aristocrats might view it, and be pleasantly formal. He had long ago rejected any plans to deflect Lady Marianne's affections by showing interest in someone else. If he must break her heart and his own, it would not be through deceit.

"You must forgive me, Lady Eugenia." He bowed to her. "My travels at present do not take me to the troubled areas."

"But, my good man," Mr. Highbury said, "surely you hear news of the war…or at least rumors." An intense look flickered in his eyes, and he leaned toward him.

Jamie smiled and lifted one shoulder in a light shrug. "Sir, the North American continent is vast. An entire war can be fought at one end without a ripple reaching the other." He observed the disappointment in Highbury's expression, but could say nothing more. The lad might indeed be sympathetic to the Cause, but his emotions were too much in evidence to invite Jamie's trust.

"Oh, bother." Moberly emitted a long sigh. "Must we talk of politics? It is beyond enough that our fathers engage in their tedious debates over such things."

"I agree, dear brother." Marianne put one arm around Lady Eugenia's waist. "For my own part, I have missed dear Genie very much these past months. We simply must have more time together. I think Mama should give a ball. Everyone has been in London since October, and here it is March. Yet she has not done her share of entertaining."

"Oh, a ball at Bennington House." Lady Eugenia's voice trilled with excitement. "Indeed, that would be lovely."

"Rather," Mr. Highbury said with a chuckle. "That is, if you don't think Lord Bennington will cast us out for disloyalty." He sent Jamie a meaningful look.

Jamie returned a placid smile and looked to Moberly to respond for them. But inwardly, he groaned. In his search for allies, the last thing he needed was a foolish young pup who might ruin everything.

Chapter Seven

"Lord, I trust You to bring them safely home." Bundled in her warmest woolen dressing gown, Marianne sat by the window of her bedchamber and watched the darkened street two stories below. Her prayer, which she had repeated countless times over the past several hours, soothed her emotions each time anxious thoughts beset her. Why this night was somehow different, she could not guess, but it seemed something sinister hung in the air.

After supper, Jamie had accompanied Robert and his friend Tobias Pincer on their nightly wanderings. Marianne had been hard put not to ask their destination, but such a question would have been beyond propriety. Perhaps they had indeed gone to a rout. In her first season, she had attended one and found it a crushing bore. But other than an occasional supper at the home of some friend, Papa preferred for Mama and her to stay home in the evenings, saying the night was for the devil and his dark deeds. Never mind that much of London's social life occurred after sunset or that many political compromises were made over a fine supper. This very evening, from Billings House across Grosvenor Square, soft sounds of party merriment reached through Marianne's slightly open window.

She yawned and snuggled into her wrap to ward off the night chill. Perhaps she was being foolish. But after going to bed she had lain awake for well over an hour, at last rising to light a candle and find comfort in the Scriptures. Her eyes fell on Psalm 27:1. "The Lord is my light and my salvation; whom shall I fear? The Lord is the strength of my life; of whom shall I be afraid?" Whether or not Robert sought God's protection, Jamie would, and in the coal-black streets of London, the Lord would be his light.

Her eyelids grew heavy, and she rested her head against a pillow on the windowsill. A cold breeze sent images of ships floating through her mind, and she dreamed of standing beside Jamie aboard his *Fair Winds* while the sails filled with wind and carried them to faraway shores.

Sitting up with a jolt, she realized that noise no longer came from the party across the Square, and silence ruled the night. But, no, distant sounds drew nearer. The muted thuds of a horse's hooves on the dirt street, the rattle of carriage wheels. Hurried whispers. Jamie's deep voice. And John the footman, who had kept vigil at the front door at Marianne's request. She shoved the window farther open and leaned out to see a hired hackney driving away and forms disappearing through the front door beneath her.

She dashed from her room and downstairs to meet them in the front entry.

"Milady, 'tis Mr. Moberly." John's bushy eyebrows met in a frown as he and Jamie struggled to half carry, half drag Robert into the light of a single candle illuminating the hall.

"Go back to bed, Marianne." Jamie jerked his head toward the stairway as he knelt and let Robert slump against his chest. "We can manage."

Jamie's breath came in deep gasps. Robert lay silent.

"Let me help." Marianne knelt in front of her brother, whose forehead bore a bloody lump. "What happened?" Did Jamie realize he had not used her title?

"Go upstairs." Jamie used a stern tone, one that must cause his sailors to quake, but only made her cross.

"I will not. John, take Mr. Moberly into Papa's library. We can tend him there." She could see the footman's hesitation. "Do as I say."

"Yes, milady." John sent Jamie an apologetic look.

Still working to catch his breath, Jamie shook his head. "To his bedchamber."

"No," Marianne said. "We would have to pass Papa's door, and he might hear us."

Now Jamie leaned toward her, and she could see the raw emotion in his eyes. "Madam, it may turn out that Lord Bennington would actually want to have some final words with his son."

Marianne drew in a sharp breath. She stared down the length of Robert's drooping form and saw a scarlet stain oozing through a slash on the left side of his yellow waistcoat. "Oh, Robert—" She clamped down on her emotions. Tears would not help him.

Jamie glanced up the wide front staircase and released a weary sigh. "You're right. To the library, John."

While Marianne took charge of the candle, the men carried Robert down the dark hallway beside the staircase to Papa's library. Inside, she pointed. "On the settee."

"Milady, the blood," John said.

"Never mind. Mama is planning to redo this room." Perhaps not soon, but she did redecorate often.

With Robert on the long settee, Jamie fell to his knees beside him, still breathing heavily.

"John, fetch clean rags and water." Marianne hurried to the hearth for more light, bringing back a candlestick with three candles. She placed it on a table in front of the settee. Robert smelled of sweat and brandy…and blood. "What happened?" She unbuttoned his waistcoat and shirt to reveal a one-inch red gash on the left side of his pale, doughy chest. Although it still oozed blood, the color was crimson, not dark as from a deeper wound. Refusing to succumb to the horror of it, she rolled his linen shirttail and pressed it against the cut.

Jamie leaned against the settee arm. "Thank You, Lord. It's not as deep as I feared." He shook his head as if to clear it, and studied Robert's forehead. "This is why he's unconscious. I feared the stab wound was—"

"Yes. No doubt the blade was aimed at his heart." Relief soothed Marianne's ravaged emotions, and she released a few tears. "What happened?" she asked again.

Jamie blinked, as if struggling to focus his eyes. "It is sufficient to say that Moberly's gambling luck did not follow him into the streets."

"Footpads?" She could not think anyone would attempt to murder the son of an earl. It must have been true criminals, not bored aristocrats up to no good.

"Aye. And a scurvier bunch I've never seen." He grimaced. "Forgive me."

She laughed softly. "I am not so fragile that I cannot bear such words. My brothers—"

"Lady Marianne." Blevins marched into the library wearing his usual black livery, but his sleeping cap instead of his periwig. Behind him, John carried the requested items and more. "Please permit me to attend Mr. Moberly."

"Yes. Thank you." Marianne stood and moved back.

Jamie struggled into a nearby chair, grasping his left

forearm with his right hand. His blue wool coat was torn in several places and lightly splattered with bloodstains.

"Jamie!" She reached toward his arm, but he pulled it away. "You must let me look at your injury."

"Just a scratch or two." His eyes still did not focus. "I'm not injured." Belying his words, he touched the back of his head and winced. "Not badly, anyway." He glanced at Blevins and John, who were huddled over Robert, and sent her a warning frown. "Please, my lady, go to bed."

She settled into a chair next to him. "When I am assured of Robert's—and *your*—health, I shall retire. Until then, you will have to endure my company." She would have given him a mischievous smirk had not Robert been lying there having his side sewn together by the incomparable Blevins.

Jamie watched the butler's doctoring methods with interest and growing respect. He himself had stitched up numerous wounds during his whaling days. But he was in no condition to do this job. He'd certainly not expected to see such violence on the streets of London, especially against the son of an earl. Jamie couldn't be altogether certain Tobias Pincer had not orchestrated the attack. At the very least, the man proved to be a worthless coward. If Moberly recovered, as it now seemed he would, Jamie would give a full accounting of his gaming companion.

After they had eaten supper at Lady Bennington's table, the three of them had attended a strange gathering at a large private home, one of those routs, during which a throng of people milled about with no apparent purpose. Jamie met several people but was never presented to a host. Afterward, Moberly and Pincer insisted their next stop must be a gambling establishment. While Jamie stood near a window in the dim and smoky room, the two sat at cards downing drink after drink. Or perhaps Pincer didn't drink all that much.

With minimal knowledge of the game, Jamie still could sense that Pincer was helping Moberly to win. When they decided at last to leave, Moberly's pockets bulged with notes and gold coins. And it was he whom the footpads attacked. If Jamie hadn't been last out the door, he might have suffered the same fate. As it was, he'd been able to drive away the scoundrels with a few blows of the ebony cane Moberly had loaned him for the evening. As many attackers as there were, perhaps three or four, Jamie thought he and Moberly had come out of it fairly well, especially since Pincer disappeared the moment they exited the gaming hall. But then, footpads generally proved to be cowards if their victims fought back.

Sitting in Lord Bennington's library generated an instinct in one part of Jamie's mind. He should be trying to locate a chest or hidden compartment where maps or plans or royal communications might be kept. But another part of him could think only of Moberly and his near encounter with death.

Jamie's dizziness began to clear, but the injury on the back of his head still pounded deep into his skull. He touched it, drawing Lady Marianne's anxious gaze. Dropping his hand to the chair arm, he decided he'd have to ignore the sticky lump until he could get to his quarters and have Quince check the damage.

Still, a surge of pride rolled through him. He'd never imagined Lady Marianne would be awake, much less that she would view her brother's injuries without swooning. His lady had courage and pluck.

His lady? Try though he might, he couldn't dislodge the

pleasant notion nor stop the accompanying warmth spreading through his chest. If not for the blood on his hand, he might have reached out to grasp hers. Thank the Lord for the blood.

Before a new day dawned, he must speak to Moberly about his eternal soul, which so far the Almighty had mercifully spared.

Marianne insisted upon overseeing Robert's transfer to his bedchamber, and informed Blevins that she would sit with her brother until morning. "You and John must retire for the night so you both can see to your duties tomorrow."

In the dimly lit room, she noticed just a tiny flicker in the butler's eyes, perhaps wounded pride, for he never failed in any of his duties no matter how late he had labored the night before. But he gave her a perfect servant's bow. "Of course, Lady Marianne. Shall I summon Miss Kendall to accompany you?"

Marianne glanced toward the small side chamber where John had gone to wake Ian, Robert's young valet. If she, Jamie and Ian were to keep watch over her brother, propriety demanded the presence of another lady in the room.

"Yes, please."

Ian soon emerged fully dressed and began to assess the situation. Like Blevins and John, he demonstrated no emotion, but Marianne could see concern in his eyes as he arranged Robert's dressing gown, pillows and covers.

Jamie excused himself to wash up, and Marianne settled into a chair beside Robert's bed just as Grace joined her for the vigil. Within a half hour, Jamie returned, but gently refused Marianne's request to check the lump on his head.

"Quince cleaned it and says it's nothing, my lady." Jamie settled into a chair across the room. When he fell asleep, with his long legs extended out in front of him and his head resting back on a pillow, Marianne spent half her time watching him and half watching Robert.

In the early morning hours, her brother became delirious, thrashing and mumbling nonsensically. Jamie awakened, and he and Ian held Robert fast so the stitches would not tear. Soon he quieted. Marianne wiped his face and freshened the cool, damp cloth on his forehead. The crisis passed, but she could not be certain another would not strike. All the while, she was aware of Grace's soft prayers…and her tears. Assured of her brother's progress, Marianne moved to the small settee where Grace sat.

A slim horizontal thread of gray appeared on the floor beneath the window, announcing dawn's arrival. Marianne looked over to see Jamie stir awake, then walk to the bedside just as Robert opened his eyes. Relief swept through her, and she clasped hands with Grace.

"Well, old man," Jamie said. "I believe you got the worst of it."

Robert coughed out a weak laugh, then grimaced and grabbed at his wound. "Ahh. Hurts. Never thought—"

"Shh." Marianne rushed to him. "Rest easy, Robert dear." She dampened another fresh cloth for his forehead. "You're safe at home."

He turned his bloodshot eyes toward her. "Merry." Then beyond her. "Miss Kendall. Ian." A wry smile lifted one corner of his lips. "I say, have you all kept vigil? Am I going to die?" A sardonic tone accompanied his gaze around the room. "What, Father did not come to bid me farewell?"

"No, Robert." Her heart aching for him, Marianne applied the compress. "We did not wake him."

"No, of course not." Robert grunted. "By all means, do not disturb the patriarch." His bitter tone cut into her. "Fine

Christian father that he is." He closed his eyes and leaned into the cold cloth as she pressed it against his temple.

She swallowed an urge to reprimand him. "Shh. You must rest."

"Hmm." He rolled his head toward Jamie. "I say, Templeton, how did you enjoy your first night out in London?" He chuckled, then coughed and again clutched at his injury.

Standing on the opposite side of the bed, Jamie glanced at Marianne and then frowned down at Robert. "Can't say I'd like to repeat it." Again he looked at her, this time with a question in his eyes.

Without a word spoken, she understood him and quietly resumed her place beside Grace. Surely after this night, Jamie would see how well they worked together. How they could communicate without speaking. How their very souls were knit together in purpose.

A sense of urgency pulsed through Jamie. Many times he'd seen a wounded man become receptive toward God's call at the height of his pain, only to recover and forget his mortality. Jamie had not a single doubt that the Lord had permitted this attack to capture Moberly's attention. But where to begin? Jamie already had learned much from Reverend Bentley's tutoring, especially that these aristocrats could take offense if wrongly addressed. But he must not lose this opportunity. *Wisdom, please, Lord.*

"You must forgive us for not waking Lord Bennington. Our main concern was tending your wounds and seeing you rested."

Moberly shrugged against his pillow. "I doubt he would have been concerned." The pain ripping across his face appeared more like damaged emotions than an injured body.

Jamie sat on the edge of the bed, hoping to set a mood of

familiarity. Hoping Moberly would not be offended. "My friend, even the tenderest of earthly fathers can disappoint us."

Moberly snorted, then cried out and grabbed his chest. "What is this? What happened to me?" Teeth gritted, he shoved away the goose down cover and clawed at his nightshirt.

Jamie grasped his hands. "I recommend you leave it alone, sir. You received a nasty knife wound, but Blevins stitched it together very nicely. Let's don't break it open."

Moberly's eyes widened. He touched the area with his fingertips. "Right over my heart. I might've died." He slumped back and looked vacantly toward the bed's canopy. "I might have died."

"God's mercy was on you," Jamie said. "No mistaking that."

"Yes," Moberly whispered. His gaze returned to Jamie. "Yes." A stronger tone. "Thank God. And you." His eyes grew red and moist. "You saved my life."

Jamie leaned a bit closer. "Perhaps. But I was merely God's instrument. You're right to thank Him."

Moberly gave out a mirthless laugh. "But why would He bother when my own father regards me as a parasite and cares not whether I live or die?"

His words slammed into Jamie's heart. How could anyone understand why Lord Bennington treated his sons so callously? "My friend, God desires to be a father to you. He longs to save your eternal soul. This is why you didn't die in the street last night."

Moberly appeared to consider the idea, and fear filled his face. "No. I have waited too long, done too much—"

"No." Jamie gripped his arm as he would a drowning man's. Moberly's words indicated he comprehended his own sinfulness. Surely that meant it wasn't too late for him. "Don't believe that lie. The blood Jesus Christ shed on the cross covers every sin. God's grace is offered as a free gift to you right now. All you need to do is accept it."

Moberly seemed to fold into himself. "No. It cannot be that simple." His gaze hardened. "There are rules and rituals and *righteousness*." His lips curled. "All the things I despise about religion and—"

"No!" Jamie prayed Robert wouldn't take his stern tone as an affront. "Christ's death and resurrection are sufficient to save the worst sinner. If we were required to do even one small thing other than accept His grace, none of us could be saved. Did He not say to the thief who was crucified beside him 'Today thou shalt be with me in Paradise'?"

Moberly's dark eyebrows met in a frown, and his left eye twitched. "I thought perhaps the man received a special dispensation."

Jamie shook his head. "I believe, in fact I am more than certain, that thief was meant for an example to us. As he was saved, so we can be saved." He leaned close again. "Believe in the Lord Jesus Christ, Moberly, and you *will* be saved."

A long, narrow swath of light shone from beneath the drapes onto the Wilton carpet at the center of the room. The smell of sweat vied with the scents of soap and lavender for preeminence. Moments passed without a sound in the room, not even a rustle. Some hours ago, a maid had started a fire in the hearth, and Ian kept it burning. A barely audible sigh came from across the room, and Jamie guessed both ladies were praying. He wondered how much longer he could sit up without rest.

"I will try," Moberly whispered.

Jamie's energies vanished, and his posture drooped. This was useless. The man did not grasp God's truth at all.

Jamie's head pounded, and he ached to go to his own chambers, his own bed. He glanced at Lady Marianne. Her eyes reflected the same weariness he felt. But Miss Kendall, who always carried herself with reserve, now sat at the edge of her seat and stared toward Moberly with her jaw set firmly and fire in her eyes. Jamie shook off his lethargy, which he realized was nothing less than the work of eternal darkness. He would, he *must,* continue his struggle for Moberly's soul.

"Faith is not something you can try, Moberly. Accept God's gift of eternal life, or reject it. There is no middle ground."

Moberly blinked. He opened his mouth…and closed it. Another moment passed. "I see. Yes, I think you are right about that."

"Well, then?"

He chuckled, but winced as if the effort pained him. "A bit pushy, aren't we?" Another chuckle, then he sobered as a tranquil expression smoothed the premature lines around his eyes. "I feel…there is…*peace*…here." He touched his chest and spoke in a hushed voice. "Peace such as I have never felt in my life. It floods me, floods my very soul." His eyes glistened with hope. "I have always known about God. I have seen His goodness in my stepmother and my sister. But now I *believe.* I accept Him. Why, Templeton, I think if I were to die at this moment, God Himself would take me up in His arms."

Jamie experienced his own flood of emotions—joy, gratitude, tranquility—and he cleared his throat. Before he could offer an affirmation to his new brother in Christ, Lady Marianne appeared at the bedside and kissed Moberly, pressing her cheek against his and blending her sweet tears with her brother's. Beyond her, Miss Kendall stood with lifted chin, her tear-filled eyes ablaze with victory. Jamie gave her a nod. When his energies had failed, her prayers had infused him with strength enough to complete his mission.

A sharp thump on the bedchamber door caused them all to jump. Before anyone could respond, Lord Bennington threw open the door and strode into the room, staring about at the occupants. Rage rode on his wrinkled brow, and his lips curled in a snarl.

"*What* is going on in here?"

Chapter Eight

Marianne stood like a shield in front of Robert's bed. Behind her, she heard his quiet groan, the sound of a man wounded deep within his heart. She had no doubt that if Papa had entered the room one minute sooner, her brother's immortal soul would still be in danger, perhaps lost forever.

"Robert was stabbed and robbed by footpads last night." She grabbed a quick, quiet breath that she might appear calm. "If not for Captain Templeton, he would have died."

Papa stared at her as if she were crazy. "Footpads, you say? Common street ruffians dared to assault a son of mine?" He strode toward the bed. "Move aside, daughter." His eyes blazed as he inspected Robert from head to toe as he would a piece of furniture. "Well, boy, are you going to live?"

Marianne saw a flash of anger on Jamie's face—fiery eyes and lips clamped shut. But she moved close to Papa and slipped her hand in his, hoping her presence might soften him. Robert's eyelids drooped with feigned laziness, and his lips formed a smirk, the bored expression he wore when Papa was present.

"I suppose I must live," her brother muttered. "If only to show my gratitude to Templeton here. 'Twould be deuced bad-mannered of me to pop off after all his trouble."

Papa looked across the bed at Jamie. "Are you injured?" His eyes blazed.

Jamie shrugged and returned a crooked grin that caused Marianne's heart to skip. "I believe we did more damage than we received, my lord."

"Ha!" Papa fisted his free hand and pummeled the air. "That's the spirit." He looked at Robert again. "Do plan to survive as best you can. With these despicable wars going on, I do not have time for a funeral."

Marianne thought she detected a tiny crack in Papa's voice, but perhaps it was wishful thinking.

"Marianne." He patted her hand. "You and Miss Kendall are dismissed. I commend your interest in your brother's welfare, but in the future, leave such ministrations to the servants."

She bit her bottom lip to keep from responding with anger. This was the closest to scolding her Papa ever came, but it was inconsequential in light of Robert's tragedy.

"Yes, Papa." She nudged past him and bent to kiss her brother's cheek. "I love you, dear one. Please rest until you are healed." The responding tear in the corner of his eye nearly undid her, and she hurried from the room to hide her own tears.

If Jamie had held the slightest scruple against spying on Lord Bennington, it just vanished. No decent man should treat a son so callously, no matter how that son behaved. But, like their king, these English aristocrats seemed to think their ranks and titles granted them the right to use all other beings in any manner they chose. From everything Jamie had seen, he could only conclude that, instead of seeing Moberly as a son to nurture and guide, Bennington had let him grow up like a weed and then despised him for it.

"Captain Templeton." His tone sounding almost jovial, the earl spoke across the bed as if Moberly were not there. "Lady Bennington has asked my permission to give a ball in your honor. She says your dancing master has given his approval for you to participate in some of the less complex dances. What do you say?"

Remember why you are here. Swallowing his bitterness on behalf of Moberly, Jamie forced a smile and a bow. "I would be honored, my lord."

"Very good. Now, I am off to Whitehall." The earl looked at Moberly with a bland expression. "See if you can keep my son from doing further damage to himself."

"Yes…my lord."

Bennington clearly did not notice Jamie's clenched teeth, for he strode from the room with his head held high, wearing his importance like a crown.

Moberly chuckled softly. "Let it go, Templeton. That's what I have to do. The old man is…what he is."

Jamie regarded his friend. Weariness once again deepened the premature lines on his face, and his pale, blotchy skin gave evidence of many late nights and much drinking. But a soft new light shone in Moberly's eyes, encouraging Jamie. He felt a pressing need to examine its cause.

"Before Lord Bennington came in, we were having a discussion—"

"Ah, yes." Moberly breathed out a lengthy sigh and tugged his covers up to his chin. "About my *new* Father…" He yawned, then winced, perhaps in pain. "We must talk about that soon…." His voice faded, and his eyelids drooped.

The young valet hovered near, so Jamie walked to the door. "I'll leave him in your good care."

More than exhausted, he trudged up the staircase to his own chamber, where in spite of his best efforts to keep quiet, he woke Quince.

"Did you learn anything?" Quince jumped up from the trundle bed and inspected Jamie's head wound, tsking his concern.

"No." Jamie waved him off and walked to the window to close the heavy velvet drapes. "The Lord seems to have altered my mission for the time being." He watched his friend, whose clownish smile hinted at some secret. "All right, then, out with it."

Quince cleared his throat, obviously pleased with himself. "If you want to learn what's going on with the aristocracy, it pays to fraternize with their servants."

Jamie threw himself on the four-poster bed, neglecting even to remove his shoes. "Brilliant. Absolutely brilliant." He rolled over and burrowed beneath the counterpane. "That's why you took leave of your considerable properties in Massachusetts and are acting as my valet." Sleep beckoned, but he could feel Quince tugging off the heavy footwear. This business of having a body servant had its advantages.

"Ah," Quince said, "but when one discovers where the master keeps his important papers…and the best time to access them—"

Jamie bolted up in the bed, fully awake and fully aware of the lump on the back of his head. He grunted, but shook off the pain and punched Quince's arm. "Good work, man. Tell me everything. How do we get to them?"

Chapter Nine

"Do listen to me, Robert." Marianne mustered the crossest look she could manage while feeling so happy. "It is far too soon for you to be riding again." Seated at the smaller of two oak tables in the sunny breakfast room, she turned to Jamie, who stood serving himself at the buffet. His dashing appearance in his newest gray riding clothes pleased her very much. "Captain Templeton, you must speak reason into my brother's barely healed head."

"Nonsense." Across the table from her, Robert waved his hand in a dismissive gesture. "I have lain about for nearly two weeks while the weather gets warmer, the grass becomes greener and everyone who's anyone is out and about." He popped a bite of toast and jam into his mouth.

The twinkle in her brother's eyes heartened Marianne. He truly did seem to have recovered, as evidenced by his voracious appetite. He would soon regain those few pounds lost during his convalescence.

"Then at least ride in the carriage with Miss Kendall and me." Marianne tilted her head toward Grace, taking in the scent of her lavender perfume.

"Lady Marianne," Jamie said, "the surgeon has given Mr. Moberly permission to resume his activities as he wishes. Doubtless he'll be happy to be out in the fresh air."

As he took his place beside her, amusement lifted one corner of his lips, and again Marianne was encouraged. And even more in love with him than before. Since Robert's injury, Jamie had spent hours with her brother every day, discussing Scriptures and other pleasant topics. The result was that, in these recent days, Robert had made every effort to be at the supper table on time, had borne up under Papa's comments well and had completely stopped drinking spirits—all due to Jamie's influence. If the good captain thought to dissuade her from her affections for him, he was certainly going about it in the wrong way.

"Very well, then." She sniffed, still pretending to be cross. "Just remember that I have advised a better course."

But she felt anything but cross. Today's early morning sunshine promised a grand April day at Richmond Park, where the four of them would meet with friends and enjoy a picnic. A longing struck her to make the most of the day, for she did not know when Jamie would be returning to East Florida. Although she could never wish him ill, she could not help but be happy that his ship required serious repairs before sailing back across the vast Atlantic. And fortunately, Papa seemed content to continue hosting him here in London.

"But since you insist upon riding," she said, "I shall ride, too."

Eyebrows shot upward, and if she was not mistaken, Grace's soft gasp held a modicum of delight. Marianne guessed she had not ridden in some time, for Mama no longer rode.

"Splendid," Robert said. "I'll warrant Templeton here hasn't ridden since our last foray to the park."

Jamie's smile flattened, and Marianne hoped she had not put him in an awkward situation.

"Of course you understand, Templeton," Robert said with a smirk, "that Miss Kendall will have Bess. We shall have to find another horse for you."

True alarm filled Marianne. Why had she failed to think this through? Bess was their gentlest horse. In fact, the only one they could depend upon always to be gentle. She noticed Jamie was concentrating on his plate and chewing his boiled eggs with fierce determination.

Without lifting his head, he shot a look of irritation her way. "I shall endeavor not to embarrass you, my lady."

Heat rushed to her face. These men would ever strive to prove themselves to one another, no matter what the cost.

She glanced across the table at Robert. He looked at Jamie, then back at her, and his eyes widened. One eyebrow lifted with an unspoken question. She could not stop her continuing blush, nor think of a single thing to say or do to divert the all-too-correct deduction written across his face. What would he do with the information? Would he protect her interests, as she had always tried to protect his? Or would he rush to Mama, or even Papa, and betray her, possibly causing Jamie to be banished from the house and Papa's good graces? Glaring at her brother across the table with her chin lifted and lips a determined line, she dared him to do his worst.

He grinned broadly and shook his head, and the tender look in his eyes washed away all her fears. But if Robert, with all his self-centeredness, could see that she and Jamie loved each other, surely others in the household could, too.

Jamie gripped the prancing gelding with his knees and secured his black riding boots into the stirrups. If he thought of the horse as a ship on an undulating sea, perhaps it would become easier to stay in the saddle. A lifetime of keeping his balance on rolling vessels had strengthened his leg muscles, a fact that now aided him as he sat on this chestnut horse aptly named Puck. The rascal was as full of mischief as Shakespeare's impish elf, not unlike Moberly.

Jamie could not fault the man for this choice of horses, for Bennington's town stable housed only so many mounts. But he felt certain Moberly chose this particular one to test Jamie's mettle. If that night outside the gaming hall wasn't sufficient, Jamie would show this coxcomb what he was made of…and enjoy every minute of it as he did. The lump he'd received at the hands of the footpads still ached from time to time, but his thick hair hid it from view. Moberly was thriving under all the attention his injuries attracted, and Jamie wouldn't diminish that by calling attention to himself.

Leading the group, Moberly rode his bay stallion next to Miss Kendall on Bess. Jamie followed beside Lady Marianne, forcing his attention away from her to the houses and businesses they passed. He'd learned that this part of London had burned to the ground over a hundred years ago, but the past century had erased all signs of the fire. The two- and three-story wooden or stone buildings were packed close together. In the streets, vendors hawked their wares, and dusty little shops hummed with customers. The smells of fish and bread, horses and garbage assaulted the senses.

"Captain Templeton." Lady Marianne nudged her spirited mare close to him. "Robert said we'll take a ride through Hyde Park before we go to Richmond Park, where the servants await with our picnic." Her wine-red woolen riding dress brought a rosy color to her smooth cheeks, and the fresh breeze carried her jasmine perfume his way. "Hyde Park has riding paths, and at this early hour, there will be no crush of riders."

"Very good, my lady." He risked a second glance in her direction, and a familiar pang struck inside his chest. His service to the Revolution notwithstanding, he was enjoying this prolonged stay in London because of the beautiful lady beside him. Perhaps it was not too wrong to permit himself the luxury of relaxing a bit in her presence.

They'd fallen into a pleasant companionship, at least when Moberly or Miss Kendall or one of Jamie's tutors was present. Under Mr. Pellam's supervision, he'd even managed to practice his dancing with her as his partner without succumbing to an excess of feeling. Of course, at that moment, his attention had been focused on his own two feet. At this moment, however, with the warmth of the April sun shining on their little group, all things seemed possible. And he confessed to himself that he loved her.

"Captain," Lady Marianne said, "may I speak to you about a matter of some delicacy?"

Had she read his heart? *Lord, please don't let her speak of it.* Jamie forced a bland expression to his face. "My lady?"

Her eyes sparkled with…playfulness? "Have you noticed that my brother and Miss Kendall seem quite compatible?"

Relief swept through him, and he shrugged. "I try not to concern myself with matters of the heart." Wrong thing to say. "Of other people's hearts. I mean—" He clamped his mouth shut, and heat shot up his neck. He rarely suffered a loss for words, except with this lady.

Her delightful laughter seemed to echo around him. "But can you say you have no concerns about your Quince and my Emma?"

He cleared his throat. "It is my understanding Miss Emma has your permission to…*speak* with Quince." How odd, the way these aristocrats ruled their servants' every move. Even if Quince were truly Jamie's servant, he could love whom he pleased. Nor would Jamie ever concern himself with his crew members' affections.

"Indeed she does." She exhaled a long sigh. "They, of all of us, have the least possibility of their hearts being broken."

"I don't understand. Why should Moberly and Miss Kendall not form an attachment?"

Marianne glanced sideways at him. "Why, now that you mention it, I cannot think even Papa would mind. But one never knows with him, and without his permission…" Her gaiety vanished into a frown. "I envy their freedom to love whom they will. Emma and Quince, I mean."

"My lady, please." Jamie envied that freedom, too, but it would be unwise to confess it to her.

"I would become a lady's maid if it meant I could marry as I wished." Her voice took on an edge, maybe even tears.

"Lady Marianne." He doubted he could withstand her crying. "You don't know what you're saying." A quick look about the street revealed that none of the inhabitants were close enough to hear them. On the other hand, some scruffy fellows stared at Lady Marianne as they rode by, and Jamie's riding crop burned in his hand at their boldness. If they dared to come near her—

"Here we are," Moberly called over his shoulder.

At last. Drawing in a deep breath as the party emerged from the crowded street into the fresh air, Jamie gazed around the park's wide green expanse edged with blooming trees and blossoming bushes.

With a wave of his riding crop, Moberly directed them to circle their horses. "Shall we walk a bit and smell the flowers?" The fond look he cast at Miss Kendall showed his preference for that activity.

"Hi ho, Moberly." Young Highbury galloped up on a fine

looking brown gelding. "Imagine meeting up with you here. Lady Marianne. Miss Kendall." He bowed to each in turn. "Hi ho, Templeton. How's our favorite American today? You look right well astride old Puck. What do you think of the news of our General Gage being driven out of Boston by your General Washington? I hear Washington generously permitted our troops safe passage to sail to Nova Scotia."

Jamie's belly clenched. If Bennington had not spilled this news the night before, Jamie might have given himself away just now with a great huzzah. "Such are the fortunes of war, I suppose. No doubt Gage will not sit idly in Canada for long."

Highbury laughed in his high-pitched way. "My father says the colonials will send all of our troops packing. What do you think?"

"I say, Highbury." Moberly reined his horse between Jamie and the pesky youth. "I care nothing for the troubles in America, but do have some respect for His Majesty's position. At least in front of the ladies."

"Very well." Highbury laughed again. "Tell you what. You and Templeton join me in a race around the park. These horses have not had a good run all winter, and my Socrates is eager to show what he's made of."

"A grand idea." Moberly's face brightened. "A race is precisely what I need."

"Most certainly not." Lady Marianne moved her horse beside Jamie. "I will not permit it."

Jamie ground his teeth. "If you please, my lady, I believe a race is exactly the thing."

Despite her continued protests, Moberly and Highbury marked out a course by pointing their riding crops.

Jamie's mouth felt as dry as last year's dead leaves littering the ground, but he forced down a swallow, forced down his fear. A familiar excitement and sense of competition began to fill him, and he set his feet more firmly in the stirrups. Puck nibbled grass, oblivious to what would soon be expected of him.

"Now," Moberly said, "since my beloved sister protests, I shall leave it to Miss Kendall to drop the handkerchief." He drew a silk one from his pocket and handed it to the lady. "When it hits the ground, we're off."

Miss Kendall's face was a mirror of Lady Marianne's, and both wore their fear like a mourning veil. The few denizens of the sparsely populated park somehow got wind of the event and gathered beside the pathways.

Her hand raised, Miss Kendall cast an apologetic glance toward Lady Marianne and dropped the handkerchief.

With merry cries, Moberly and Highbury dug in their heels, and their horses sprang away. Jamie swatted Puck's flank, but the gelding merely danced around in a circle. Lady Marianne reined back her own horse, which seemed eager to join the party. She eyed Jamie and shrugged, then swatted Puck across the flank with a cry of "Off you go, you silly nag."

Puck lurched into a run, knocking Jamie off center. He felt his upper body careening toward the ground, but tightened the grip of his knees and grabbed the opposite edge of the saddle to right himself. Again in the saddle, he crouched low on Puck's neck. The pain rattling his lower back soon numbed, and he gasped for breath, pulling in the odors of horseflesh with an occasional whiff of the nearby flowers.

Puck now seemed to realize what it was all about, so Jamie trusted the race to him as he would trust his ship to a seasoned helmsman. They galloped after the other two horses and soon gained on them. Cries and cheers met Jamie's ears as he thundered past a blur of people.

After what felt like an endless chase around the park, Jamie saw Lady Marianne ahead. Throwing up a prayer that Puck would know when to stop, Jamie felt a mad desire to win. He slapped the crop against Puck…to no avail. Highbury's horse pulled away and soon crossed the line scratched across the dry pathway by some enthusiastic by-standers.

Jamie tugged on the reins and brought Puck to a stop some twenty yards beyond the finish. Energy pulsed through him, almost lifting him from the saddle with the same elation, the same sense of victory he'd felt after a successful whale hunt. He'd done it. He'd conquered his fear and run the entire course. If he'd known riding a horse could be so invigorating, he would have taken up the practice long ago. Excitement, a sense of personal accomplishment and pure joy crowded his mind and heart as Puck trotted back to their waiting group.

Once there, he slid his feet halfway out of the stirrups and began his dismount. On the way down, he discovered his left boot would not come free. Puck shifted his massive weight, and Jamie felt a jolt of panic as he rolled toward the ground. The back of his head hit the hard-packed dirt in the exact spot where he'd been struck by the footpads, and pin-points of light stabbed his eyes. The last thing he heard was Marianne's voice.

"Jamie!"

Chapter Ten

"So there Templeton lay, dazed as a duck, with my sister and Miss Kendall nearly undone thinking we'd murdered Father's protégé."

Even Marianne found herself joining the laughter as Robert regaled their friends at Mama's ball. For Jamie had recovered and was none the worse for his accident, as evidenced by his flawless dancing in the first two sets.

"Permit me to say—" Jamie lifted his hands to quiet them "—landing on one's back in the ocean, even surrounded by thrashing whales, is much less dangerous than landing on hard English soil."

Laughter erupted again, and Marianne felt a measure of pride in how well he blended into this exalted company. Wearing his new periwinkle silk coat and white satin breeches, and his long blond hair held back in a queue with a black satin ribbon, he looked every bit as noble as any titled man in attendance. Perhaps even more so, for his sun-browned skin bore a healthy glow and set him apart from the powdered, foppish men around him. His dark brown eyes gleamed as he spoke, his American accent was giving way to English pronunciations, and his every gesture was filled with grace. Papa had outdone himself with Jamie Templeton. He had made him into a true gentleman and proudly introduced him to several exalted politicians and lords this very evening, each of whom had commended his loyalty to the Crown.

"Do tell us more about whaling, Captain Templeton." Miss Martin, the pretty daughter of a baron, who would one day inherit her own fortune, stood near Jamie sipping ratafia. Her green-eyed gaze never left his face, even when Robert was speaking. Marianne felt a twinge of annoyance. Last season Miss Martin had played with Robert's affections, then cut him. Everyone knew she was looking for a titled husband, but she would ever torment those whom she considered unsuitable. The game was played by several of the young ladies in this crowd. Jamie's good looks and graceful dancing brought them buzzing around him like bees, but not one would think twice about stinging him merely for her own amusement.

Jamie appeared to consider Miss Martin's question about whaling, but before he could answer, Mr. Highbury wedged himself into the group.

"I say, Templeton, I'm all keen on the happenings in America. Have you heard anything new?"

Several ladies tittered. Several gentlemen groaned. Marianne gave Jamie a sympathetic smile, for he blinked at Mr. Highbury as if he were some odd creature.

"Mr. Highbury," she said, "do you have any idea how difficult it was for me to secure an invitation for you and Eugenia? If my father hears you spouting your Whig opinions, he will be most displeased."

Robert nudged him with his elbow. "Indeed, perhaps you should stay out of Bennington's vision altogether." He tilted his head toward Papa, who stood across the room talking with Lord Purton.

As the musicians began another tune, Mr. Highbury winked at Jamie and ducked away. A surge of anger swept through Marianne. Mr. Highbury was more than a little obnoxious, and his casting aspersions on Jamie's character was simply too much. He would not even have been invited if not for his sister Eugenia, whom Robert now approached to claim a dance. The very idea. Thinking Jamie was disloyal to the Crown simply because he was an American.

The others dispersed, most taking their places on the dance floor. Marianne had declined an invitation so she could remain beside Jamie. She sipped her lemonade and moved closer to him, almost brushing his sleeve with hers as they watched the dancers.

"A very fine ball, Lady Marianne." He smiled down at her, but his eyes held caution. "Lady Bennington seems to be having a grand time."

Marianne saw Mama, with Grace Kendall beside her, chatting away in the midst of the older women seated in the far corner of the ballroom. "Yes, she does. And so does Papa." She noticed Papa chatting with his friends and laughing heartily, a good sign. "But I have not stayed with you to speak of them."

His smile dimmed. "Indeed? Then how may I be of service, madam?"

His formal tone, as devoid of emotion as John the footman's, stung her. "I require nothing. But I should like to warn you that Miss Martin and her friends may decide to make sport of you. Please guard your…your heart."

"Guard my—" Jamie gazed at her, and his formal facade melted into tenderness. "My lady, thank you for your concern. And please be assured that my heart is…well-guarded." A light sparked in his eyes, then vanished as he turned away and cleared his throat.

If she had even the slightest doubt about his love, it now disappeared. But even more, she stood in awe of his confidence and poise, surely the results of his being a self-made man. In this society, where birth and rank meant everything, her wellborn friends might scoff at such a notion. But she saw within Jamie something they would never possess. Now more than ever she knew she would give up everything for him. Could he not do the same for her? Could he not cease this foolishness and confess his love?

Jamie wondered how long he could stand beside Marianne—*Lady* Marianne—without surrendering to the constrained emotions swelling within his chest. Her curly black hair framed her porcelain cheeks, and her modest pink gown outshone the garish, wide-skirted fashions of many other ladies in the room. She wore jasmine perfume tonight. He liked the jasmine better than the rose, but the rose also—

Think of something else, man. Of the *Fair Winds* now being serviced across the Thames in the Southwark shipyard, under the watchful eye of his worthy first mate, Saunders. Of his crew, who had sworn themselves to good behavior as they awaited their return to East Florida. Of the cargo he would deliver there—fabrics, leather goods, perfumes, plows and harnesses, dishes…and several dozen crates of muskets from Spain that Lord Bennington knew nothing about.

"Have I commended you on your dancing, Captain Templeton?" Lady Marianne interrupted his thoughts with more than words. Her sweet smile contrasted with the tears at the corners of her eyes.

He looked away. "You have, my lady. Thank you. And you may thank Mister Pellam for his fine skills in teaching me."

"Yes, I shall do that." She lifted the delicate lace fan hanging on her wrist and began to wave it slowly.

The ladies of East Florida would appreciate fans. Fans, parasols, bonnets in the latest fashion—

"Have you recovered from your fall?" Her voice took on a higher, softer pitch.

"Yes. Very well, thank you." *No.* Sometimes his head pounded like Puck's hooves on the dry ground, especially at the end of the day. Especially when he was in her presence. Perhaps he'd suffered a concussion. He'd seen a man succumb to such repeated injuries—

"You cannot imagine how frightened I was when you fell off of Puck."

Yes, I can. You've shown me nothing but kindness and goodness. Your concern is everywhere in evidence, even to the protection of my heart against your friends. He forced a chuckle. "I was a bit alarmed myself."

Her responding laugh was more like a squeak. His resolve almost shattered.

"Would you excuse me, my lady." His own voice sounded thin. He knew it was bad form to leave her alone. But as he bowed to her, he looked into those blue, brimming eyes and knew he could not stay in her presence.

"Yes. Of course." She returned a curtsy. "Lord Goodwyn will soon claim his dance."

Unreasoning jealousy joined the warring emotions within Jamie's heart. "Ah, yes. The thin fellow." *Whom I could break like a stick.*

She smothered her laugh with her fan. "Shh. Here he comes."

The young viscount, dressed in green and blue, strutted toward them like a peacock about to spread its tail. He greeted Jamie, then offered his hand to Marianne, and off they walked to the dance floor. While her expression was pleasant enough, Jamie could see her sway away from Goodwyn when the man leaned near to speak to her. *Lord, forgive my unreasoning jealousy.*

With a mixture of relief and a sense of loss, Jamie forced his attention away from her to concentrate on the large ballroom's decor. The polished wooden floor gleamed in the light of hundreds of candles whose flames were magnified by exquisite girandoles, ornate candlesticks hung before tall mirrors to intensify the light. The tall windows had been opened wide, and red-and-gold-liveried servants waved large feathered fans to keep the crisp night air moving. The room was awash with the scents of countless perfumes. A table laden with punch, cakes and various liqueurs offered refreshment to the guests between dances. And among the powdered wigs and ceruse-covered faces were some people who had eschewed those hideous, impractical fashions. But with or without their masks, he could not discern the political leanings of any of them. Except for Highbury, who was becoming a serious nuisance. Fortunately, he was busy with the newly begun country dance in partnership with some young lady Jamie hadn't met.

The ballroom itself had seemed much larger during Jamie's dance lessons, but now, despite the brightness, the walls seemed to close in around him. In the midst of this mass of people, he longed for the open sea, where he could breathe again.

Across the room, Lord Bennington had lost his pleasant demeanor and waved his hands about, as he did when expounding on the Revolution. Even if that was not his topic, his familiar gestures brought to Jamie's mind his purpose for being here. This would be the perfect time to slip away and locate the secret desk drawer Quince told him about. Earlier, Jamie saw Lord Shriveham hand a document to Bennington, who treated it like a treasure and briefly retreated to his study.

No one seemed to notice Jamie move toward the large double doors and into the hallway, where another crush of people milled about or stood talking in groups. He slipped through, not looking directly at anyone, but focusing beyond and smiling as if his destination was a particular acquaintance. With only two friendly greetings from those he passed, he managed to make it down the wide staircase to the brightly lit first floor.

He kept a casual pace, stopping to admire a painting hanging in the hallway leading behind the stairs, stopping to adjust his silk cravat in a mirror a few feet away. He had his hand on the study door when he felt a sharp tap on his shoulder.

Stifling his alarm, Jamie feigned calm as he turned around.

"Hi ho, Templeton." Hugh Highbury stood there with a wide grin. "I'm so glad to have found you alone. We simply must talk about the war in the colonies."

A mix of relief and irritation swept through Jamie. He knew he should pretend to be insulted. But something in the younger man's eyes stopped him. He rested one shoulder against the study door, praying he would be able to find the right words. After all, this man and his father supported the Revolution in open defiance against their king and powerful men in Parliament, and he might know something of value. Jamie would be foolish to make him an enemy.

"Highbury, I came down here for a short rest." He

touched the back of his head. "That blow when I fell off the horse still has me a bit off balance."

"I'm terribly sorry, my good fellow." Highbury reached up to pat Jamie's shoulder. "Had I known you did not ride…" He smirked. "I no doubt would have challenged you, anyway."

Jamie winced and offered a weak chuckle designed to confirm his need for rest.

Highbury glanced around the candlelit hallway and up the stairs, then sniffed the air and cupped a hand behind his ear. "Can't see anyone. Can't smell anyone. Can't hear anyone. We're in the clear. Why don't we step into the privacy of Bennington's library, and you can tell me what old Washington and his friends are up to. Is it true this entire rebellion began in a Boston tavern?"

Jamie swallowed a groan. Those words revealed far more than Highbury could possibly realize. If he knew anything of value about the Revolution, he never would have asked such a foolish question. Nor would he be so flippant about it.

"Listen, Highbury." Jamie stood to his full height, head and shoulders above the other man, and leaned toward him like the sea captain he was. The shorter man blinked and his jaw went slack, just the effect Jamie had hoped for. "For you this is a game. But I could be accused of treason merely for meeting privately with a Whig. Surely you realize, as Lord Bennington's guest, I will defer to him in all things. Now, I don't have anything against you, lad, but if you have any decency, leave me alone so I can rest." For further effect, he once again put his hand on the back of his head.

"I—I say, Templeton, easy on." Highbury's shoulders slumped. "I'm merely looking for diversion." He waved in a dismissive gesture. "You cannot imagine how boring life can be when one is on the outs with the cream of society."

Comprehension swept through Jamie. He'd almost trusted this man. This silly, pampered pup. He clamped one hand on Highbury's shoulder harder than he needed to, and was rewarded when panic swept over the man's youthful face. "But look around, lad. You are right here among that cream of society tonight. Why are you wasting time with me when fifty eligible young ladies are no doubt awaiting your attention upstairs?"

Highbury shrugged. "I suppose." He brightened. "Yes, that's just the thing. I believe the minuet is up next, and I would loathe to miss it. You see, Miss Martin actually promised to dance with me, and she would never speak to me again if I stood her up."

Jamie gave his shoulder a hearty shove. "By all means, go. You must not keep Miss Martin waiting."

Grinning broadly, Highbury dashed toward the stairs and ran up them two at a time. Jamie waited until certain the young pup was gone for good, then ducked into the library, praying no one else would accost him.

The dark, quiet room was cool, with just a hint of Bennington's favorite tobacco in the air. Outside the velvet-draped windows, torches lit the street so guests could make their way to the door. Jamie could see drivers tending their carriages and footmen standing by to assist latecomers. At any time, one of them might peer in the window. In the torchlight, Jamie saw his own shadow flicker on one wall, but when he moved to Bennington's desk, darkness covered him. He sat on the tapestry seat of the ornately carved white chair and felt around the edges of the drawer. Quince said it was well known among the staff that this desk had a secret compartment where the earl stowed his latest missives from the king. In fact, Jamie had seen such a hiding place in the desk of Bennington's youngest son in East Florida.

Underneath the drawer, toward the back of the desk, he felt a latch and tried to open it. *Locked*. But a small bit of paper stuck out through the tiny slit between the compartment and the drawer. Jamie eased the sheet through, careful not to tear it, and slipped it under his waistcoat. He felt again to see if he could unlock the latch. A click echoed throughout the room, but instead of coming from the desk, it sounded from across the library. The wide door opened slowly, and a dark form entered, eerily lit from behind by the hallway candles.

Chapter Eleven

Jamie eased down in the chair, rested his head against the carved back and stretched out his legs. Surely no one would believe he'd chosen this place to sleep, but he had no other option but to pose that way.

As if in a familiar place, the person moved to the center of the room without bumping into any furniture.

"Jamie?"

He bolted to his feet. "Lady Marianne?"

She hurried to the desk and found a candle to light. "Mr. Highbury said you were ill." The flame revealed her lovely face pinched with worry. The scent of flint blended with her jasmine perfume.

He ached to comfort her, to reassure her, but shoved away that impulse. "And so he sent you instead of your father or brother or a servant?" Jamie thought he might strangle Highbury.

Lady Marianne laughed softly, but a little catch in her voice cut it short. "No. I asked him if he had seen you, and he told me you came in here to rest." She lifted the candle high. "Do not be alarmed. No one knows we are alone."

His heart pounded as if it would leap from his chest. If they were discovered, all would be lost, especially if the paper in his waistcoat was found. "And we shouldn't be alone, so I'll just say good-night, my lady." He strode toward the door.

"Jamie."

He stopped, all senses heightened by his near discovery. But he would not turn back to face her. "My lady?"

"How long must we pretend?" Her voice thick with tears. "My love for you did not diminish in your absence. It has grown stronger with you here." The sound of her soft footsteps on the Wilton carpet drew nearer. "And I believe you love me still."

Her tears had ceased. Jamie wished that gave him more relief than it did. But her words shattered the last of his reserve. "Yes, I do love you still." He still would not look at her, though at this moment he could cast his entire future to the wind just to proclaim that love to the world. *No.* One of them must be strong.

She touched his arm, and he covered her hand with his—an instinctive gesture he could not undo.

"Jamie." Her voice caressed his name.

He turned and pulled her into his arms, resting his chin on her head. Ah, the comfort of her responding embrace swept through his entire being, even as his heart ached for their impossible situation, even as he feared she might notice the crinkle of the stolen letter.

A soft, shaky laugh escaped her. "Will you kiss me?"

Shoving away every thought of intrigue, he pressed his lips against her smooth white forehead. "My beloved."

"But I meant—"

He cut her short, bending to kiss her lips gently, then firmly. "Will that do?"

Another shaky laugh. "Yes. It tells me what I wished to know." She moved out of his embrace and took his hand, leading him to the settee in front of Bennington's desk.

And now he sat there holding her white-gloved hands and thanking the good Lord they both had a strong measure of self-control. But it was those very hands that made marriage impossible for them. If he took her back to East Florida, no matter how his business prospered, she would have work to do, as did every person in that wilderness, whether wealthy or poor, master, mistress or servant. She would not be able to wear gloves for her work, and soon her hands would become callused like everyone else's. He could not do that to her.

"What are we to do, Jamie?" The innocence and trust in her voice stabbed into his heart.

He reached out to caress her smooth cheek. "Beloved, you realize there is nothing we *can* do, don't you? We are not well suited. Therefore, we must pray for strength to follow the paths God has chosen for us. For as surely as we sit here, He has ordained separate paths for us."

"No." She gulped back a sob, and he could see she was trying not to cry. It was no use. A flood of tears poured down her cheeks, and she grasped his hand tighter. He bent close and touched his forehead to hers. *This too shall pass,* he told himself. *One day this pain will subside.* But he'd never been successful at lying to himself.

Marianne could not stop her tears, but with deep breaths, she managed not to sob. She would save that for later in her bedchamber. Despite her denial, she knew Jamie spoke the truth, although it stirred a bitter rebellion within her. There simply must be a way for them to share a future together.

"I do wish to follow God's path." She reached for the handkerchief in her sleeve and dabbed her cheeks. "But I am not convinced His will is to separate us."

Jamie took the handkerchief and finished the job of patting away her tears, a tender gesture that calmed her. "He's already separated us through our births, and the work He's given each of us will take us to different places." Sorrow creased his broad forehead.

"Yes, you have important work to do. But what work has God given me? I am pampered by my parents and society, and I know full well my uselessness on this earth."

"How can you say that?" He reached out as if to touch her cheek again, but then withdrew his hand. "Your charitable work among London's orphans is an example to that same society, and I know it comes out of a true Christian heart."

"But are there not poor people everywhere? I can minister to the needy wherever the Lord sends *you*."

"Not at sea. Not to my crew." His words were a whisper, yet she flinched at this truth.

"But will you always sail your own ship? As you prosper, will you not hire others to import your wares so you can settle in comfort either here or in East Florida?"

He started to speak, but she touched a finger to his lips. "Would we not have a lovely life there? You and I, Frederick and Rachel. Oh, Jamie, I so dearly long to know my brother's wife, my own dear sister. Will you not take me there to meet her?"

Jamie moved back, staring beyond her as if contemplating her words. But then he shook his head. "Lord Bennington will never approve our marriage."

"Perhaps we should give him a chance to approve or disapprove. He surely thinks well enough of you. He has made you like a son, even favored you over his own." She felt like a traitor to Robert for saying it. William, Thomas and Frederick had all found their places in life, but dear Robert was still far from it, even with his recent improvements. "We have not been fair to him. We must give him a chance to say yes or no."

"But what if it's no, as it likely will be?"

"I cannot think he would deny me my happiness when he himself has been so happy in marriage with Mama."

A loud sneeze came from the room's other settee, which faced the hearth. Marianne jumped, and Jamie drew in a soft breath. The man chuckled as he peered over the settee back. His face was shadowed, but the well-formed shape of his head was unmistakable.

"Well, isn't this a pretty pickle?"

"Robert!" Marianne thought she might faint. "What are you doing here?"

Robert sat up and scratched his jaw. "I came to escape the ball."

"But you were having such a grand time." Marianne feared some lady had wounded him.

"Perhaps I should say I came to escape trouble." He rose and crossed the room. "The brandy looked all too inviting, and Tobias Pincer was there waving a glass under my nose." He gave Jamie a weak smile. "I turned him down, but somehow I do not feel as if I entirely won that battle."

"Pincer." Jamie's voice resounded with disdain. "I thought you got rid of him."

"I did, but his father has some influence with Bennington, so I certainly could not avoid him." Wearing a teasing grin, Robert sat on the chair next to the settee and looked back and forth from Jamie to Marianne. "So my suspicions are correct. What are we going to do about this fine mess?"

Jamie cringed. Things were getting far too complicated. He'd nearly lost his life—twice. His love for Marianne had no future, he felt the burn of an important document against his chest, and now Moberly was putting himself in the mix. Had he heard Jamie examining the desk? What a fool he'd been for not searching the dark corners of the room first. Moberly hadn't made a sound, nor had the scent of his bergamot cologne carried across the room.

Jamie must turn this conversation away from delicate matters of the heart. "Why don't you feel as if you won the battle against the brandy?"

Moberly slumped in his chair. "Strange, is it not? I turned away from it, but I wanted it very badly. I went away feeling deprived and cross that other men can drink and I cannot. Once I begin, I cannot stop." He rested his elbow on the chair arm and propped his chin on his hand. "Even now, my mouth waters at the thought of brandy."

"Oh, Robert." Marianne reached out to squeeze her brother's arm. "I am very proud of you. I had the lemonade. It is quite tasty and has a splash of strawberries. Will you not have some of that?"

He gave her a paternal smile. "Yes, I should do that. Next time I will." He straightened and patted her hand. "But for now, here we are, and you two still have not answered my question."

Jamie permitted himself to feel a bit relieved. Moberly didn't seem in any way suspicious of him. The best way to handle the other situation was straight on. "If you heard our conversation, my friend, you know of our feelings for each other. But you also know the impossibility of our being any more than friends. Please help me convince your sister of this painful truth." How he regretted his confession of love to her. He should have walked right out of the room...

"Well…" Moberly drawled the word. "You could elope. There would be a bit of a scandal, but then, society needs one of those from time to time. Eventually it would die down, and you could live on in bliss, oblivious to it."

Jamie stiffened. "Lord Bennington has done nothing but good for me. I would never do that to him." Except for advising the king to send thousands of soldiers to quash the Revolution.

Moberly's laugh was sardonic. "Ah, my good man, I would do *that* to Bennington. But then he would disown me completely, and my ladylove would suffer for it."

"Speaking of your ladylove." Jamie grasped this diversion. "You and Miss Kendall enjoy each other's company." He glanced at Marianne for her confirmation.

She nodded and gave Moberly a mischievous smile. "You do indeed."

Moberly snorted. "And how will penniless I provide for penniless her?" A pained, wistful look overtook his shadowed countenance. "Indeed, how?" Again he snorted. "I should have gone into the church. Father could have found me a living among his friends. But alas, I came to faith far too late."

"Why too late?" The idea pulsed through Jamie. "You have your Oxford education. You know your Scriptures. With the proper mentor from among the clergy, you could become a very fine minister."

Moberly's frown lessened. "I was joking, but—"

"But why not?" Marianne's face glowed with love for her brother. "Do you have any idea how long Grace has prayed for you?" She bit her lip. "Oh, do not tell her I told you. She would be mortified. But if anyone would suit for a minister's wife, it is she."

A smile broke over Moberly's entire face. "I will…it seems strange for me to say this…*pray* about this matter. Yes, I will pray, first, that the Lord will show His will regarding my future. And second, that He will make Miss Kendall a part of that future."

"Well reasoned," Jamie said. "I'll pray likewise for you."

"And I, too." Marianne stood. "Now, we must return to the ball. Mama will be disappointed to find us shirking our hosting duties."

Jamie and Moberly rose, each offering her an arm. With a laugh, she took both of them, and the three proceeded to the door. "We look like a trio of conspirators, do we not?"

Her words sent a chill down Jamie's spine.

Marianne lay abed that night thinking of all that had transpired. Although Jamie had confessed his love, they had not settled anything. But if he thought she would give up on their future, he was quite mistaken. Robert's suggestion about elopement had long ago occurred to her, but that would ruin Jamie's partnership with Papa. Somehow she must find a way either to break his resolve against asking Papa for her hand, or throw all to the wind and follow him back to East Florida, which would protect Jamie and put all the blame on her shoulders.

How could it be accomplished? Her brother Thomas was an officer in His Majesty's navy. Perhaps he could see to her passage. No, Thomas was all rules and order. He would never help her against their father.

She stared through the darkness toward the little chamber where Emma slept. When Marianne came upstairs after the last guest left the ball, her servant seemed particularly happy. Upon examination, she'd confessed to a pleasant visit with Aaron Quince under the watchful eye of Mrs. Bennett, the housekeeper. As surely as Marianne trusted Jamie's integrity, she trusted his Quince not to play with Emma's heart. She fully understood that if they married, Emma would return to East Florida with him. While Papa might be mildly displeased to have a servant desert his household, he would not go against Mama, who had brought the orphaned Emma into their home.

Feeling far from sleep and more than a little envious, Marianne let her imagination wander. She could see herself bundled up in a plain brown cloak, boarding the *Fair Winds* as Emma's lady's maid. No one would know the difference, even Jamie, until they were far out to sea. She laughed into the darkness at the silly idea. Then sat straight up in her bed.

Perhaps the idea was not so silly, after all.

Chapter Twelve

The message, informally scrawled on foolscap, held helpful information, some of which General Washington might already know. The King's 60th Regiment of Foot, which the general might well have fought alongside during the French and Indian War, had been serving in the West Indies in the ensuing years. Now they would be removed to East Florida and serve under Colonel Thomas Browne, a colonial from Georgia who'd suffered at the hands of Patriots for his loyalty to the king.

Jamie chafed at not being able to get this vital information to Washington as soon as possible. But until his ship was seaworthy, he must remain in England. He and Quince often reminded each other that they were doing what they'd been sent to do, and must trust God to open opportunities where He willed. After copying the missive in the early morning hours, Jamie left it to Quince to slip back to the library with the stealth of his Shawnee grandfather and replace it in the desk. Now that they knew where information was to be had, they would check often. In the meantime, boredom often set in for both men.

Although Quince had worked his own farm in Massachusetts, with leisure times only in the dead of winter, Jamie was more used to long stretches of inactivity while his ship sailed from port to port. After crew drills and other exercises, he filled his time by reading the Scriptures or lighter fare, and keeping busy about the vessel. But most of these aristocrats seemed to have honed their skills at indolence. While they found contentment in sleeping half the day, visiting and gossiping with one another, and attending parties and balls, Jamie's hands ached to work. He feared that by the time the *Fair Winds'* hull and mast were repaired, his hard-earned calluses would be worn away.

He managed to spend some of his time traveling to various suppliers and arranging the goods he would take back to East Florida. In addition to household goods and luxuries for the wealthy, the plantation owners needed metalworks to build their own foundries now that they could not do business with the northern colonies. Jamie could supply some of their needs, such as the Swedish bar iron on order from Birmingham. The *Fair Winds* was being reinforced even now to carry the heavier cargo. But it would take many more ships and many more trips between the continents to import everything the burgeoning colony required to be self-sufficient.

Sometimes his divided interests wore him down, especially since he seemed not to be able to get back into Bennington's library alone. The earl had invited him to read any of the countless leather-bound books that lined two walls floor to ceiling. But when Jamie did so, Moberly or Miss Kendall or Marianne or the ever-present Reverend Bentley would also be reading there. Many evenings during supper Bennington would mention progress in the war against the colonists. But Jamie could not detect anything further regarding the Crown's plans for defending East Florida, or any helpful information about troop action in the northern colonies.

At least Marianne seemed to have reconciled herself to the impossibility of their going beyond friendship, for she no longer cast wistful glances in his direction, glances that cut into his soul and distracted him. In fact, her cheerful disposition had brightened the entire household these past weeks. For his own part, after those brief sweet kisses the night of the ball, he felt something settle in his own heart. To know such pure and tender love, though denied its fulfillment, was still a gift from the Lord. Jamie would treasure the remaining time with Marianne and thank God for every moment they spent together, however formally they must conduct themselves.

"How do you stand for it, my friend?" Quince folded Jamie's new gray jacket and placed it in a trunk. "If anybody told me Emma and I couldn't marry, we'd elope in the middle of the night."

"That's exactly what I'd expect of you, and I'd not fault you for it." Jamie stared out the window into the bright May sunshine. "But can't you hear me telling Bennington 'by the by, old man, in addition to my using our partnership to spy on you, I'm also stealing your daughter'?" He looked down on two servants sweeping the back terrace, and envied their industriousness…and the simplicity of their lives. "If spying on the man strains my sense of honor, elopement would destroy it altogether."

Quince grimaced. "Under the circumstances, it would be reprehensible, wouldn't it?" He brought another jacket from the wardrobe. "Are you going to help me with this?"

"You're the valet, not I." Jamie crossed his arms and leaned against the wall. "I think you've found your calling, my friend."

Quince glared at him, but there was mischief in his grin. "Shall I dump it all on the floor and let you pack for yourself?"

"Now, now. Let's not take offense." Jamie crossed the room and began to carry items from the wardrobe to the trunk. "I must say, I never expected to own so many clothes, nor such fine ones. Have Ian or Greyson told you what I'll need for country living?" Jamie laughed at his own words. "Lord, what've You brought me to? An orphaned boy and lowly whaler playing with the aristocracy."

Quince clapped him on the shoulder. "And you play the part well, Cap'n Jamie." He surveyed the growing stash of clothes. "Yes, we should take all of it. Ian says the family's months at the country manor are filled with even more activities than their season in the city."

"I suppose it depends on what you consider 'activities.' Other than their frivolous nonsense, they don't seem too full of activity," Jamie said. "I'll arrange with Moberly to have horses available for us to return to the city and see to the *Fair Winds*. When I was at Southwark yesterday, she looked well on her way to being mended. They can step up the mast in another month and start the rigging. What's our old friend François said about the arrival of the muskets?"

Quince snorted. "Who could have guessed that arrogant fellow hates the English so much? When he brought the gray jacket yesterday, he told me his sources require anonymity. But he also said his latest news from France indicates some important people are backing our Revolution. Of course, young Louis will want us to succeed if only to needle the English…and repel their interests on the Continent."

"That kind of help will be a blessing indeed. But what about the weapons?"

"We'll have the details of where to get them by the time the ship's ready to sail."

Jamie felt a sense of reprieve. Once he had the Spanish muskets, he might not be able to return to Lord Bennington's hospitality. And he was not yet ready to say goodbye to Marianne.

Seated in the family carriage with Mama and Grace, Marianne watched the passing scenery of the Surrey countryside with a mix of joy and sorrow. She longed to return to Hampshire and Bennington Park, for she preferred the country over the city. But she had no doubt this would be the last time she ever visited her childhood home. With this in mind, she treasured each sight, each fragrance, each moment with Mama and Robert.

With Robert especially. Her dear brother seemed a different man since Jamie had convinced him to trust in God's mercy. He confided his lack of confidence in approaching Papa regarding service in the church, but he did spend many hours with Grace. Marianne could see them growing closer, could see Robert growing in his faith. And while he said nothing more about her relationship with Jamie, he did his best to arrange times when the four of them could be together. Perhaps Mama sensed a romance for Robert, too, for she granted Grace an unusual amount of freedom.

On May Day, they had at last enjoyed their picnic at Richmond Park. What a lark it had been to spread out linen tablecloths on the green grass and enjoy cold chicken, salad, hothouse strawberries, and cakes, and to greet their many friends. With the social season soon to end, everyone seemed eager to gather as often as possible, and the next two weeks had seen a flurry of parties and balls, few of which members of Bennington's household attended. Marianne found she did not miss the events in the slightest.

Now, as the end of May neared, the closed carriage wended its way home through the pine forests that shrouded the Portsmouth Road, while Robert and Jamie rode alongside, their guns and swords at the ready in case highwaymen dared to attack. Papa would join the family as soon as Parliament adjourned.

Marianne experienced several moments of guilt over being glad for her father's absence from the family circle. Without pressing duties to king and country, he often bore down a bit harder on his family and might notice how often she and Jamie were together. She must find ways to avoid his scrutiny. Glancing out of the window, she watched Jamie riding beside Robert. Pride filled her over how well he had learned to manage Puck, and even seemed to have formed a friendship with the frisky horse.

As she watched, Robert reined his Gallant near Jamie. "Can I interest you in a race to Portsdown Hill?" He pointed with his riding crop. Marianne could hear her brother's teasing tone.

"Oh, Robert, do not—" She started to put her head out through the open window.

"Now, now, my dear." Mama touched her arm. "Do let the men have their fun. Moberly is the picture of health these days, and I'll warrant Captain Templeton has learned to stay astride by now."

As the thunder of racing hooves met her ears, Marianne's heart dipped to her stomach. She glanced between Mama and Grace, and her face grew hot. Mama's mild expression revealed no deeper meaning beyond what her words conveyed. But Mama could surprise a person, and Marianne knew better than to assume anything. If she were twelve years old again, she would confess everything and cast herself upon Mama's mercy. But to do so would destroy everything. No, if Marianne planned to follow Jamie to East Florida, it must be without Mama's knowledge, for she would never approve of such a scheme. She had been heartbroken when Papa sent Frederick to the colony, and she would be devastated when Marianne left.

With a soft laugh that she feared sounded more giddy than casual, Marianne conceded Mama's assertion. "Yes, Robert has never been healthier…or happier." From the corner of her eye, she could see Grace's pink cheeks. "And I suppose the captain's riding has improved. But tell me, Mama, what plans have you made for our entertainment these next months?"

Mama's eyes lit up. "The viscount has accepted our invitation to summer at the Park. He and Lady Mary are bringing the children, so we may expect some lively games every day."

"How grand. I shall be delighted to see my nephew and nieces." Marianne's oldest brother, William, and his viscountess, Mary, were a bit stuffy, but their children made up for it with merry antics that amused the entire household.

"And you, my darling." Mama's eyebrows rose. "What are your plans?"

Marianne started. "My plans? What do you mean?"

Mama blinked. "Why, do you plan to have your usual parties for the village children? The sweetmeats for them after church each Sunday?" Again, her expression betrayed nothing.

And again, Marianne's laugh sounded a bit giddy in her own ears. "Oh, yes, of course. I would not wish to disappoint the children." *This will be the last summer I see them.* The thought made her heart ache. "And I'm looking forward to our traditional garden party in June."

"Ah, yes. The highlight of our summer."

The carriage emerged from the forest and slowed, soon to be surrounded by a flock of fluffy, bleating sheep.

Marianne waved her fan. "Ah, yes, the distinctive sounds and smells of Surrey."

Mama smiled but also tilted her head in a chiding fashion, for she felt that ladies should never complain. "But can you not also smell the rich fragrance of the earth? See how green the grass and trees are." She waved a gloved hand toward the window, which framed a view of Surrey's verdant hills. "Ah, how I look forward to working with my roses once again. And once Bennington comes home, summer will truly begin for me." Her eyes shone with anticipation. Mama always presented a picture of grace, but summers in the country brought out her very best.

Marianne forced a responding smile, but felt it waver, so she stared out of the window at the landscape. No doubt Jamie and Robert had completed their race and awaited the ladies at the top of Portsdown Hill, where they would disembark from the carriage to take in the view before making their descent. Crossing from Surrey into Hampshire was Marianne's favorite part of the ten-hour trip from London each spring. After months away from Bennington Park, she never failed to be awestruck over the beauty of God's creation visible in the vast panorama laid out before her. But this year, she felt only heartache. How could she leave it all behind?

Chapter Thirteen

If the invigorating race up Portsdown Hill wasn't enough to make Jamie breathless, once he and Puck reached the crest at Devil's Cleft, the spectacular scenery of the green, rolling hills of Hampshire viewed from this nearly five-hundred-foot elevation caused him to inhale in wonder. Then, with the intake of air, the familiar scent of the ocean met him, causing a painful ache in his chest. To his left lay Portsmouth, where the Royal Navy's vast fleet lay anchored. The sight was so impressive he could not help but question how the colonies' few ships would have any success against them.

A few miles beyond lay Southampton, where merchant vessels docked. The sight of countless vessels in both ports made him long for the *Fair Winds,* made him long to sail across the wide Atlantic toward home, where he could take a more active part in the Revolution. Perhaps he would offer to have his sloop more heavily armed for use in the war, for with his present defenses the smallest British man-of-war could sink him. But those thoughts were for another time. Right now, the splendor of the setting before him served as a reminder of all the beauties in England claiming a large portion of his affection.

"I say, old man." Moberly, equally breathless, reached the summit and reined his Gallant beside Jamie's Puck. "'Tis not wise to run a horse up such a hill."

Jumping down from his heaving, sweating mount, Jamie cringed. "Bad form on my part. I should have realized…" As captain of his own ship, he knew when to ease up on his crew. How foolish not to grasp the needs of this magnificent animal.

Moberly dismounted and came to check Puck's eyes and legs. "There, boy, you're all right. Never mind, Templeton. No harm done. I'm the one at fault. Should have warned you. Old Puck likes to run full out, but he's not always smart about hills and such. Do not give it another thought." He nodded toward their right. "Bennington Park, over there."

Only a little relieved by his words, Jamie followed Moberly's gaze toward a vast manor house in the distance, set on a lesser hill but nonetheless imposing. Once again, wonder stole his breath. So this was where Marianne grew up, where she became the genuine soul he loved so dearly. Even London's snobbish, irreverent society could not damage the purity of her character. In this place, Jamie would be hard put not to abandon all his resolve to maintain his emotional distance from her. But of course he must.

Rolling, grass-covered hills stretched before them to the north and east, with occasional rock and chalk outbreaks jutting to the surface. In the distance, countless sheep appeared as white dots on a carpet of green. At the sight of it all, peace swept through Jamie, and an assurance that all would be well.

The black-red-and-gold Bennington coach lumbered up

beside them and stopped, its four horses echoing Puck's labored breathing. Wiggins, the driver, set the brake, and three footmen descended from the top.

"Lady Bennington." John the footman approached the coach door. "Will you walk down the hill today?"

The lady appeared in the window. "Yes, John. Thank you."

The footmen assisted the ladies from the conveyance, and Jamie and Moberly joined them. His senses already heightened by the race and spectacular view, Jamie felt a mad impulse to claim the right to escort Marianne down the steep incline ahead of them. Before he could put the plan into effect, Lady Bennington smiled up at him from beneath her broad-brimmed hat.

"Captain Templeton, may I take your arm?"

"It will be my honor, my lady." Indeed, it would. And he felt more relief than disappointment over not accompanying Marianne. Surely the Lord had intervened to keep him from a situation in which he might be tempted to say too much. Furthermore, in his two months as a guest in Lady Bennington's home, he had yet to have a private conversation with this kind, elegant woman.

Taking particular care to guide the lady to the smoothest parts of the rutted road angling down the hill, Jamie permitted himself to relax. He felt certain that manners dictated he should wait for her to address him, but words of praise for the landscape before them burned inside him.

"What a lovely day for travel." Lady Bennington spoke his very thoughts. "Tell me, Captain, what do you think of our Hampshire countryside?" Only a hint of pride edged her tone, and her face beamed. Without doubt, Marianne's gentle nature and flawless grace came from her mother, as did her beauty.

"Very fine country, indeed, madam."

She glanced up at him with eyes as blue as Marianne's. "Tell me about your home. Nantucket, I mean."

Jamie drew her off the road while the coach rumbled past. Two of the footmen walked beside the lead horses and held their harnesses, while Wiggins kept a hand on the brake. Dust flurried about them, and Lady Bennington brought up her fan to wave it away. Once the coach had passed them, they resumed their walk.

"Nantucket is a fine piece of land. Though it is more sand than grass, it still provides sufficient pasture for our sheep." He nodded toward the grazing flocks in the distance, and an unexpected thread of homesickness wove through his heart. His beloved sister still resided on the island of their birth. Now that the British navy had impressed most of the Nantucket whalers into English service, Jamie feared Dinah and his childhood friends would suffer terribly despite their neutrality toward the war. But he would not mention such unpleasantness to Lady Bennington. "The Quakers who settled the island in the last century have bequeathed it a legacy of faith."

"Ah, yes. The Quakers." Lady Bennington continued to wave her fan. "I have known several fine Christians who are Friends." She glanced at his brown riding clothes, complete with brass buckles and buttons. "May I assume you are not of that persuasion?"

"No, ma'am." Jamie's heart warmed. If the discussion was to be about his faith, he would gladly tell her everything. "While I respect their interest in seeking an inner light for spiritual guidance, I endeavor to depend upon Scripture to guide me, lest my heart mislead me." His own words reminded him that only in Scripture would he find strength for the days ahead.

"Ah, very good." Her smile was placid. "I noticed your enjoyment of the services at St. Paul's. I hope you will equally enjoy Reverend Bentley's sermons at Bennington Park."

Jamie stepped over a slight dip in the road. "The good reverend has been most helpful in guiding me through the complexities of the social graces." He wanted to laugh, thinking of how his crew would mock his fancy new manners on their return voyage. "I'm certain he will prove equally proficient in his pastoral duties."

"You will not be disappointed." Lady Bennington peered over her shoulder, and he followed her gaze. Several yards back, Robert escorted the other ladies, while John the footman walked at the rear, leading Gallant and Puck. John's diligent perusal of the surrounding landscape was no doubt meant to check for any highwaymen who might be lurking nearby.

"And now you must tell me about East Florida." Lady Bennington's eyebrows lifted, as though her words held more than a surface meaning.

"'Tis quite a wilderness, madam, though not totally uninhabitable." Jamie turned away with a grimace. These were not soothing words for her. "But you may be very proud of your son, for he is proving to be an excellent force for good in St. Johns Towne."

"Indeed?" A tiny catch marred her melodious voice.

Her maternal tenderness brought a twinge to his chest, and he wondered how it would have been to grow up under his own dear mother's care. "Indeed, my lady. Under Frederick Moberly's watch, civilization spreads deep into the land. His father's plantation prospers under his management, and all of the people along the St. Johns River, whether plantation owner, merchant, slave or indentured servant, find him the most just of magistrates."

Moisture rimmed her eyes even as she smiled. "Yes, Frederick has always been diligent in his duties and fair to those under his care."

Ahead, at the bottom of the hill, the coach awaited them, but Jamie felt a strong impulse to tell her more. "My lady, please permit me a kinsman's pride over the good woman your son has married."

She gasped softly. "Why, yes, Bennington told me she is your cousin." Her smile grew radiant, and her face a lovely older version of Marianne's. "That makes us related by marriage. Dear Captain Templeton." She gave his arm a gentle squeeze. "If your cousin Rachel is anything like you—"

"My lady," Wiggins called from atop the coach. "Will you ride now?"

Jamie assisted Lady Bennington back into the coach, and the rest of the party all clambered back to their earlier places to resume the journey to Bennington Park. But as Jamie remounted Puck and urged him to follow the others, he felt an odd confusion stirring within him. Was it merely wishful thinking, or had Lady Bennington been interrupted just as she was about to bestow her approval upon him?

As they continued toward Bennington Park, Marianne could barely keep from squirming on the coach's red velvet seat like an ill-mannered schoolgirl. Questions and speculations scurried through her mind as she wondered what Mama had said to Jamie. Of course, Marianne could never ask Mama, but their little visit must have been pleasant, for when Jamie assisted Mama into the coach, they exchanged earnest pleasantries emphasized by sincere smiles. At the first opportunity, she must try to ferret out the information from Jamie.

Calming herself so as not to draw Mama's scrutiny, Marianne turned her thoughts toward Bennington Park. Unlike some of her friends, she found life to be much more engaging and enjoyable in the country than in the city. In anticipation of a last summer of gaiety, she longed to stick her head out and see the manor house as they approached it. The most she could do was lean close to the window as the coach hastened along the winding, tree-lined lane as if the horses and driver were as eager as she to be home again. Familiar woodlands, gently sloping downs, the private lake, and the village beyond the manor house all beckoned to her.

At last the coach broke from the last stand of trees and the gray stone mansion appeared in all its beauty. Marianne's heart jolted as never before. Home, if only for a few more months. And she had much to see, much to cherish before she said goodbye to it all forever.

Chapter Fourteen

"Bertha." Marianne hurried into the musty-smelling attic room of the manor house. "We are home for the summer." As she knelt by the heavy upholstered chair where her old nurse sat, her voluminous skirts puffed with air and then settled about her. There, light beams from the single window shone on airborne dust particles, sending them into a swirling tempest.

"Lady Marianne." The nearsighted woman dropped her knitting to her lap and reached out to take Marianne's face in her soft, wrinkled hands. "Oh, my child, how I have missed you." Tears slid down her lined cheeks, but her smile was radiant.

"And I have missed you, my darling." Marianne's heart ached at the thought of the sorrow Bertha soon would feel. Once Marianne left England, it was doubtful they would ever see each other again this side of heaven.

"Now, you must tell me all about your season." Bertha picked up the woolen scarf she had been knitting and resumed her work. "Did you meet any fine young gentleman worthy of my little girl?"

Marianne laughed. "No, dear, I did not meet anyone new." Her nurse had asked the same question for the past four years upon the family's return from London. But despite her gift of discernment, she had failed last year to realize Marianne's heart had been claimed.

"Ah, no one *new*." Bertha's eyebrows rose in thick gray arches. "But there is something you are not telling me."

Marianne seldom did well at keeping secrets from Bertha, who was more like a grandmother than a servant to her. But this time she must hold her own counsel.

"What I will tell you is that the orphans at St. Ann's were delighted with the wonderful mittens and scarves and hats you knitted for them. Many a child keeps warm because of these hands." She reached out to envelop and still the busy fingers that had cared for her since birth.

A glow softened the wrinkles on the old woman's face. "God is more than generous to permit me to perform this service in my last years. One longs to be ever useful, you know." Her gaze, while a bit unfocused, settled on Marianne's eyes. "You have not diverted me, my little lady. But I am so pleased to see you that I shall not press you." She reclaimed her hands and set to knitting again. "When you are ready, I will be grateful to hear it all."

Marianne leaned close and nudged aside the woolen scarf, laying her head on Bertha's lap and closing her eyes. How good it would be to have a confidante in her plans. But Bertha's loyalty extended beyond Marianne to Mama and ultimately to Papa, whose generosity provided her a home for as long as she lived. She would be bound by honor to report such a scheme as an elopement. Well, not exactly an elopement. A runaway? Marianne's insides quivered at the thought of what she was planning.

"Shh, my dear one." Bertha must have set aside her

knitting, for she placed both hands on Marianne's head as she always had when praying for her. "Seek God's wisdom, and let Him guide your path," she whispered.

Even through her thick coiffure, Marianne felt the tender touch of those guiding hands. Warmth spread through her like the blessing of a biblical patriarch, sweeping aside her embattled emotions and replacing them with peace.

This is the man you will marry. Thus had her prayer been answered two long months ago, and thus she continued to believe. She had searched the Scriptures for some example of what to do, but none was to be found there. With no other recourse but to stow away aboard Jamie's ship so that honor would require him to marry her. How else could God's will be accomplished?

She permitted herself a few tears, enough to dampen Bertha's gray muslin skirt. But she would not burden the woman with her secrets. Lifting her head and brushing away the moisture from her cheeks, she patted Bertha's hands.

"Take up your knitting, for I have many stories to tell you." Marianne rose and fetched a straight-backed chair to sit beside her nurse. "Now, do not be alarmed, but Robert had quite an adventure. In the company of Papa's guest, a Captain Templeton from America…"

For the next half hour, Marianne recounted to Bertha the long winter's many happenings. She took care not to mention Jamie's name too often, but when she did, she noticed Bertha's eyebrows wiggling. Could the old dear discern her feelings for him? If so, Marianne feared that her heart might give away her plans.

"A common sea captain."

A woman's harsh voice brought Jamie to a halt outside the open door of the manor house's drawing room.

"And not even in His Majesty's navy." The voice continued within the chamber. "A merchant and an *American*. Really, Bampton, could your father not choose someone of rank, or at least an Englishman for his current pet?"

As quietly as he could, Jamie inhaled a deep, calming breath. So far Lord Bennington's friends had viewed him as just that, a powerful aristocrat's "pet," whose acceptance in their society was due to his sponsor's influence. He had an uncomfortable feeling he would not find that same acceptance from the earl's oldest son and heir.

"Now, now, my dear," a languid male voice responded. "We must let the old boy have his fun. And after all, the man did save Robbie's life."

"Humph." The woman sniffed. "Whatever else should a servant do? 'Twas his duty."

"He could have run." Moberly's voice. "As your good friend Mr. Pincer did."

Jamie ground his teeth. He'd been summoned to the drawing room to meet the viscount and his wife, but he would have difficulty managing his temper if they treated him with the contempt he now heard in their voices.

"Jamie?" Marianne appeared beside him and touched his arm. "We should go in."

He recoiled, moving several feet away from her, then regretted it when dismay covered her lovely face. "Forgive me, my lady," he whispered, "but we cannot enter together."

She winced but nodded. "Of course not." She moved past him and walked into the room. "William. Lady Bampton. How wonderful to see you."

A painful ache tore through him. He couldn't bear to hurt her, yet couldn't avoid it. Nor could he fail to notice the differences in her address to her oldest brother and to his wife.

In her life of so-called privilege, Jamie's ladylove was forced to play many games.

He leaned against the wall and gazed around the vast entry hall. As grand as the Grosvenor Square town house was, this vast hundred-year-old mansion outshone it by far. Daylight streamed in through tall, narrow windows onto pale green wallpaper framed by dark oak woodwork. The requisite life-size ancestral portraits lined the wide, elegant front staircase, and brass candlesticks and delicate figurines sat on every table. The air smelled of roses, fresh from Lady Bennington's gardens. Jamie looked forward to touring the grounds, for Moberly had hinted at the many interesting sights and activities the Park afforded.

A footman walked past carrying a tray of refreshments, and cast a curious look in his direction. Jamie shrugged and rolled his eyes, playing on the camaraderie he'd established with that particular rank of servant. The man puckered away a smile. Waiting a few seconds, Jamie followed him into the drawing room. Or, rather, he followed the aroma of coffee wafting from the carafe on the tray. Although he rarely chose that drink, a good jolt of the dark brew should fortify him against the coming interview.

"Ah, here he is." Moberly rose from a brocade chair and strode to greet Jamie, shaking his hand as if it had been a week since they'd seen each other instead of merely since breakfast not an hour before. "Come, my friend, I want to present you to my elder brother and his wife."

Moberly's voice held a hint of strain along with its jollity. Could it be he feared his older brother because one day William would hold the title *and* the power? Jamie pasted on a smile, but not a wide one. He must perform a delicate balancing act in this company.

"Lord and Lady Bampton." Moberly guided Jamie to

where the others sat in a grouping of furniture in front of a great stone hearth. "May I present Papa's…and *my* particular friend, Captain James Templeton."

"I am honored, Lord Bampton, Lady Bampton." Jamie bowed to each to the same degree he would to Lady Bennington, and cast a quick glance at the viscountess's hand to see if she would lift it to be kissed. She did not. Jamie tried to recall Reverend Bentley's instructions about such things, but nothing came to mind to indicate an error on his part. So he bowed to Marianne, who was seated in a nearby chair. "My lady." He then moved to stand by the hearth until invited to sit, though he guessed such an invitation would not come. He didn't want to sit, anyway, but rather to walk out into the fresh air and be away from all this stuffiness.

"Well, I must say…" Lord Bampton stared at Jamie up and down through a quizzing glass. "These Americans do grow tall." Though seated, the viscount appeared not to have inherited his father's height nor his slender frame. Like Moberly before his stabbing, he owned a well-rounded form and a pasty complexion.

"La, such height seems unnatural to me." The viscountess was her husband's mirror image in feminine form, although her round, smooth face did hint at the beauty she must have been in her younger days.

"Why, Lady Bampton, whatever do you mean?" Marianne held out a cup of coffee to her sister-in-law. Again, her use of the woman's title told Jamie much about their relationship. No wonder she wanted to go to East Florida and meet Rachel, who would be a dear sister to her. If only he could grant her desire.

"Why, nothing, Lady Marianne." Her voice edged with disdain, the viscountess used *her* quizzing glass to study Marianne before accepting the coffee. "What a question."

This couple was quite a pair. Jamie could only guess what tortures they put the earl's younger offspring through. He could not keep his gaze from straying to Marianne to see if the other woman's tone had hurt her feelings. Marianne wrinkled her nose so quickly Jamie thought he might be mistaken. He had difficulty not laughing. His sweet lady would take nothing from this pompous woman. All the more reason to love her.

"Well, then." Moberly moved closer to Jamie rather than sit back down, but he addressed his brother. "What shall we do today?"

"Oh, la," the viscountess said. Jamie wondered if that was her favorite word. "I must rest from the journey. Swindon is entirely too far from Hampshire. I shall be glad when we take up permanent residence here."

Marianne's jaw dropped, and Robert choked on his coffee. Yet the woman seemed not to realize what she'd said. Nor did her husband, if his approving nod indicated his attitude. Even Jamie comprehended that they would not inherit Bennington Park until Lord Bennington died. Yet how could they act as if the patriarch's death counted for nothing?

Jamie bowed his head as guilt crowded judgment from his chest. Was betrayal a lesser sin than wishing someone dead?

Chapter Fifteen

"Georgie." Marianne waved to the children on the far side of the duck pond, where her nephew and nieces frolicked on the lawn under the watchful eyes of their nurse, a maid and two footmen. "Katherine. Elizabeth."

"Aunt Moberly! Uncle Robbie." Eight-year-old Georgie ran around the pond. Behind him six-year-old Elizabeth raced to catch up, while twelve-year-old Katherine kept a more sedate pace.

Georgie slammed into Robert, nearly knocking him over, and Elizabeth leaped into Marianne's outstretched arms. Amid much laughter, the children traded targets and lavished kisses on the two. Even Katherine let down a bit of her reserve to embrace them with open joy. Then she glanced beyond Marianne and stood up straight, a perfect lady.

"Good afternoon, Miss Kendall." Katherine's sweet, inclusive manners sent a surge of pride through Marianne. Most people, and certainly Lady Bampton, utterly ignored Grace because of her status as a mere companion to Mama.

"Good afternoon, Miss Moberly, Miss Elizabeth." Grace curtsied to the girls and Georgie. "Mr. Moberly."

"I say, Aunt Moberly." Georgie smiled up at Jamie. "Who is this tall chap?"

"This, Georgie, is your grandfather's good friend Captain James Templeton. He is an American sea captain."

"I say, a sea captain. How dashing." He stuck out his hand. "Pleased to meet you, Templeton."

"My honor, Mr. Moberly." Jamie's bemused expression as he shook Georgie's hand made Marianne want to laugh. She had never asked him if he spent much time around children. And no doubt he wondered how many more Mr. Moberlys he would be meeting.

After all the proper introductions were made, Marianne beckoned to the children. "We were about to go visit the Roman ruins and—"

"Oh, do let us go."

"Please take us with you."

"What fun!"

The children jumped up and down and clapped their hands.

"Not this time," Robert said. "We will plan a picnic for you there soon."

Their whines and fussing ceased at his stern frown. Marianne wondered how long they would show such respect to this uncle when their parents treated Robert so shabbily. She wanted to give an extra kiss to each of them for their courtesy to Jamie. In fact, Katherine's gaze had not left Jamie's face. This pretty niece would soon become a young lady and already showed an interest in her future social life.

"Now run back to your play, my darlings." Marianne gave little Elizabeth another hug. "You will see us often enough this summer."

The four adults walked toward the downs on the north-west end of the Park. Jamie and Robert had brought walking sticks, and each offered an arm to assist his lady with the ups and downs of the inclines. Once past the thatch-roofed outbuildings beyond the manor house, over a rise and around a stand of trees, they paired comfortably without a word or look, as if all were in mutual agreement.

Indeed, Marianne guessed that another silent concurrence had been reached, for she felt certain Grace was aware of her love for Jamie. Yet as much as Marianne longed to ask for Grace's prayers regarding her plans to follow Jamie, she dared not. A deeply spiritual woman, Mama's companion would surrender her claim on Robert before doing anything so drastic to marry him. If Marianne confided in her, Grace, like Bertha, might feel bound to speak to Mama or at the least urge Marianne to abandon her scheme. If they did not speak of the matter, Grace could honestly say Marianne had told her nothing. Thus, Marianne must be content with these stolen moments and find solace in her own prayers.

Enjoying the fresh spring breeze that carried the fragrance of honeysuckle and new-mown hay, the group ambled over the grass-covered chalk downs to a small cluster of trees a half mile from the manor house, wherein lay a clearing of hard-packed clay.

"Right there." Robert pointed to the familiar enclosure rising some eighteen inches from the earth. "This is the site of a Roman settlement of some sort."

"At least we think it is Roman." Marianne felt a rush of childhood memories. She and Frederick had discovered the outline of the stone structure during a family picnic. Their three older brothers proclaimed it a Roman ruin, and they all dug furiously to reveal how deep it went into the earth. Later, servants exposed the entire eight-by-eight-foot square with an opening on one side and even evidence of ancient fires that had burned within it. "Father said it might have been a forge built by earlier settlers whom the Romans conquered."

When Marianne and her brothers played here under the watchful care of servants, they'd dug around, trying to find other ancient structures. Those times of exploration had been happier days for the family, and Marianne could never discover what had changed…or when.

"Interesting." Jamie bent down to touch the rough surface of the wall. "What stories must dwell in these stones. Yet the people who built this structure are lost to history."

"How like the verses in Psalm 103," Robert said. "They speak of a man's days being as the grass of the field, flourishing one day until the wind passes over it, and it is gone. I think one of the loneliest sentences in all of Scripture is 'and the place thereof shall know it no more.'" His face grew sober.

Marianne felt so pleased with his new interest in the Holy Bible, and her heart warmed to think of this new spiritual depth, even though the passage seemed to depress him.

"But the verse continues with a hopeful promise." Grace hooked her arm around his and gave him a sweet smile. "'The mercy of the Lord is from everlasting to everlasting upon them that fear Him, and His righteousness unto children's children.'"

"Well quoted," Jamie said. "I'm sure you both recall that the promise is to those who keep His covenant and do His commandments." He stood and stared beyond the ruins in the direction of Portsmouth and the sea beyond, as if deep in thought. "It seems we have all been moved by those Scriptures to realize how transitory our lives are and how important it is to obey His laws."

Laws such as honor thy father and thy mother. Conviction bore down upon Marianne, but she stiffened her back. Or perhaps it was not conviction at all, but guilt, when she had nothing at all to feel guilty about. Did not the Lord create marriage? Did not her father and mother have a rich and happy marriage to a person chosen of their own free will? Should she not have the same privilege?

"Are you all right, Marianne?" Robert's gentle questioning interrupted her inner turmoil.

Jamie and Grace turned her way, and tears scalded her eyes at their concern. She raised her parasol as a shield against their concern. "We should not stay out in the sun much longer."

"No, we should not." Grace's voice lost its cheerfulness. "And perhaps I should return to the house to see if Lady Bennington requires anything from me."

"My dear stepmother will not mind if we stay away a bit longer." Robert drew his linen handkerchief from his pocket and dusted portions of the wall. Jamie followed suit, and soon all were seated, Grace and Robert close together on one wall and Marianne and Jamie across from them—a full two feet apart.

The ever-present breeze rustled Marianne's muslin gown and blew black strands of hair from her already loose coiffure. She glanced at Grace, who was, as always, a picture of modesty and control, with her muslin skirt smoothed beneath her and her dark brown hair tucked perfectly under her white cap. Only a frown marred her lovely appearance.

At this rare mood, Marianne cast off her own concerns. "Grace, you must tell us why you have grown melancholy. Is something amiss?"

Grace shook her head, but tears formed as she looked at Robert.

"What is it?" Marianne studied her brother's face.

He shrugged. "She is put out with me because I did not speak to Father about a living before we left London."

"I am not put out, Mr. Moberly." Even Grace's protest was gently spoken. "Merely sad. You are a new man in Christ and, as such, you must not let fear keep you from doing God's will."

Marianne withheld a laugh at this new assertiveness, but Robert grimaced.

"Let me see if I understand." Jamie's eyes lit with playfulness. "You expect to have the boldness to preach the gospel to sinners, yet you can't gather enough courage to ask for your own father's sponsorship for your studies?"

"You know Bennington." Robert's wry expression matched his tone. "Why would he give me an egg when he can give me a scorpion?"

"Mr. Moberly." Grace shook her head.

"Robert!" Marianne would have smacked his arm if he had been closer.

"Now, now, ladies." Robert's light laugh held no mirth. "You well know Bennington showers you two—and Lady Bennington, of course—with nothing but kindness. But not one of his four sons will ever live up to his high standards, nor will we even comprehend what those standards might be."

"Nevertheless, Moberly," Jamie said, "you *must* ask him to sponsor your bid for a church post. Just ask yourself whether, at the end of your life, you'd rather have pleased your earthly father or your heavenly Father."

"Well put, Captain Templeton." Grace clapped her hands, another unusual display of emotion that surprised Marianne. "You see, Mr. Moberly, we are all with you in this. That is—" Her face grew pink. "I have said too much."

"Nonsense, my dear." Robert grasped her gloved hand and kissed it. "Very well, then, since I can count on all your prayers, I shall speak to Father as soon as he arrives from London."

"Perhaps the morning after, brother." Even Marianne had received a sharp retort when approaching Papa too soon after his arrival from a long journey.

The others laughed, and in the corner of her eye, she noticed Jamie looking at her. With all his talk of courage, she longed to ask why he could not exert the same daring and speak to Papa for her hand. "Now we truly must go home." She stood, and the others joined her.

As they left through the small opening in the stone enclosure, Robert chuckled. "I have been meaning to tell you all a very fine joke, but thought it best not to speak it within the hearing of others." His laughter grew. "Ah, if only those who think they are wise had any comprehension, they would discover us all too soon."

Marianne eyed him with curiosity. "Whatever are you talking about?"

"Why, do you not know, sister?" Robert clapped Jamie on the shoulder and reached out to pat Marianne's cheek. "Your lovely mother and our exalted father think Miss Kendall and Templeton here have formed an attachment." More laughter, real and deep from his belly. "Isn't that rich?"

Marianne stared first at Robert, then Grace, her gaze landing at last on Jamie. "So that is why they permit, even encourage, the four of us to spend time together. Why, they expect Robert and me to be your chaperones."

Grace's smile held a great deal less amusement and a great deal more worry as she looked around their circle. "Oh, dear. Now what shall we do?"

Robert moved closer to her and captured her arm. "We shall enjoy our little secret, Miss Kendall. That is what we shall do."

So Jamie needed only to focus his attention on Miss Kendall when others were around, and no one would discern the true object of his love. The idea tantalized him. To think he could set aside his guilty feelings over the hours spent in this merry little group. He could feel free to enjoy Marianne's company as long as they were all together. After all, until Lord Bennington returned to his country home, bringing the latest news about the Crown's plans for defending East Florida, Jamie had nothing to do but wait for word that the *Fair Winds* was ready to set sail.

Halfway back to the manor house, the couples changed partners, and Jamie offered his arm to the compliant Miss Kendall. He gave her a teasing wink to lighten her mood. But the scarlet blush on her fair cheeks sent a dagger of conviction into his heart. Clearly their scheme did not please this Christian lady. And Jamie felt the same old guilt gnawing at his soul.

In the days following their excursion to the ruins, Jamie permitted himself to appreciate country living. Each morning he rode around the shire with Moberly and his brother, finding Bampton much more pleasant when not in the company of his snobbish wife. As weather permitted, afternoon walks afforded much-needed exercise. And each evening the adults gathered in the drawing room after supper to play whist or to read poetry.

The night before Bennington was to return home, Marianne brought out a leather-bound volume. "The sonnets of Sir Philip Sidney rival those of Shakespeare." She opened the book. "I have a favorite, and should I ever find a man worthy of my affections, I shall embroider it on a sampler for his wedding gift."

"Do read it, my dear." Lady Bennington's eyes lit with interest. "And do not despair over love, for the man of God's choosing will come into your life one day."

Jamie swallowed hard and turned to study a figurine on the table beside him, praying Marianne's audacity would not cause them both further heartache.

She settled in a chair and glanced around at her audience, pausing briefly to give Jamie a smile that sent his ravaged emotions tumbling. "'My true-love hath my heart, and I have his, By just exchange one for the other given.'" Her voice wavered, and she cleared her throat. "'I hold his dear, and mine he cannot miss. There never was a bargain better driven.'"

The tender words spun through Jamie's mind and reached his soul, pulling the breath from his lungs until he thought he might have to leave the room—an unforgivable affront.

She continued. "'My heart was wounded with his wounded heart; For as from me on him his hurt did light, So still, methought, in me his hurt did smart. Both equal hurt, in this change sought our bliss, My true-love hath my heart and I have his.'"

Marianne closed the book, and her eyes glistened. Sweet, brave girl, she didn't look at Jamie. Yet for one mad moment, he longed to shout "amen." For she truly had his heart…and would have it forever, no matter how much it hurt.

Chapter Sixteen

Marianne ached for the pain in Jamie's eyes. Perhaps she should not have read the sonnet. But this was the closest she could ever come to announcing her love for him to her family. After everyone retired for the night, she lay abed as usual, reexamining all her plans. Tomorrow she would begin that sampler. And perhaps one day soon, everyone would know that Lady Marianne Moberly loved the American sea merchant, Captain Jamie Templeton, for he had her heart, and she had his.

Upon waking the next morning, she learned from Emma that Papa had arrived late the night before and retired to his apartment. As she expected, the morning atmosphere in the manor house became formal, almost somber. The house-maids hastened to clean common areas, then scurried out of sight, no doubt to avoid encounters with their early-rising employer. Footmen wore blank expressions rather than pleasant ones. The children stayed out of sight with their nurse until such time as their grandfather should summon them, an annual family ritual everyone dreaded. Marianne hoped this year their good behavior would win Papa's approval, but they often misbehaved in front of their parents. But her greatest concern was that Papa would somehow notice the unplanned, affectionate gazes she sometimes traded with Jamie. Of all the denizens of Bennington Park, it seemed only Mama was happy to have Papa home.

Jamie, Robert and William went out riding, a custom they had acquired of late and one which generally pleased Marianne. She hoped her eldest brother's better nature might show itself when he was away from Lady Bampton. But today she would find Jamie's company reassuring, and missed him terribly. As it was, Mama and Lady Bampton slept late, and even Papa did not come downstairs as early as usual. So Marianne and Grace ate a quiet repast in the breakfast room before taking up their needlework in the bright light of the south parlor.

"Bother." Marianne searched her sewing basket. "I have used all of my blue."

"Hmm." Grace held out a small ball of thread. "Will this do?"

"Thank you." Marianne laid the twine next to the indigo stitches on her sampler. "'Tis a bit too light, do you not think?"

"Indeed, yes." Grace could always be counted on to agree.

Marianne studied her new project, but last night's inspiration eluded her. In truth, she did not want to sew, and longed to be out riding with the men. Or out anywhere. "Nothing will suit but to take the carriage down to Portsmouth and shop."

"Or we could go to the village, which will not take as long." Grace's eyes twinkled. "We want to be back to welcome Lord Bennington."

"I suppose so." She truly loved Papa and always tried to

please him. Never before had she feared or avoided him. But now she began to understand some of her brothers' foolish behavior in their vain attempts to satisfy their patriarch.

She looked at Grace, seated in the adjacent chair wearing a peaceful smile as she concentrated on her sewing—the very picture of serenity, much like Mama. She would be content with whatever God chose for her, even if it meant giving up Robert and breaking her heart. Yet, just as Marianne knew God had spoken to her about marrying Jamie, she believed Grace and Robert should be married. But how could either couple be wed when Papa stood before them all like the angel with the flaming sword who had kept Adam and Eve from reentering the Garden of Eden? In her own case, if she could not persuade Emma to help her board Jamie's ship, what other recourse did she have? Dress as a sailor? Hide in a barrel?

"Ridiculous." What a mad course her thoughts had taken.

"What is ridiculous?" Grace's fair face creased with concern. "Are you unwell?"

"I am well, thank you." Marianne released a long sigh. "But I shall be much better after we take our walk to the village." She set aside her sewing, grasped Grace's hand and stood. "Why waste a lovely day by staying indoors?"

Returning to her chamber, she summoned Emma to bring her walking shoes and shawl in case the day grew overcast and cool. As her maid helped her tug on the heavy leather shoes, a thought occurred to Marianne. At sea, this lace shawl would not keep her warm. She must have a new hooded cloak, heavily lined and black. A nervous thrill swept up from her heart to her throat at the idea of doing something tangible for her "flight."

Outside, the sun shone brightly, and a fresh breeze carried the fragrance of roses from Mama's garden to the narrow village road. Soon the musty smell of sheep became the stronger scent, and Marianne and Grace covered their noses with linen handkerchiefs. John the footman followed behind in case last year's gypsy band had again set up camp in the woodlands.

The small settlement of thatch-roofed cottages and businesses had been tidied up, probably in anticipation of Papa's arrival. Shop signs had been repaired and painted, and the single, rutted lane through the center of the village had been raked clean of debris and evidence of animals. Although Papa seldom went there, the citizens always took pride in being prepared in case their landlord varied his routine. Like a feudal thane, Papa served the king while his own tenants worked his land. Marianne had never considered such a thing before, but in truth they all were descendants of that time long ago when a serf could never leave the land of his birth, and daughters of the wellborn grew up to become bargaining tools in the world of politics. While these villagers were still dependent upon Papa's goodwill, at least he had never tried to force her into an unwanted marriage.

As though wafted on the wind, news of Marianne's approach must have carried from one building to the next, for in each doorway men bowed and women curtsied, all smiling their greetings. She waved and called each by name, stopping to inquire about a newborn infant or a child's progress in reading or the health of an aged parent. Each tenant seemed as pleased by her interest as if Father Christmas had paid a summer visit.

In the tiny mercantile shop, which sold a surprising array of fabrics, buttons, stays and needles, Marianne found her indigo thread, and Grace a card of buttons. Marianne also found a set of shiny brass shoe buckles engraved with three-masted ships, but resisted the temptation to buy them for Jamie. Then, while Grace chatted with the shop owner, Marianne gave whispered orders to his wife for a hooded black cloak made of wool from Papa's large flock of sheep. The woman, comprehending Marianne's need for secrecy, discreetly wrote down the order, her eyes twinkling. "A gift for yer mum's birthday, eh, milady?" she said. "Never you mind. We'll make it up good and proper and deliver it on the sly."

Marianne smiled and tilted her head in a noncommittal gesture, but felt as if she had just told a lie. Swallowing back her guilt, she thanked the woman. "Shall we go, Miss Kendall?"

As she and Grace walked back toward home, several children skipped along beside them. Marianne promised sweetmeats after Sunday services for any who could recite their catechism, and a party for them all one day soon. She thought one or two of them might have followed all the way to the manor house if their parents had not called them back.

"What an invigorating walk." Marianne inhaled the fresh spring air. "We must bring Mama next time."

"And perhaps Lady Bampton."

Marianne cast a glance at Grace, then a quick look over her shoulder. John the footman followed at a discreet distance, so she could be free in her conversation. "I doubt my sister-in-law would care to walk so far." She did not intend to be unkind, but the viscountess could make life insufferable, especially for Grace, whom she treated as a servant instead of Mama's poor but wellborn companion. Grace's inclusiveness of the woman revealed her sweet spirit.

Yet while Marianne admired Grace's Christian character, she could not help but think there were times when a person, even a woman, did not have to accept so submissively the pains and disappointments life meted out to her. Grace might find such thinking a sin, but Marianne was not so certain. Having ordered the cloak, she felt more than ever that her plan was right.

"How's this?" Jamie stood tying his cravat before the long mirror in his bedchamber, a larger, sunnier room than the one he'd inhabited in London.

Quince lounged in a brown leather chair. "You're getting better. Make it look good, because my reputation as a valet is at stake." He yawned and rolled his head and shoulders, as if waking from a long sleep.

"Get up, Aaron." Jamie took his gray jacket from the bed and shrugged it on. "You know how these servants come in to tend their duties with barely a scratch on the door. If one of them caught you sitting down while I'm dressing myself, it'd be all over the house in five minutes."

Quince groaned. "How much longer do we have to play this game? I'm ready to marry my Emma and take her home." He stood and stretched, then found a clothes brush and began to whisk nonexistent lint from Jamie's jacket and breeches.

A familiar ache throbbed in Jamie's chest. He longed to wed, too, and take Marianne back to East Florida, but that could never be. "Saunders'll send word when the *Fair Winds* is ready to sail. I've been thinking. Instead of our returning to London, I'll tell him to gather the crew and sail over to Southampton."

"Sounds pretty risky, if you ask me. After François delivers the muskets, do you really think Saunders should sail past Portsmouth and the Royal Navy docks?"

"Under the Union Jack and Bennington's flag, we shouldn't have a problem." Jamie pointed to his shiny black shoes with their large brass buckles. "Don't forget the footwear." He smirked at his friend.

Quince rolled his eyes but bent to brush the shoes. "I must confess I'm tied in knots now that the earl has shown up. Lady Bennington told Emma she would speak to the old man about our getting married. Of course, we'll get married with or without his consent. But if he gives permission, it might mean he'll give Emma a wedding gift." Aaron finished his job and rested an elbow against the mantel. "Of course, I don't need the money, but she doesn't know that, and it'll give her a measure of pride to bring something to our marriage."

"That's decent of you, my friend." Jamie punched his shoulder, then took a final glance at himself in the mirror. "How do I look?"

"Ready for an audience with the king, milord." Quince grinned.

Jamie chuckled. "From what Moberly and the viscount have said, it's very much like a king holding court when Bennington gathers his family here at the Park. Apparently the old man sits in his high-back chair as if it's a throne, and makes personal comments to each of his offspring. Bampton likened it to a whaler in the midst of a pod of whales. Harpooning, he called it." Jamie shook his head. "And not one of his sons escapes the lance."

A scratch on the door brought their conversation to an end. John the footman entered. "Captain Templeton, sir, the earl has summoned the family and requests your presence."

Jamie almost sent a knowing look to Aaron, but stopped himself in time. Gentlemen, Reverend Bentley had taught him, did not engage in such camaraderie with their servants. Instead, he nodded to John and strode from the room as if summoned before a king.

As with his bedchamber, the drawing room on the first floor was larger than the one in town. Jamie had enjoyed the evenings he'd spent there with Marianne and her family for these past few days as they waited for the earl's return. Her reading of Sir Philip Sidney's sonnets would always be a fond memory, and Jamie thought he might have liked that noble Elizabethan courtier. Lady Bampton cooled their laughter somewhat, but all in all, it had been a pleasant start to the summer.

What was he thinking? He'd become entirely too relaxed while he lived with this ruling class. He had a duty to perform, and the success of the Revolution, or at least his small part in it, depended upon his completing that duty. And yet the niggling sadness over his approaching separation from Marianne would not cease.

The afternoon sun beamed through the tall west windows and heated the drawing room, which would doubtless intensify the misery of the coming assembly. Only the fragrance of the long-stemmed red roses in six or seven vases around the chamber mitigated the closeness of the air. Jamie could only conclude that the earl liked to see his children sweat.

"Ah, Templeton, there you are." Moberly entered and strode to Jamie, his hand outstretched. "Well, here we go. The dreaded annual judgment day."

Jamie pumped his moist hand, an unmistakable sign that Moberly was already nervous. "Surely it can't be that bad." He clasped his friend's shoulder. "Buck up. You know what you have to do."

"Yes. My father's agreed to speak privately with me after

he's finished with the family." Moberly's eyes gleamed a bit too brightly. "You cannot know what your support means."

"Three others are praying for you, friend." Jamie moved to the hearth, his usual perch. "And don't forget God Himself cares deeply about this. It is He whom you desire to serve."

Moberly's expression softened. "I have felt your prayers *and* the Lord's touch." He tapped his chest. "I must admit that feels far better than the 'touches' of brandy I've depended upon these many years."

Footsteps sounded outside the door. The younger members of the family entered in a group, all wearing solemn faces. Marianne sent Jamie a sweet smile, causing a swirl of emotions to churn through his chest. He put on a sober expression and gave her a formal nod, stopping himself in midwink. He really must drop that habit, at least in this company.

Everyone took their places, each seeming to know where they were expected to sit. Lord and Lady Bampton were more subdued than Jamie had ever seen them, and he was surprised to see the usually active children sitting primly on a settee, their hands folded in their laps. Even he felt his chest tighten in expectation, and for the first time in weeks, he worried that Bennington might have found him out. To ease such ground-less speculation, he struck a careless pose, resting a foot on the pedestal of a five-foot statue of Zeus standing sentinel beside the hearth, and his elbow on the Greek god's shoulder.

Some minutes passed without a word among them, until at last the earl entered, a scowl on his noble visage, while the countess followed close behind, dispensing a beneficent smile to each person in the room. Facing the rest of the fur-niture, the earl's ornate wooden chair had a red leather cushion and a high back with a wild boar carved in the center, presumably to force its occupant to sit absolutely erect. Jamie wondered why a person would choose such a seat when he could have any of the comfortable chairs in the room. But the ways of these English nobles never ceased to perplex him. Did the man prefer to be as uncomfortable as he made his children?

Only seconds after Bennington settled in, and before he could begin his comments, little Georgie started to grasp Elizabeth's hair. As he pulled, Jamie coughed and let his foot slip from the pedestal so that his hard leather heel thumped loudly on the hearth's stone floor. All attention swung to him, with several gasps coming from the ladies. But Jamie kept his focus on Georgie, narrowing his eyes for the briefest instant. The boy snatched back his hand, sucked in his lower lip and stared down.

"Your pardon, my lord." Jamie gave the earl his best boyish grin. "Clumsy me."

The earl's eyebrows shot upward. "Do not give it a thought, my boy." As if the sun had emerged from behind a cloud, the man's expression brightened, and he gazed around the room. "Ah, 'tis good to be home with all of you."

"Welcome home, sir," Bampton said on the wind of a long-held breath.

"Father, dear." Marianne hurried over to kiss his forehead, and the children clambered after her before their parents could stop them.

The earl lifted Elizabeth up on his lap, tousled Georgie's hair and pulled Miss Moberly into a one-armed embrace. "And what mischief have you three been up to?"

The children spoke all at once, regaling their grandfather with their stories while the adults looked on. Bampton sent Jamie a grateful nod. Lady Bampton stared at him up and down through her quizzing glass, her expression unreadable.

"All right, now, let us see how tall you are." Bennington put Elizabeth off of his lap and stood, then measured the two younger ones against his waistcoat buttons. When it came to Miss Moberly, he shook his head. "Whom have we here? Where has my little Katherine gone? Who is this elegant young lady?" She giggled, still a child.

More clamoring ensued, with the earl laughing out loud more than once. Everyone in the room appeared surprised, relieved, even relaxed. Jamie noticed Moberly's hopeful expression, and Miss Kendall's serene smile. Marianne sent Jamie a wistful look, stirring his emotions again. Were they all thinking the same as he? In this pleasant, generous mood, perhaps the earl would grant each and every one of them their hearts' desires, if they would but ask him.

Jamie reined in his thoughts and turned from Marianne's sweet gaze to stare up at the painting above the hearth. While he could not ask for his own wish to be granted, he could pray that Robert Moberly would have the courage to ask for his.

Chapter Seventeen

Marianne gazed across the room at Jamie, her heart over-flowing with love. This dear man had brought nothing but good to her family, and she longed to tell Papa how much she loved her American sea captain. How marvelous that a simple pretense for awkwardness could alter the entire atmosphere and everyone's frame of mind. Neither she nor her brothers would ever have tried such a trick to change the mood of the room, or to rescue their nephew from scolding and disfavor. Perhaps that was their trouble. They feared Papa needlessly.

She put herself in Papa's place, coming home to a family that seemed to dread his company, just like some of his opponents in Parliament. With all of them cowering before him, no wonder he had always been critical of his sons. Of course, she and Mama never had anything to fear, but they both always sympathized with the misery of their loved ones.

Now, in this moment of family amiability, she could envision herself asking Papa's favor for Jamie to court her. She looked again at her beloved and saw the longing in his eyes, which he quickly shielded from her by staring up at the painting over the mantelpiece. Tears scalded away her confidence, and prudence gripped her once more. And yet perhaps, just perhaps, if Robert's interview with Papa turned out well, she might dare to ask for her own heart's longing.

"There now." The earl slumped back in his chair and swiftly bucked away from that silly wild boar designed to force good posture. She winced for him, but his stoic facade gave no hint of pain. "You have wearied this old man." He patted Georgie's head and gave the girls another hug. "Run along now. Find your nurse. The adults must have some peace and quiet once in a while." His jolly tone belied his words.

The nurse must have been hovering outside the door, for she hurried into the drawing room and whisked the children away.

Immediately, Marianne sensed caution falling over the room like a curtain. But Papa merely asked after everyone's health, going from one to the next around the circle. He expressed regret over missing William and Lady Bampton in London during most of the season, but recalled their pleasant time at Christmas last. He brought news of Jamie's ship, which had been careened, scraped and recaulked, and would soon sport a new mast of sturdy live oak, a fact that startled Marianne, for it meant her beloved must soon sail away. Jamie thanked Papa, but she thought she detected a hint of hesitation in his eyes. Was he thinking her thoughts? Once his ship was loaded with the gathered cargo from the warehouses, nothing remained to keep him here.

Papa told Marianne that Tobias Pincer missed seeing her in town. She thanked Papa, but wanted to gag at the thought of Robert's former friend and all of his treachery.

Next, with the gentleness of a loving parent, Papa

promised to enlist Grace's commentary on Reverend Bentley's upcoming sermons, for the minister would henceforth have the living at Bennington Park now that the old vicar had retired, something they had all expected and approved of. At last, he stood and kissed Mama's hand.

"And the happiest news, my dear, is that my son Thomas will soon arrive in Portsmouth, perhaps even in time for your summer garden party."

"Oh, Bennington, how delightful." Mama reached up to kiss his cheek. "Do you suppose he has been promoted?"

Father's countenance clouded. "I shall be greatly displeased if he has not been. With all our trouble with France and that nonsense going on in the American colonies, His Majesty's navy will need good commanders. Of all my sons, only Thomas possesses the courage of a military man." He pointed at the painting above the mantel, one Marianne had always loved, which showed Papa mounted on horseback in battle beside the late King George II. "When I served with His Majesty at Dettingen back in '43, we knew what a man was. We knew how to fight." He beat the air with his fist. "Yes, Thomas has what it takes to show those brigands who their master is."

Marianne could see William and Robert wilt, and she sent up a heartfelt prayer that Robert would not let these comments defeat him.

"Well, now," Papa said, "you are all dismissed except Robert." He strode over to Jamie and shook his hand. "Good to have you here, lad. Have my sons kept you entertained?"

A soft gasp escaped Lady Bampton, and Marianne puckered away a smile. Her sister-in-law had never spoken a civil word to Jamie, yet he saved Georgie—and all of them—from Papa's sour mood. No doubt the viscountess felt some degree of indignation over Papa's favor toward Jamie.

Well, the disagreeable woman would simply have to endure it.

Yet another thought struck Marianne. One day William would ascend to the title and Lady Bampton would become Lady Bennington. How would she treat Mama, who would become the dowager countess? Marianne reminded herself that it would not do to make her an enemy. But if Marianne followed Jamie to East Florida, she would have no say in how anyone treated her mother back home in England.

As the company disbursed, Jamie escorted Miss Kendall from the drawing room, and they joined Marianne beside the wide staircase in the entry hall. Miss Kendall bowed her head, and Marianne chewed her thumbnail, a habit she had taken up of late. Jamie longed to grasp her hands to reassure her, but his own feelings were loose from their moorings.

He'd had good friends all his life, but his friendship with Robert Moberly had been perhaps the most rewarding, a fact for which he could take little credit. God truly had touched Moberly, changing him from a drunken prodigal to a man who desired to serve Him. Jamie had no doubt that with further studies and Reverend Bentley's mentoring, he would make an excellent minister of the Gospel. But everything hinged on Bennington's approval, and Jamie's nerves skittered about his stomach in anticipation of the outcome of this interview.

The earl's deep, hearty laughter rang from behind the drawing room's closed door. A good sign? Jamie and the ladies traded looks, mirroring each other with eyebrows raised in expectation. The drawing room was silent for several moments. Now the door opened and slammed against the entry wall. Moberly stalked out, his eyes wide and wild, and swiped the back of his hand across his lips, a gesture Jamie had not seen since the man quit drinking.

He stopped to stare at them briefly, yet no recognition lit his eyes. Then he strode down the hallway, cutting through the house toward the back. Marianne huffed out a cross breath, while Miss Kendall's sigh held a note of heartbreak. Anger roared up inside of Jamie, and he turned toward the drawing room, his jaw and fists clenched. He would tell that fool of a father what a mistake he'd just made.

"Jamie."

"Captain Templeton."

Marianne and Miss Kendall grasped his arms.

"You must not." Marianne's eyes swam with tears. "I will speak to Papa."

Jamie chewed his lip. "You're right. I'd only make matters worse."

At the slam of a door, Miss Kendall's gaze turned in the direction Moberly had taken. She turned to Jamie. "Please, will you…?" Her voice sounding clogged with emotion, but the plea in her eyes was clear.

He squeezed her forearm. "I'll look after him." With a nod to Marianne, he hurried down the hallway. He'd managed to figure out the maze of halls, rooms and staircases comprising the manor house. Guessing that Moberly had headed for the stable, he descended a small flight of stairs and exited through a back door. Across the wide backyard, where geese and chickens pecked the ground for bugs and a servant sat at a grinding wheel sharpening knives, Moberly entered the low-roofed stable. Jamie quickly closed the distance between them, entering the darkened building just as his friend slung a saddle onto Gallant's back.

"Mr. Moberly, sir." A slender, mop-haired young groom reached out to help him. "I'd be honored to saddle 'im for you."

"I can do it myself." Robert's bitter tone cut the air, and

he waved the boy off with a sharp gesture that did not make contact, but nevertheless sent him reeling backward. "I *am* capable of a few things."

"Very well, sir." The groom watched with widened eyes.

Jamie clapped the boy on the shoulder. "Would you saddle Puck for me, lad?"

The groom gave him a quivering smile. "Aye, sir, be glad to."

"I do not require a nursemaid, Templeton." Moberly jerked the girth around Gallant's belly, and the massive horse snorted and danced on his heavy back hooves. "Hold still." His words came out through gritted teeth, but at least he'd not cursed, as had been his former habit.

"Of course you don't." Jamie stepped forward and rubbed Gallant's forehead, something Moberly had taught him to settle a horse down. "But I, too, would like an outing this fine afternoon." In truth, sullen gray clouds had begun to roll over the sky as if following the sun as it wended its way westward—a promise of rain if Jamie had ever seen one. His new jacket and shoes, neither made for rain or riding, might be ruined. But it was a small price to pay for his friend's well-being.

Moberly finished with the saddle. "You will not want to go where I'm going." Again he brushed the back of his hand across his lips. Jamie had seen many a drunkard do the same thing in his desperation for a drink.

He followed as Moberly led Gallant out of the stable, then watched him leap into the saddle, dig in his heels and gallop away. The groom seemed to take a long time to bring Puck, and Jamie paced about the yard, his nerves tightening as the minutes passed. The boy still looked stricken as he handed over the reins. "Here you go, sir."

"Thank you, my lad." Jamie lifted his foot to place it in

the left stirrup, but Puck pranced around in a circle. He had the urge to swat the mischievous animal's flanks, but realized that would only make matters worse.

"Here, sir. Let me 'elp." The groom grabbed the bridle and secured it to a post, then gave Jamie a leg up into the saddle.

"Thank you, lad." His pride was a bit bruised by his needing help to mount this rascal. But pride was unimportant now, for Jamie had a far more important concern. He dug his heels into Puck's flanks and reined him toward the road to Portsmouth, where the dust from Gallant's hooves still stirred in the air.

"We must not stay here." Marianne could hear the sound of Papa's footsteps crossing the drawing room floor. She grasped Grace's hand, and the two of them scurried up the wide front staircase like frightened mice. Once they reached Marianne's bedchamber, they fell into each other's arms and wept. Marianne had never seen Grace so discomposed, but her own anguish was so severe she had no words to comfort her friend.

"My lady." Emma appeared from her little room wringing her hands. "Whatever is the matter? How can I help you?" She brought forth two fresh linen handkerchiefs and fetched glasses of water from the crystal pitcher on a side table.

"Thank…you…Em…ma." Struggling for control, Marianne sniffed and dabbed at her tears. In love herself, surely Emma had long ago noticed the other romances blooming in the shadows of the household. While Marianne had not yet confided her plans to her little lady's maid, she had not denied the girl's veiled remarks regarding her affections for a certain American nor her open remarks about Grace and Robert.

Grace breathed out a long shuddering sigh. "Forgive me," she whispered.

Marianne started to say there was nothing to forgive, but realized her friend was praying. Still, she could not think God would mind these heartfelt tears on Robert's behalf. Infused with a sudden fervor, she grasped Grace's and Emma's hands and led them to the chairs in front of her hearth. "We will pray together. Has the Lord not said that wherever two or three are gathered in His name, He will be with us?"

Grace gave her a trembling smile, and Emma's eyes grew round, as if she was startled by this unsettling elevation from lady's maid to lady's confidante.

"It is all right," Marianne said. "We are all equal before our Heavenly Father."

"Yes, my lady." Emma's eyes sparkled, and her smile held a bit of mischief. Marianne could not guess why.

With her head bowed, Marianne prayed first for Robert's and Jamie's safety, then for Papa to have a change of heart regarding Robert's future. The others lifted the same petitions in their own words. Emma added her request that, while the Lord was in the business of speaking to Lord Bennington regarding matters of the heart, He might also grant Aaron Quince favor in the earl's eyes. Then she gasped. Marianne and Grace raised their heads to look at her.

"I did not mean to be impertinent, my lady." Emma's round cheeks were pinched with worry.

Marianne shook her head. "Be at ease, Emma. I did not think you were at all impertinent."

However, the answering gleam in her maid's eyes threw up a caution in Marianne's mind. Mama had always taught her that God loved every person the same, whether rich or

poor, mistress or servant, but each had her place in His plan.
Servants who were granted too much liberty might one day
misuse it, even a grateful orphan like Emma. Marianne must
walk a delicate path while keeping Emma in her proper
place, for one day soon her own happiness, her own future,
would depend on Emma's good feelings for her.

Chapter Eighteen

Jamie bent low on Puck's back and urged him to a full gallop, taking care not to plow into people walking or driving carts on their way home from a long summer day's work. At least he did not have to stop to ask directions. In his early morning rides with Moberly and Bampton, he had seen Portsmouth in the distance, some five or six miles over numerous hills from Bennington Park. Late at night, from his bedchamber window, he could see the flickering lights of the growing naval town and Southampton to the west, where he must make arrangements at one of the public wharves for the *Fair Winds* to dock. Now that Bennington had informed him the ship was ready to sail, he would have to follow through on those plans, and the sooner, the better. Yet this evening, God had clearly shown him his work in England had not yet been completed.

Mindful of the danger he'd put Puck in a few weeks earlier, Jamie slowed the horse when the road rose over the hills, then gave him his head when they descended. As always, Puck seemed to enjoy their outing. Jamie wished he could say the same for himself this time.

Portsmouth had all the clutter of a town growing so fast it kept popping its seams. Some semblance of planning appeared in the residential area Jamie passed through. Fine brick homes and straight, tree-lined streets graced these outer edges. But that quickly gave way the closer Jamie got to the narrow, winding streets along the waterfront, where he hoped to find Robert.

Jamie prayed good sense would prevail, yet he had a foreboding that he'd find his friend already "three sheets in the wind," as they said in Nantucket, especially since Jamie had no idea where to find him, giving Moberly more time to drink to excess.

A typical navy town, Portsmouth boasted in what should be its shame—countless taverns large and small, and countless immodestly dressed women calling to sailors or any passing man in decent clothing to come into their lairs. Again, Jamie had cause to pray, for Robert had confessed an occasional visit to such places before he'd placed his trust in Christ. If Jamie found him returning to his old haunts, he'd beg Moberly on Miss Kendall's behalf not to return to such a vile custom.

In his many years among seafaring men, whether whaler, sailor or merchant, Jamie had learned that self-righteous preaching never accomplished anything. In the first few taverns he visited, he ordered a drink, then asked the serving wench about Moberly. Everyone in Portsmouth knew Bennington's second son, but he'd not been that way. Jamie paid his coin and left the rum on a table. In each place, he noticed how quickly someone grabbed his abandoned tankard. Finally, a clear-eyed wench who seemed entirely too young for her occupation said Moberly had been there, but had moved on to the Stowaway, unless he'd changed his mind.

Jamie hooked a finger under the girl's chin and stared into

her pale blue eyes. "God loves you, child. I will pray He will show you a more worthy profession." He pressed a silver coin into her hand and enjoyed the shock and, perhaps, conviction covering her sweet face.

Outside, he took Puck's reins from the boy he'd engaged to tend him, paid the lad a coin, and continued down the street. This evening was becoming very expensive for a sober man who generally held on to his money. How much might it cost a drunkard whose pockets were filled with his father's guineas?

The Stowaway stood two blocks in the distance. As Jamie jostled his way through the masses, he saw a young man struggling to free himself from several sailors with clubs. *Press gang.* Jamie's heart hitched thinking of the terror he'd felt as a lad when the warning came that the British navy had sent out ruffians to gather crew members for their ships. Torn away from friends and family without warning, given no chance to say their goodbyes, the hapless victims seemingly disappeared, some never to return. Jamie looked closely to see if the young man was from Bennington's village. If so, he would intervene, warning the sailors of the earl's displeasure and reprisal. But the lad was not familiar, and although Jamie pitied him, he felt the Lord's prompting to continue on his mission.

Rain began to splatter the dust at his feet. The shoes would be ruined, all right. He'd never be able to talk Quince into cleaning them up, and it would be dangerous to ask the earl's valet how to do it. Greyson already eyed Quince as if he were an inferior servant. No need to give him reason to learn Quince employed servants of his own back home.

Ducking into the tavern just as the heavens opened in a deluge, Jamie saw Moberly seated in a corner, his back to the wall. He looked up and met Jamie's stare. But instead of a sullen or angry greeting, he gave a lazy smile and beckoned to him. Apparently, the drink had already done its job. As evidenced by the expression on his face, Moberly was feeling nothing but mindless bliss, from which he would come crashing down in the morning.

Ignoring the smells of sweat, rum and cooking cabbage, Jamie wended his way through the roomful of drinking men, and sat adjacent to Moberly. "You're a hard man to keep up with."

"Ha." Robert tossed down the last drops in his tankard, then lifted it toward a wench serving the next table. "When you can, Betty."

"Right away, milord." The plump woman left the other men, common sailors who apparently knew who Moberly was, for they made no complaint. Well past her prime, she gave Jamie a sliding look up and down and puckered her lips suggestively. "My, aren't you a pretty one. What can I do for you, milord?"

"I have all I need, thank you." He gave her a little smile, remembering Christ's kindness to women like this one, even as revulsion churned within him.

After she left the table, Jamie studied his friend, who closed his eyes and rested his head against the wall. "Miss Kendall sends her best wishes."

Moberly glared in his direction with unfocused eyes. "How dare you mention her name in a place like this?" His words were slurred, but his anger came through.

"How dare you come to a place like this when you have the love of such a good woman?" Jamie had never truly crossed his friend, and questioned just how far he should go. If he'd learned nothing else in the country, he'd learned not to speak rudely to the aristocracy. Yet these were the words God had given him, and he would not back down.

Rage reddened and creased Moberly's cheeks, and narrowed his eyes. "He laughed at me." He pounded the table, splashing rum from the fresh tankard the wench had brought. "All I have done, working like a fiend to prove myself to that old goat, and he *laughs* at me. Said I am not fit to be a minister."

Jamie prayed his next words were from the Lord. "And so you promptly go out and prove him right. You're *not* fit to be a minister."

Thunder crashed overhead and a bolt of lightning lit the street, turning the raindrops into a million fireflies. Jamie would haul this sorry sinner out into the deluge if not for the lightning. As it was, he hoped the lad caring for horses here had taken Puck to the tavern's stable. What had Moberly done with Gallant? Jamie had more than one creature to care for this evening.

"Grace…" Moberly stared vacantly across the room.

"Now who's saying her name unsuitably?" Jamie's temper was rising, and he longed to pummel this man who seemed all too willing to abandon his faith.

"No, I do not speak of Miss Kendall." Moberly's voice sounded weary. He ran his finger around the rim of the tankard, but did not drink. "Grace from God. The prodigal son and all that. But when *I* returned home, my father never noticed." He slumped on the table, propping his head on one hand. "I've always wondered why the older brother became so angry. Did not everything belong to him? All the younger son wanted was his father's approval. Yet, in our family, 'tis the third son who's all the rage now because, like our august father, he fights for king and country."

Jamie could not quite follow Moberly's musings, but conviction for his own self-righteousness cut into him. He'd been willing to dispense grace to the young wench at the other tavern, but not to his fallen friend. *Give me words, Lord.* "Our fathers are human, even one as exalted as yours."

Robert's stare bored into him. "Did your father treat you like worthless baggage?"

Jamie shrugged but held his gaze. "No. My father died when I was six."

Moberly snorted. "Fortunate you." He put his head in both hands. "No, I do not mean that. Forgive me."

The rain abated somewhat, and Jamie decided they'd leave when it slowed a bit more.

"You're right, Templeton." Moberly gave him a crooked grin. "I am not fit to be a minister. But, as you have said, we've all sinned and come short of the glory of God. And—" he held up his index finger to stress his point "—as you also said, God will be a father to me. I will never, as long as I live, *ever* expect anything else from Bennington." He shoved the tankard away, put his hands to his temples and blew out a long breath that nearly knocked Jamie over for its smell of secondhand rum. "Lord, forgive me. Why did I drink all of that? And so quickly. And without anything to eat." He belched and placed a hand over his mouth.

In the dim daylight of the tavern, Jamie could see Moberly's face grow pale. "Come. I'll take you home." He gripped his friend's arm to pull him to his feet.

"Oh, no." He shrugged away. "Cannot go home drunk." He leaned away and deposited the contents of his stomach into a cuspidor beside the table.

Jamie wiped Moberly's face with a handkerchief and grasped him again. "Come on, then, we'll get you sober." He began to move the two of them toward the door.

Moberly's lucidity seemed to have passed. "Shall we sing a song? How 'bout 'Rule, Britannia' or 'God save the king'?" He staggered along beside Jamie and would have fallen without support. "Rule, Britannia—" For a drunk, his baritone was not bad.

The sailors in the room lifted their tankards high and joined his song.

Jamie swallowed a retort. He and nearly every other American had suffered far too much of Britannia's rule. "I heard a new song. 'Amazing Grace.' Do you know it?" They reached the door none too soon for him with all that riotous singing behind them.

Moberly stopped and shook his head, as if trying to clear it. "No, but it sounds like an excellent song. Will you teach it to me? Perhaps Marianne can play it on the pianoforte. She is very good at playing, you know."

Jamie chuckled. No, he hadn't known that. He would have to ask her about it once this debacle was over. So many things he did not know about her, and so little time to learn it.

Outside, the rain slowed to a drizzle. The stable boy informed them that their horses were safely sheltered behind the tavern. Paying out yet another coin, Jamie started in that direction. On the way, he noticed a watering trough newly filled with rainwater. "Come along, my friend." He tugged Moberly toward it.

Robert must have guessed his plan, for he dug his feet into the mud. "Oh, no, you don't."

"Oh, yes, I do." Jamie gripped him around the waist and forced him forward, plunging his head into the cold trough and holding him there for a few seconds before releasing him.

Moberly came up gasping. And laughing. He tried to force Jamie into the trough, but slipped in the ankle-deep mud, grabbing Jamie's arm and pulling him down, too.

The two of them sat there in the mud for a few moments, then both burst out laughing. Jamie's new gray jacket and breeches were stained with splotches of brown and black dirt, and the buckles on his new shoes might never regain their shine. Indeed, neither the clothes nor the shoes would ever be fit for fine company again. But somehow, that no longer mattered to him.

What did matter was getting Moberly home and tucked into bed without the earl seeing him in this condition.

Chapter Nineteen

Marianne's stomach felt tied in knots. Papa expected the family to join him promptly at nine o'clock for his first supper at home. Like the drawing room gathering each year, he demanded strict adherence to these rituals. She cast about in her mind, trying to think of how to appease his anger when Robert and Jamie did not appear. It was bad enough for her brother to bring trouble on himself, but she was quite put out with him for Jamie's sake. Did he not realize Jamie was again risking his standing with Papa in order to rescue him from his mischief?

As the supper hour drew near, Marianne and Grace changed their gowns for the occasion, then watched together from the second-story parlor window for signs of the two men. On these long summer days, daylight lasted until late in the evening. While the afternoon storm had darkened the landscape, once the rain stopped, the sun burst through the clouds to cast its golden rays upon the green hills.

"The roads appear dreadfully muddy," Grace said. "Even if Captain Templeton found Mr. Moberly, they will never make it home in time to freshen up."

Marianne nodded as she searched for riders on the lane. More than once a distant horse lifted her hopes, only to pass by the Park entrance.

"There." Grace pointed. "Two riders. I think…yes, they are coming." She clasped her hands to her chest, as if struggling to contain her joy.

Although they were far down the lane, their identities were unmistakable. "Oh, thank You, Lord." Marianne embraced Grace. "But undoubtedly they are covered in mud."

"Whatever shall we do?"

Marianne chewed her thumbnail for a moment. "Go to Robert's room and fetch Ian. Tell him to bring fresh clothes. We have just forty-five minutes to save my brother."

Grace released a giddy laugh. "Oh, my. Do you truly think we can accomplish this?"

Marianne tried to contain her rioting emotions, but a laugh escaped her nonetheless. "Yes, yes. But hurry. I shall fetch Quince for Jamie. Um, for Captain Templeton."

Grace gave her a knowing smile. "Yes. Captain Templeton." She hurried from the parlor with Marianne close on her heels.

Marianne raced up the stairs to the third floor and down the hallway toward Jamie's room. There outside his door stood Quince and Emma in a chaste embrace. At her hurried approach they broke apart. Quince looked oddly defiant. Or perhaps annoyed. Emma blushed scarlet. Marianne did not have time for this.

"Quince, you must come immediately and bring Captain Templeton a change of clothes. He will need everything." Marianne stopped to catch her breath. "He must be presentable and in the dining room by nine o'clock sharp. Is that clear?"

The man blinked, but did not move.

"Really, Mr. Quince, I cannot think why Captain Templeton retains you." Marianne's temper flared as it had not in
many a year. "Do see to your duty and rescue your master, or
I shall find someone who can." Only briefly did she think of
how much her own future depended on the good opinion of
these two people. For now, Jamie must be saved. "Will you
come?"

"Aye, milady." Quince grinned, then tugged at a lock of
his hair, a customary respectful gesture from an underling
to a superior that somehow seemed impertinent coming
from him. She would deal with that later.

"Very well. Hurry. Meet us at the back entrance nearest
the stable." She rushed back down the stairs, her heart racing
faster than her feet. "Please, Lord, help us to accomplish the
impossible."

Jamie enjoyed the leisurely ride through the rain-washed
countryside. The fragrance of wildflowers filled the air, and
nuthatches sang their loud, simple songs, no doubt pleased
to have survived the storm. Even the mud clinging to
Jamie's hair and plastering his shirt to his body didn't spoil
his appreciation for the glorious sunset over the distant hills.
He noticed the cool breeze, which cut through his clothes
and sent chills up his spine, seemed to have cleared
Moberly's head. That and maybe his dunking in the water
trough. What a lark that had been. Jamie enjoyed the
friendly rowdiness. And now a good night's rest should
cure the last of his friend's drunkenness. He felt certain
Moberly would think seriously before drinking spirits again.

As the tall, gray stone manor house came into view, lit
by a brilliant sunset of orange, purple and red, Jamie's chest
filled with an unexpected and bittersweet pang. In the midst

of all this beauty and in the aftermath of an event that might change the course of Moberly's life for the better, he knew nothing in this place held any future for him. With the *Fair Winds* repaired and seaworthy, he must send word to Saunders to load the ship with the goods from the earl's warehouse. His capable first mate would also complete the unwritten order to meet their Spanish allies and store the muskets and ammunition in the lower deck's secret hold. All of that and a short voyage from Southwark to Southampton would take perhaps a fortnight, perhaps a bit more. Then, after a short side trip to Boston to deliver his report about the troop movements, he would sail to East Florida, conveying a shipload of goods but an empty heart.

"I say, what is that?" Squinting, Moberly pointed his riding crop toward the east side of the manor house, where three people stood in the shadows, waving vigorously at them. "I pray nothing is wrong, but they seem a bit overwrought, do you not think?"

Without waiting for an answer, he urged his mount to a gallop, and Jamie followed suit. The horses' hooves flung up mud from the wet road, with Jamie being the recipient of Gallant's generous offerings. He'd not thought he could be any dirtier, but sure enough, now he was. He laughed into the wind. As long as he was here, he would toss away his gloom and enjoy himself.

Marianne permitted herself only a moment of horror as Jamie and Robert drew nearer. As they rode up the lane, she saw their clothing was caked and splattered and their hair grimy. But she had no time for emotions, only action. Nor had the men any time for baths, only cold buckets of water showered over them before they entered the house.

The instant they dismounted, she pointed them to the two

footmen waiting beside her. "They will wash you by the back door. Your valets have your clothing ready in a room just inside, to save your going all the way upstairs. Make haste. You have a mere twenty minutes before Papa will expect you in the dining room."

"What—" Jamie stared at her in confusion.

"Oh, bother," Robert said. "Sorry, Templeton. The old man demands a strict routine here in the country. Family custom and all that. I quit paying attention years ago, but if I am to improve my lot, I'd best make an appearance on time."

Jamie grimaced. "You go ahead." He dismounted and handed Puck's reins to a waiting groom. "I'll take a light repast in my room."

"No, no," Marianne said. "He will expect you, as well. You saw today how Papa holds court. He will expect us all at the table at the chime of nine o'clock." Her pulse raced with anxiety. Jamie simply did not comprehend.

He had the audacity to laugh. "But shouldn't country living be a bit more relaxed?"

Marianne lifted her skirts and marched across the damp grass, glad that she had put on her leather walking shoes before coming outside. "Captain Templeton, you must defer to my father in this if you expect the rest of the summer to hold any relaxation for any of us."

"Indeed." He stiffened slightly and raised his eyebrows.

She had never spoken sharply to him, and she regretted it. It was she who was at fault for not informing him about the family tradition. "Please."

A glint of comprehension crossed his eyes. "Very well." He followed Robert around the side of the house, with Marianne not far behind.

The footmen had already begun to strip off Robert's

jacket and shirt and loosen his muddy hair from its queue. Marianne hurried past them through the back door, praying the task would be completed in time.

Wafting up from the kitchen belowstairs came the aroma of roasted lamb and apple pie. She could picture the cook adorning the platter with sprigs of mint leaves, and the liveried footmen donning their white gloves in preparation for serving the sumptuous dinner. This was Papa's formal welcome home celebration, a custom passed down in the Bennington household since feudal times, and she prayed Robert had not ruined the whole thing for all of them.

She found Grace in the upper parlor and reported the homecoming. "The footmen are doing all they can to help. Do I look all right?"

Grace studied her up and down, reaching out to tuck a stray curl into Marianne's coiffure. "Except for your shoes."

"Oh, dear." Looking down, Marianne felt a merry tickle inside and could not resist a laugh. "I have tracked mud all the way in here and shall have to apologize to the upstairs maid."

The mantel clock read ten minutes before nine, so the two ladies descended to the drawing room, where the rest of the family had gathered, except for the children, and Robert and Jamie. Surprised at her own thoughts, Marianne tried to remember when she had begun to think of Jamie as part of the family. Would that Papa could regard him in the same light.

At the chime of nine o'clock, Blevins appeared in the drawing room doorway. "Lord Bennington, Lady Bennington, dinner is served."

Marianne and Grace shared a regretful look as they followed Papa and Mama, William and his lady from the room. But as the procession crossed the wide entrance hall,

Robert and Jamie slipped around the staircase and, forefingers to lips to forestall any reaction, offered arms to her and to Grace, each choosing his friend's lady to escort. Although damp around the edges, with their shiny hair pulled back in wet queues, both men looked every bit the gentlemen they were. She did notice that Robert's eyes seemed somewhat blurry, but at least he could walk straight. Well, he did wobble a bit on her arm, but she managed to hold him up.

Papa seated Mama and then started toward his end of the table. At the sight of the two latecomers, Mama smiled serenely, William snorted out a laugh and Lady Bampton harrumphed. But all attention turned toward Papa. His eyebrows wiggled slightly, as they did when he was surprised. Then a slow smile crept across his lips, and a glint filled his eyes—a gleam that appeared only when he planned to skewer one of his sons with cutting remarks. Marianne knew that Grace was praying as hard as she that Papa would not be too cruel to Robert. For indeed, how much crueler could he be than to laugh at his son's desire to serve God?

Chapter Twenty

"East Florida is a fine place for a new beginning." Jamie walked beside Moberly around Bennington Pond, a long, narrow lake edged with cattails, ferns and weeping willows, and inhabited by swans and ducks watching over their hatchlings. In the distance, a man from the village sat in a rowboat and fished the black depths. "Marry Miss Kendall and come with me. Your brother Frederick would be pleased to see you, and there's no end of possibilities for new businesses." Even as he spoke, he questioned the wisdom of his invitation. Moberly never expressed any serious views on the Revolution other than to say it would be interesting to see how it all turned out. Yet Jamie felt God's urging to encourage him.

"You are a true friend, Templeton." Moberly found a rock and flung it sideways into the lake. It skipped several times across the water, scattering a group of ducks, who quacked in protest. "But Miss Kendall and I have decided the Lord would have us stay here. These past days, through her insights, I've come to realize my desire to go into the church was the misplaced zeal of a newly converted man.

Thus, I shall have to find a way to support us before we can marry." He exhaled a long sigh. "Of course, it will require another lengthy period of good behavior on my part so my next endeavor will meet with my father's approval. In the meantime, I shall plumb the depths of my interests and talents to see if anything pops to the surface."

"I understand." Jamie nodded. "You know we'll sail in just over a week. If you change your mind, I'll give you a berth aboard the *Fair Winds*." He found a smooth, flat stone, but once he threw it, it sank beneath the surface, much like his heart each time he thought about leaving Marianne. Up to now, his determination had held strong. Now that resolve wavered like the oak leaves fluttering in the wind on a branch above him. Somehow he must distract himself. "Tell me more about this garden party. Who's coming? What do you do?" Since Bennington had come home, the evenings in the drawing room had become more than boring. He hoped the upcoming event would be a good diversion.

"You may have noticed Lady Bennington loves to throw a party." Moberly chuckled, and his eyes lit with fondness. "This one began as a replacement for the annual Midsummer Eve festival, which of course is pagan in origin. Neither my stepmother nor Father could countenance such celebrations, yet they desired some sort of summer entertainment. They hit upon the idea of a garden party the week after Summer Solstice, so as to make a distinction. Theirs was to be decidedly more sedate—bowling, billiards, riding, grouse hunting, that sort of thing—an enjoyable way to gather like-minded friends for a week or so. They've hosted this event these past three and twenty years."

"Ah, what a fine idea." Jamie again considered the earl's contradictory ways—faithful in his religion, generous to his friends and to charity, but cruel to his sons. "Christians

can always find ways to enjoy themselves without partici-
pating in godless merrymaking."

Moberly laughed ruefully. "I'm beginning to truly understand that…thanks to you."

Jamie shrugged. "More thanks to the Lord, I'd say." He
looked across the lake toward the fisherman. "Any good fish
out there?"

Moberly followed his gaze. "Sometimes. Want to give it
a try?"

"I would. I haven't been on water since March, a sorry
thing for a sailor to admit."

They found a rowboat and fishing equipment in the gray
stone boathouse and rowed out to a likely spot. In the lazy
quiet of the afternoon, both dozed beneath their wide-
brimmed cocked hats, not minding in the least that no fish
tugged on their lines to disturb their sleep.

Marianne threw herself into helping with the preparations
for the garden party, as did everyone in the household.
Mama spent a great deal of time with Cook planning a
week's worth of menus to serve the expected thirty-seven
guests. The men practiced their marksmanship in anticipation of the grouse hunting. Servants scoured the house until
not a spot of dust could be found, nor a scuff mark on the
floors, nor a frayed edge on chairs or drapes. The guest wing
was opened, furniture uncovered and linens aired. Mama
assigned Marianne the duty of planning for the evening entertainment of the younger set.

Papa did not permit the hanging of bunting or evergreen
bows, but he approved of flowers, as many as could be
gathered to decorate the house. Marianne and Grace enlisted
Jamie's and Robert's help and secured the use of a dogcart
to bring wildflowers from the woodlands and fields, and

blooms from Mama's garden. The servants filled vases and scattered them around the manor, filling every room with delightful and varied fragrances. As much as Marianne loved Mama's roses and carnations, her favorite flower was the sweet pea, imported from her maternal grandparents' villa in Tuscany.

For all their enjoyment of Bennington House in London, it was Bennington Park the family claimed as home. And when Marianne considered all she was sacrificing for love, and how few days remained before she left, never to return, she found herself grieving the loss. But she had many more moments of giddy happiness—mixed with terror—over her own audacity. The ups and downs of her emotions left her exhausted at the end of each day.

In the evenings, she stared out of her bedchamber window, her gaze caressing the beloved countryside. She imagined her coming voyage and prayed she would not succumb to seasickness. She must secure some powdered ginger root from the kitchen. And, with a single small bag for all her possessions, she must decide what to take and what to leave. Some items she'd once considered treasures now proved to be foolish luxuries. She decided to take only two plain dresses. Would that she could ask Jamie which ones he preferred to see her wear.

But first she must get past the garden party. She drew out her volume of Shakespeare to design word games. In a moment of mad defiance, she considered presenting the elopement scene in *A Midsummer Night's Dream* to tease Jamie or to give a hint to her parents of her plans. Papa could play his counterpart, the heartless Egeus, while she and Jamie were well suited to portray the fleeing lovers, Hermia and Lysander. She could hear Jamie repeating Lysander's line, "'The course of true love never did run smooth.'" But such foolishness would ruin her flight. In any event, Papa did not care for that particular play because of its pagan setting. Instead, he preferred the Bard's histories, especially *Henry V,* which he likened to George II's courageous leadership in fighting for England and making the throne secure for the House of Hanover.

As her musing continued, a startling thought occurred to her. Jamie had never asked her to marry him. Did he love her as Lysander loved Hermia enough to risk his entire future for her? What if, when they were far out to sea and he found her aboard his ship, he brought her back home in disgrace? Papa might be hurt by her desertion, but he would be destroyed to see his only daughter behaving like certain infamous society women whose affairs he had widely condemned. Before Marianne ran away to sea like a boy longing to be a sailor, she must force from Jamie the truth about the depth of his feelings for her, even as she gave no hint that she planned to sneak aboard his ship.

Chapter Twenty-One

As the carriages began to roll up the lane in a procession, Jamie grew morose. He'd become tired of these aristocrats with all of their frivolities. Yet he knew his irritation came more from a mixture of heartache over leaving Marianne and the limited information he'd gathered for General Washington. The best he could do for the next four days was watch the unfolding spectacle and try to enjoy himself in this hodgepodge of people.

Servants rushed around taking care of the incoming guests and their baggage. The aroma of cakes and meats wafted up from the kitchen, making Jamie's mouth water. Bennington's mastiffs—spoiled beasts—barked incessantly, while the children got loose from their nursemaid and ran about causing mischief. Through little Georgie's efforts, more than one vase of flowers crashed to the floor, causing extra work for the harried servants. But Lady Bennington insisted the children must not be punished, for everyone felt the excitement of the day.

In the midst of it all, Thomas Moberly came home to announce he had indeed been promoted and given command of a forty-four gun frigate christened HMS *Dauntless*. Jamie had hoped *this* Captain Moberly would be delayed until his own departure. But as numerous guests gathered in the drawing room, and Robert drew Jamie into the family circle, he was presented to a man who one day might very well try to blast his own ship out of the water.

"Another one of Father's pets, eh?" Captain Moberly, in an indigo uniform replete with brass buttons and gold braid, stood as tall and slender as his father, with broad shoulders, straight posture and a lift to his chin that suggested the man was full of himself—a younger version of the earl by some forty years. Like Marianne and Robert, he had thick black hair and sky-blue eyes. But whereas Marianne's eyes exuded gentleness, and Robert's earnestness, Thomas's icy stare bored into a man like a cold steel blade. Jamie could not fault him too much. He'd used the same stare himself on insubordinate sailors.

"Your father is a generous man." Effecting a humble bow, Jamie glanced beyond Captain Moberly and noted Marianne's dismay. The dear girl loved all of her brothers.

"Indeed." Captain Moberly turned away to speak to another guest. Several unattached ladies hovered nearby, but his stiff demeanor seemed to indicate he didn't welcome their attentions.

Marianne sent a quivering smile Jamie's way, and he returned a wink. If anyone but Robert or Miss Kendall noticed, he no doubt would have been sent on his way forthwith.

In the afternoon, the younger set moved outside to bowl on the leveled lawn. Jamie had bowled in Nantucket and Boston, and if invited to join the aristocrats, he would not embarrass himself. For the first hour or so, he had to be content to watch, until Marianne dragged him in to replace a wearied young lady.

"'Tis quite easy, Captain Templeton." Marianne placed the black wooden ball in his hands. "You only have to roll this ball across the lawn and try to knock down as many of the ninepins as you can." Her tutorial tone and the twinkle in her eyes sparked high spirits in him.

"Like this, my lady?" He held the ball in both hands over one shoulder, as if he would lob it through the air like a cannonball.

"No, no. Just one hand." She reached for the ball. "Let me show you."

He lifted it higher. "Ah-ah. 'Tis my turn, is it not?"

Murmurs erupted around them, intermingled with a few titters from the ladies. Had he gone too far to tease a lady of her station in front of them?

Marianne moved back and crossed her arms. "Very well. You have seen us play. Do it right." Her lips puckered, as if she was containing a laugh.

He longed to wink at her again, to secretly convey his love to her while everyone looked on. But he dared not risk such an affront, as they all would see it. Instead, he bowed. "I shall do my best not to embarrass you, my lady."

Gripping the ball in both hands, he held it up and eyed the pins some twenty-five feet away. He moved the ball to his right hand, swung it back and whipped it across the closs-cropped grass, knocking down all nine pins.

"Well done, captain." Marianne applauded, as did several others. "You have played before. Tell me, what other hidden accomplishments do you have?"

Some in their audience again murmured their disapproval, but Jamie threw caution to the winds. "My lady, I have ridden the back of a whale in the South Atlantic and shot a bear in the wilderness of East Florida." He put a finger on his jaw in a thoughtful pose. "I have climbed a tree and rescued a kitten for your niece, Miss Elizabeth." His audience now began to chuckle. "But my most difficult accomplishment has been to dance the minuet without tripping over my own large feet and falling flat on my face."

The laughter grew, and the bowling continued, with others taking the center of attention. Marianne pulled up the fan on her wrist and waved it lazily. "After all of those amazing deeds," she said softly, her eyes sending a silent plea, "do you suppose you could brave the dangers of escorting me to the refreshment table?"

Not twenty feet away and near the house, servants had set up a long, linen-draped table and filled it with beverages, cakes and sweetmeats. The temptation to speak to her alone was too great. Perhaps this would be the last time they could talk privately before he left. Jamie bent low in a formal bow. "My lady, it will be my pleasure."

He offered his arm, and she set her dainty gloved hand on it. He couldn't resist the urge to cover it with his own. If anyone found this closeness inappropriate, he would declare himself a boor, and she would be blameless. He longed for the courage—or stupidity—to put an arm around her waist and draw her close to his side, where he wished to keep her forever. The ache he always felt at the edges of his chest now moved to the center, cutting deep into his heart.

At the table, they each took a crystal cup brimming with lemonade, then, as if they'd planned it, turned and walked the pathway down the hill toward the lake. One of the rowboats lay available for use at the water's edge. Nearby, in the care of nursemaids and footmen, Georgie and his sisters played with the dozen or so other little lords and ladies, offspring of the various adults who amused themselves around the vast estate.

The weather had bestowed its approval on Lady Bennington's garden party. Warm enough for outdoor activities, cool enough not to overheat the guests. Sunny enough to provide a profusion of light softened by a few puffy white clouds. The gardens bloomed in abundance, filling the air with varied pleasant scents and showing no evidence that many flowers had been plucked from them to grace the house.

If Jamie were a poet, he would pen the sentiments of his heart. At most, he could only think of Shakespeare's sonnet, "Shall I compare thee to a summer's day? Thou art more lovely and more temperate—" He could not remember the rest, and felt the fool for it. Perhaps he would memorize the Sidney love sonnet Marianne had read.

Now was the time. Now he must tell her how deeply he loved her, how leaving would be the hardest thing he'd ever done. Did she long to hear those words as much as he longed to say them? Or had their love been a mere pastime to her, the game of a bored, wellborn lady? Yes, she'd proclaimed her love and shown all the courtesies and generosities of such a sentiment. But had that merely been an amusement, safe for a young lady of her station to engage in because he would leave one day?

They came to a weeping willow and found refuge beneath its abundant tresses, a bower wherein he might speak the overflowing emotions of his heart. He turned to her and drew in a quick breath. Her eyes seemed like sparkling sapphires in her porcelain face, and tiny teardrops clung to her long black lashes. A rush of protectiveness overwhelmed him. He set both of their cups on the ground and pulled her into his arms.

"Marianne." He sighed.

"Oh, Jamie." Trembling, she laid her head against his chest and encircled his waist with her arms.

He held her for some time. When she tilted her head back

and gazed up at him, he kissed her. The sweet softness of her lips, the innocent trust in her eyes, made him realize all the more that he *must* protect her from every danger, including himself. "If someone should see us—" He tried to move back.

She clung to him. "I do not care."

He brushed his hand across her cheek and kissed her again, breathing in her sweet jasmine perfume. *Lord, help us. How easy it would be to fall into the world's ways. But I will not corrupt her or myself, as difficult as it may be to resist the temptations of the flesh.* He lifted his head. "We must not do this, my lady."

Marianne gave him a playful smirk. "Yet you do not push me away."

"No, my lady, I would never do that."

"Enough of 'my lady'." She tapped his lips with one finger. "Have I not told you? I am your Marianne, and you are my Jamie. 'My true-love hath my heart, and I have his.'"

He shoved away his fond remembrances of Sidney's poem. "That was long ago in a dream world. Now we must live in reality."

Her broken sigh cut into him. "Would you marry me if you could?" In her eyes, he read the same despair his own heart held. Somehow, for both of them, he must lighten this mood.

"Yes, my darling daughter of a lord. If I were the eldest son of a prince or duke or whatever you English consider worthy, I would marry you." He gently removed her arms from around him and gripped both of her hands. "But I am not. I am a simple merchant sea captain, your father's business partner, a working man." He pulled off one of his gloves. "Do you see these calluses? I've worked hard all my life, and I'm proud of them." She reached out to touch his hand, but he pulled back and put the glove back on. "Please don't think me vulgar for it, but that is the essence of who I am. And I will never be what your family and your station require."

She stepped back and crossed her arms. "Lady Weston married her footman."

"Lady Weston was a widow whose reputation set no example for a Christian girl."

Marianne stared at the ground for a moment, then lifted her gaze to meet his. "But you do love me, and you would marry me if Papa gave his permission?" A strange gleam flitted across her eyes.

Jamie blinked. "Yes, of course. I've already said that."

She seemed to suppress a smile and instead released another long sigh. "Very well. I am content with that knowledge."

"Good." Yet he didn't feel very good. The conversation had shifted without warning, and he had the strange feeling she was neglecting to tell him something important. But he dared not ask what it was. Perhaps reality had settled in her heart at last, as it had in his, and she'd decided to make the best of it. But if she went to her father and declared their love, he'd simply have to beg the earl's forgiveness. "May I escort you back to the others?" He offered his arm.

As they walked beside the lake, her mischievous smile further unnerved him, making him reconsider his conclusions.

Suddenly she peered around him toward the water and gasped. "Georgie!"

Jamie followed her gaze.

There in the middle of the bottomless lake, the rowboat was foundering, and the earl's grandson flailed and splashed his arms.

"Help me!" The boy's gurgling wail sounded across the water.

Chapter Twenty-Two

"Georgie!" Marianne cried out and started toward the water, but realized she had no power to save her nephew. The horror of the drama before her swept away all thoughts of her own happiness. "Lord, save him."

Beside her, Jamie was already stripping off his gloves, shoes and jacket. He splashed into the lake where, several yards out, he dived in and swam with powerful strokes toward Georgie. Jamie would save the boy. She knew it as certainly as she knew he loved her.

She looked along the shore, where the family and guests had become a wailing throng. Nursemaids and footmen paced the edge, and John the footman stood knee-deep in the lake. Marianne ran to them. Tears ran down Lady Bampton's cheeks, and she wrung her hands. Marianne pulled her into her arms. Oddly, the woman held fast to her. Papa stood at the water's edge, his hand pressed against his chest and his legs drenched. Like the footman, he appeared to have stepped into the water, but must have drawn back when Jamie plunged in. She heard prayers around her and joined in with all her heart.

Near the water, Georgie's sisters held on to each other, and both were crying. "You see, Betts," Katherine said, "if you had gone with Georgie, you would be drowning, too." Elizabeth wailed all the louder.

Thomas came running from the house, with William close behind. Marianne had not seen her plump oldest brother run since they were children. While he took his wife into his arms, Thomas kept going, splashing into the lake several yards before he stopped, apparently realizing, like Papa, that Jamie was capable of the rescue. He turned to the earl. "We just heard what happened." He waved impatiently toward the footmen. "Can't any of those blokes swim?"

Papa's shoulders slumped, and he looked his age. "I have no idea. 'Twas never required of them…until now."

Jamie swam toward shore using one arm, while holding Georgie's head out of the water with the other. He stopped and gained footing fifteen yards out, then lifted the unconscious child and brought him to land. Breathing hard, he fell to his knees, gently laid the boy on his side and pressed a fist against his stomach.

The throng clustered close until Robert shoved in front of them. "Get back. Give him room to breathe."

The footmen seemed to remember their calling and herded the guests away, while the family knelt around Georgie. Lady Bampton—Mary—prayed. William prayed. Robert prayed. Even proud Papa pleaded with his Maker for his heir. Mama appeared and knelt beside Papa, and he accepted her comforting embrace. Thomas leaned over Jamie's shoulder, yet did not interfere with his ministrations.

Georgie's pale face frightened Marianne. In truth, he looked dead. Yet Jamie calmly rolled him on his back and breathed several long breaths directly into his mouth. A spasm shook Georgie, and he coughed out a stream of water, coughed some more, then started to cry. "Annie," he called in a choking voice to his nurse.

Mary scooped her son into her arms. "No, my darling boy, not Annie, but your dearest mummy, who loves you so very much."

Georgie rewarded the effort by coughing more water onto his mother, and then clinging to her. Mary did not appear to notice her ruined gown, another uncharacteristic behavior.

Great sighs of relief filled the air, along with giddy laughter, as the family rose to their feet, each member reaching out to touch the boy's back, or embracing someone else.

Assured of her nephew's recovery, Marianne went to Jamie, who was still on his knees, inhaling deep breaths after all his exertion. "You saved him." She knelt and kissed his cheek.

As if her touch burned him, Jamie jerked away and jumped to his feet, then helped her up. "By God's grace, my lady." He warned her with a stern look, but she returned a warm smile. Surely his courage in saving Papa's only grandson would change everything.

"Ask what you will, Templeton, and it is yours." Lord Bennington sat in his kingly chair in the drawing room, surrounded by family and guests, and chuckled a bit uncomfortably. "As the rulers in the Scriptures used to say, 'Up to the half of my kingdom.'" The lines on the old man's face had deepened since the afternoon's near tragedy, even after Captain Moberly sent to Portsmouth for his ship's physician, who declared the boy recovered from his ordeal. Jamie had not disputed the physician's word, but he had seen drowning victims seem to recover, only to die later of a brain fever. He prayed that would not happen to Georgie.

Jamie noticed the crowd leaning forward for his answer, and he surmised he truly was expected to ask for something. A flippant laugh rose from his belly and tried to escape, but he swallowed it. What would this august group do if he asked Bennington for his only daughter's hand? What would the earl do? Jamie tried not to look at Marianne. But she stood just behind her father's chair, and her widened eyes and hopeful smile made clear her hope. She knew how to manage her father, but on this one matter, Jamie did not trust her judgment. Like David in the Bible, he dared not ask the "king" for his daughter.

"My lord, if you would keep that fine gelding, Puck, in your stable for me, I shall enjoy riding him upon my return."

The crowd applauded and breathed out their approval, but Marianne's jaw dropped and the fine arches of her eyebrows bent into a frown. Jamie shrugged ever so slightly. Even the earl seemed a bit disappointed, if his "harrumph" was any indication.

"I see you are a diplomat, my boy." He leaned one elbow on the chair arm and rested his chin on his fist. "Well, it will not suit. What do you want? Money? Land? That's it." He snapped his fingers. "I shall arrange with His Majesty to grant you some land near St. Johns Towne, a plantation near my own. You are a friend of my son Frederick—"

"A friend of all your sons, Father," Thomas Moberly said, a sentiment echoed enthusiastically by the viscount and Robert Moberly.

Jamie had no desire for a plantation, for he would never own a slave. Nor did he wish to settle anyplace until he'd succeeded in bringing East Florida into the Revolution, and all of the colonies were free from English rule. But he felt particular discomfort at the naval captain's praise. How could he call this man an enemy now?

"Yes, a friend of all my sons." The earl stood and clapped him on the shoulder. "And if a plantation does not suit you, we shall find something that will." He glanced around the room. "Well, now, everyone, go about your games." He waved one hand in a dismissive gesture. As the wellborn crowd disbursed, he stared into Jamie's eyes and squeezed his shoulder. "My boy, we must get you a wife." His pale blue eyes twinkled. "May I recommend Miss Kendall, whose company you seem to enjoy so much? While she is above you in rank, her lack of fortune precludes a more advantageous match. No doubt, the dear, compliant girl could be convinced that life in East Florida would suit her very well, for she has no other prospects."

Jamie opened his mouth to speak, but no words would come out. Bennington clearly thought he'd given Jamie a compliment by offering his wife's companion, and indeed the sweet lady would make the man of her choosing an excellent wife. But the earl had said far more than he realized. Did the man not comprehend how he had insulted both Jamie and Miss Kendall? Yet such was the attitude of these English lords and their king. Jamie thanked the Lord he'd not spoken for Marianne's hand.

After an awkward moment, he managed to find his voice. "Thank you, sir. I am deeply honored. But while Miss Kendall is a fine Christian lady, I would not burden her with the life of a sea captain's wife." He wished he could add that the earl would find a willing husband for the charming Miss Kendall among his own sons. "Nor would I settle such a gently reared lady in the wilderness of Florida." He glanced at Marianne, praying she comprehended the declaration was meant for her. Instead, she lifted her chin and wrinkled her nose in that quick little gesture he found so charming, despite its rebellious nature.

Lord Bennington chuckled. "You know your own mind, do you not, Templeton?" He wagged a finger at Jamie. "I shall continue to search for an appropriate reward for you. I am proud of my pedigree and my progeny. But a man my age with four sons should have a dozen grandsons by now. Thomas's young wife died with her child, and who would have Robert?" He coughed out a snort of disgust. "Of course, Frederick has received everything I'll ever give him, and his offspring will have nothing from me. But these others have not done their jobs in continuing my legacy. Even William should have more sons. So you can see why all my hopes for the family heritage lie in little George."

"Yes, my lord." Jamie's stomach turned at the earl's arrogant speech. This interview had done much to help him cut the cords of friendship binding him to this old man.

General Washington had insisted that Jamie maintain all his ties in England, which might mean he would have to return here to spy. But he would pray without ceasing that he might serve the Revolution in some other way.

Chapter Twenty-Three

"It would *seem* dreadfully scandalous," Miss Porter said. "But in truth, it would be completely innocent." The young heiress, Marianne's friend, sat primly in her chair, but her eyes were filled with mischief.

"Oh, dear." Marianne pretended shock. "My papa will be livid. The whole purpose of having Mama's garden party the week *after* Midsummer Eve is to avoid any association with pagan revelries, most of which take place in the middle of the night." Seated in the upstairs parlor with the younger, unmarried guests, she hoped no one would discover this entire game was her idea and Miss Porter her unwitting partner.

"Pagan revelries, ha," said Mr. Smythe, who everyone knew aspired to win Miss Porter's hand. "My father will think nothing of it. He has told me about some of his own youthful pranks, and this will be nothing compared to them. I rather think the old boy wants me to do something delightfully silly so he can brag about it to his friends."

"But is it fair to spoil the villagers' festivities?" Marianne looked at Robert, hoping he would contradict her. "Their summer fair takes place this Wednesday, and their feast is in the evening."

"I do not see that it would spoil anything at all," her brother said. "'Tis a grand idea, a treasure hunt in the forest between here and the village. We will not disturb their merrymaking." He frowned and puckered his lips thoughtfully. "However, to maintain propriety, the ladies must go in twos or threes, with at least one gentleman as an escort."

Marianne's heart sank. If she was required to have a partner and an escort, how could she make her escape?

"I say, what a good idea." Mr. Smythe nodded with enthusiasm. "We can have teams."

Others chimed in with suggestions that came near to ruining Marianne's plan, and she scrambled to think how to amend it. "Very well. Since my brother gives his approval, I, too, shall play. But should we not wear masks?" She eyed Miss Porter's blue gown. Perhaps her friend would trade clothes with her. "Part of the fun can be not knowing who our fellow players are."

Everyone shouted agreement, and someone found pen, ink and vellum and began a list of the rules. With great care, Marianne added a few more ideas, all the while plotting her very different course. The treasure would be divided in many parts, and every item must be found before the hunt was declared over. Surely that would last until dawn. Some time before midnight, dressed as Miss Porter, she would whisper to someone that she had grown tired and would return to her room. After a night of games, none of the younger set would be expected to rise until afternoon. With Jamie sailing just after sunrise, no one would miss her until too late.

Excitement filled her chest and made her breathless. Now she had only to enlist Emma's help, and her plan would succeed.

"I say, Moberly," Mr. Smythe said to Robert, "too bad your brother and Captain Templeton will be gone by then. They seem the sort of chaps who would enjoy such a romp."

Marianne smothered a gasp. She had not heard that Thomas would sail so soon, but this was all the better. Now, if Papa suspected her of going off with Jamie, Thomas could not pursue them. On the other hand, how else could she disappear other than to go with Jamie? Only one idea came to mind.

"Yes, it would be good to have extra men, for one never knows when the gypsies will return to the forest." She put on a worried frown. "Do be on the lookout, all of you."

Had she thought of every detail? Would something else come up to prevent her flight? Frequent twinges of guilt had struck her in the past few days, as if she had devised something evil, so Marianne had left off praying about her plan. Yet she could not help but think that God was directing her every step of the way.

"Flying Bennington's flag should keep you from unpleasant encounters with His Majesty's ships." Thomas Moberly, dressed in the full regalia of a British naval captain, stood with Jamie while the rest of the family began to gather in the entrance hallway. "If some officious fellow accosts you, you must use my father's name and mine and the letters we provided. But if you follow the heading I charted for you, you should reach East Florida without difficulty."

"Thank you, sir." Jamie forced a calm smile. If this man knew of the hundreds of muskets and the ammunition hidden in the *Fair Winds'* secret hold, or if he knew Jamie would sail to Boston to deliver them before returning to East Florida, he would sink the ship before she reached the open seas.

"How many guns do you have?" Captain Moberly's dark eyebrows bent into a frown.

Jamie coughed to cover his shock. "Guns?" Had this man read his mind?

Captain Moberly snickered and chided him with a friendly shake of his head. "Cannons, man." He clapped Jamie on the shoulder. "Surely you do not sail unarmed when the seas are filled with pirates and privateers who are eager to seize your cargo."

Jamie shrugged and huffed out a sigh, trying to hide his relief by sounding annoyed. "Ah, yes, the bane of every merchant captain. I have ten six-pounders—five port, five starboard—a twelve-pounder at the bow, and a crew that knows how to use them, sir."

"Hmm. I suppose that will have to do. 'Tis better than none at all." Thomas leaned closer. "You will be pleased to know that Governor Tonyn has been granted an admiralty commission and is issuing letters of marque to a dozen or more Loyalist sloops to protect the St. Johns River and the inland passage from Georgia." A measure of controlled anticipation filled his eyes. "A former Royal Navy officer, Captain Mowbray, has been contracted to lead the waterborne defense. This will deter the rebels from invading East Florida. In fact, on your next voyage, no doubt Tonyn will commission you to carry naval stores to the area. What do you think of that?" Patriotic pride shone from the captain's eyes. "We'll rout those scoundrels soon enough and put an end to this rebel nonsense."

"Very good, sir." During Captain Moberly's little speech, Jamie somehow managed to maintain his calm. This was the very information he needed to complete his mission. Now the Patriots would know what they were up against—that Tonyn had the orders, power and means to fully prosecute the war in East Florida—and could plan their assault accordingly. "And I'll deliver these letters to Governor Tonyn and tell your brother Frederick all you've said." Jamie sent up a prayer of thanks and contrition. He should have known the Lord would supply everything he needed to complete his mission for General Washington. Once again he knew without doubt God was on the Patriots' side.

While Marianne and the others clustered around Captain Moberly, Jamie played the part of a servant, bowing away to leave the family to their private adieus. Strange how he had grown used to effecting such poses, except when he and Marianne, Robert and Miss Kendall, had gone beyond sight of the manor house. But soon he could fully straighten his shoulders and once again be the captain of his own ship, an American Patriot answering only to God, conscience and the Continental Congress, with fealty not to a feudal-like lord but to a new nation of free men.

That afternoon, Jamie, Marianne, Robert Moberly and several household servants accompanied Quince and Emma to the church at the edge of the village, where Reverend Bentley led them in their marriage vows. Jamie stood beside his friend while Marianne stood beside her maid. More than once he gazed at the woman he could never have, to see tears glistening in her lovely blue eyes. Even though he rejoiced at seeing his friend happy, his own heart felt like a cannonball in his chest.

Afterward, they walked back toward the manor house, where a small wedding celebration was to take place in the kitchen among the household staff. Then Jamie would gather his belongings and travel to Southampton. Quince and Emma would follow later in the evening, after Emma had seen to the last of her duties as Marianne's lady's maid.

Chafing at the misery soon to visit Marianne and him,

Jamie offered his arm to her and fell back behind the others. His heart overflowed with love, as it had a few days before beneath the willow trees. Who knew the wedding of a friend could move a man so deeply?

"What a lovely bride Emma makes." Marianne's own loveliness was enhanced by her affection for her servant.

"Yes, and I've never seen Aaron…Quince grin so broadly." His emotions rioted within him. Grief must not cause him to slip from his role as Quince's master. "My lady…"

"Yes, my Jamie." She looked up and gave him a smile that was strangely serene.

"Tsk. Be careful." He winked at her, not feeling the slightest bit playful. "I won't have another private moment with you, but if you will permit, I'd like to tell you something."

"Of course." Her perfect eyebrows arched with expectation.

He cleared his throat, fearing he was treading on dangerous ground, fearing his words might inspire her to some foolish action. Yet he could not restrain himself. "If the course of history should ever level the ground beneath us to permit an equality made clear in Scripture, then perhaps by God's grace we can somehow be united." He prayed she would not notice the rebellion implicit in this declaration.

She stared at the ground before them as if hiding her widening smile. "What will it take to level the ground? Will you perform some gallant deed for His Majesty and be made a knight?"

"You know that's not possible." Why had he said anything? "I merely meant…it is my way of saying…I shall never love another."

She tugged him to a stop and faced him, no longer smiling or teasing, but staring up at him with misery in her eyes. "Nor shall I. And you must know this—if I cannot marry *you,* I shall not marry at all." Her lovely, full lips formed a pout of determination.

He stared down at her for only an instant before pulling her into his arms and kissing her with all the fervor burning in his heart. Right here on the village road. Right here where they could be seen, should someone look out of a manor house window. This moment of bliss could not be wrong, at least not before God, not when they had just pledged eternal love to each other.

A harsh whistle met Jamie's ears, snapping him out of his euphoria. He and Marianne looked up the road. While Moberly stared at them with fists at his waist, the others continued their walk toward the house. Now he beckoned sharply, his every move a warning. So this was it. Jamie might never see his love again. But he would carry her in his heart forever. *My true-love hath my heart, and I have hers.*

Chapter Twenty-Four

"**M**r. Saunders, you have done your duty admirably." Jamie's heart swelled with pride as he gazed at the *Fair Winds*. The ship had arrived in port the day before, but events at the manor had kept him from coming to Southampton any sooner to greet his crew. "She looks trim and fit, more than ready to take us home tomorrow at sunrise." In addition to recaulking and scraping and sporting a new mast, the ship wore fresh coats of paint inside and out. Her sails had been mended or replaced, and sheets and halyards restored good as new. "You've done a fine job all around." He eyed Saunders, his sea-weathered first mate, whose response to this praise seemed strangely subdued. "Is there something you're not telling me?"

"Well, sir…" Saunders scratched his brown-and-gray-bearded chin and stared up at the new mainmast, then over toward another merchant ship, then toward the town, his eyes seeming not to focus on any of them. "Ye see, sir, uh, well, sir, I—I've taken me a wife. Sir."

"A *wife*." Jamie thought the top of his head might explode. "What do you mean you, you've taken a wife?"

Saunders's pained grimace and cowering posture, so uncharacteristic of him, sent a wave of nausea through Jamie. He'd always prided himself on having a good relationship with his crew, especially someone as responsible as his first mate, who could very well captain his own vessel. "Does that mean you plan to stay here in England?" This man's patriot fervor had always been unmatched. Had some clever wench turned his mind from the Revolution?

"Well, sir, that all depends on you, sir." Saunders rolled his hat in his hands.

"On me?" Jamie could not think of losing this valuable sailor. "What—?"

"Well, ye see, sir, I want to bring me wife along." He moved closer to Jamie in a confiding pose. "Ye see, sir, Molly wants to go to America. She's willin' to throw her lot in with us, if you know what I mean, sir." He tapped the side of his nose to indicate he could say no more.

Jamie huffed out a cross breath. First Aaron and now Saunders. His friends could marry their ladyloves, but he could not. "What does the rest of the crew think of taking a woman aboard?" He looked around to see several other men standing close. They tried to look busy, but bent near, as if all too interested in this conversation between their captain and his first mate. A thread of worry wove into Jamie's chest.

"Well, sir, it seems there was several ladies of the same mind as my Molly." Saunders shrugged, and twisted his pie-shaped cap so hard it resembled a sausage.

"Several?" Now true horror swept through Jamie, that and a large measure of anger. "Do you mean to tell me that all this time you and the men have been *courting?*" Could it get any worse? He shook his head and exhaled a hot breath.

"Well, sir—"

"Saunders, if you say 'well, sir' one more time—" Jamie fisted his hands at his waist "—I'll not be responsible for my actions." Indeed, he felt like pummeling someone or something.

"Sorry, sir. But ye have to know a healthy man can't be expected to lie low in a town such as London and not seek out the comforts of a lady's presence." Saunders gave Jamie a gap-toothed smile.

"Just exactly how many 'ladies' are we picking up in London?" More nausea gurgled in Jamie's belly. Had his entire crew been bamboozled by tavern wenches? They should get out on the open sea right away, not sail back to London.

"Well, sir—" Saunders clapped a hand to his mouth, a gesture Jamie had never before seen him employ. "I mean, well, we don't need to pick up our wives in London. They're already aboard. All four of 'em."

"Four!" Rage filled Jamie, and he thought he might breathe out fire. Swinging away from Saunders, he strode to the gunwale and gripped it with both hands. Beyond Southampton lay Portsmouth and the vast British navy, countless sloops, frigates, ships of the line and men-of-war, vessels that could sink the *Fair Winds* if any hint of its true cargo and mission should be discovered. And, as if bringing Aaron's Emma weren't enough, adding four more souls, *female* souls, to this voyage made Jamie even more responsible to his Maker for their care. He took off his round-brimmed hat and brushed a hand over his hair down to his queue.

"Captain Templeton." Saunders came alongside him. "Jamie." He set a hand on Jamie's shoulder. "I can't say I'm sorry, sir. We're honest men, and our wives are the decent sort. Christian ladies, every one of 'em."

Jamie gave him a sidelong glance, this plain, muscular, bowlegged fellow who'd weathered the change from whaler to sailor to patriot without so much as asking for a single boon, except that he might remain in Jamie's crew. Seeing his friend's crooked grin, Jamie thought he might like his Molly for loving this homely but stouthearted man. Yet he could not stop the grief that gripped his own chest so hard he almost couldn't breathe. Why, if he must love a lady, did she have to be someone so utterly unattainable?

"Very well, Saunders." A dull ache of resignation rolled through Jamie's chest as he turned to complete his survey of the ship. "Just keep the women below and out of the way until we set sail." A true gentleman would call them forth to be introduced, but Jamie wasn't feeling much like a gentleman right now.

"Aye, sir." Saunders strode toward the crew, all of whom were grinning like fools. "Avast, me rowdies. Let's get this ship ready to sail at sunrise."

At their cheer, Jamie swallowed hard, as if this action could dislodge the cannonball in his throat.

"Emma, do you have room in your trunk for some of my things?" Marianne had pared her belongings down to the essentials, but they still made a bundle too heavy for her to carry.

"No." Quince answered for his bride, and without so much as a "my lady" to soften his curt tone.

Marianne stared across her bedchamber at the couple. If she ordered Emma to obey her, they doubtless would leave her behind.

"No, of course not." Tugging her new black cloak about her, she gave them a trembling smile. "Forgive me."

Quince came closer, and in the shadowed room, his dark

visage appeared ominous. "If not for my good friend's happiness, we would not risk taking you. If you cause even the slightest trouble, we'll say you forced us to take you with us."

"Your friend?" Marianne recalled some of this man's actions, hardly those of a well-trained valet. Yet Jamie defended him. Perhaps this was an American custom, to treat one's servants as friends. "Yes, of course. And do not be concerned, Mr. Quince, I shall follow our plan—"

A knock sounded on the door, and she gasped. Before anyone could move, Mama opened it and entered. "Emma, I brought you a little gift…Marianne!" She looked from her daughter to Emma to Quince. "What's this?" Even in the shadows, Marianne could see comprehension come over her mother's face.

"Oh, my lady," Emma trilled, "Lady Marianne is so kind to interrupt her games to see me off."

"Ah, I see." Mama looked down at Marianne's bundle, then stared at her, tears filling her eyes. "Well, then…" She closed the door behind her, swallowed hard and crossed the room to take her in her arms. "My darling girl." Her voice was thick. "I have known…I could see. I understand." She held Marianne in a death grip. "I was prepared to console you after his leave-taking, but you seemed so strong. I did not think you would… Why did you not tell me?"

Marianne sobbed against her mother's shoulder. "You know why."

Mama nodded. "Yes, I am grieved to say I do." She moved back and touched Marianne's cheek. "Now I understand why you embraced your father and me so fervently this evening." She laughed softly. "We thought it was gratitude for letting you and your friends have your treasure hunt." Another laugh, a sad one. "But you go to seek another treasure."

"Yes." Marianne felt a rush of anxiety and tried to pull away. "We must go, Mama. I love you…and Papa."

Mama held her fast. "Tomorrow I shall divert him as best I can. I will not tell him anything until absolutely necessary."

"You would face his wrath?"

Mama nodded again. "If I must. But I will also remind him that many frowned on our marriage because of my lower birth." She drew back, her eyes wide. "He will marry you, will he not?"

"Jamie Templeton is a man of honor." Quince stepped closer, "He'll do what's right. Now, my lady——" his every word conveyed anxiety "—we must go."

Mama gripped Marianne quickly, then released her and stared down at her bundle. "Oh, mercy, is that all you are taking?"

She shrugged, refusing to look at Emma or Quince.

"Gracious, child, take a valise or even a small trunk."

"There's no time, Mama." Marianne felt her knees quiver. For all the emotional benefits of Mama discovering her plan, would she now ruin the whole escape?

Emma hurried to the small chamber where she had slept for seven summers, and brought out a satchel. "Here, my lady." She quickly stuffed Marianne's extra belongings in it, in spite of Quince's fearful glances toward the door.

"Mr. Quince," Mama said. "I came to bring this one last gift to Emma." She retrieved a small leather bag from her pocket. As she handed it to him, the coins within it clinked, and his eyes rounded. "From Lord Bennington and me."

"Oh, thank you, my lady." Emma curtsied.

Quince blustered briefly. "Thank you, my lady." This time, his tone held true respect.

Mama kissed Emma's cheek. "Despite Lord Bennington's crossness at losing such a fine servant from his household staff, he sends his blessing on your union." She eyed Marianne wistfully. "I wonder if we'd had more courage, he might not have come around for another marriage. Oh, dear." Her eyes widened. "Do you have money?"

"Yes. I have been saving my pin money for some time." Marianne flung herself into her mother's arms. "I shall miss you, my dear one."

"I shall miss you, my darling girl." Mama sniffed back tears. "But I knew one day I would have to surrender you to some good man." She brushed a hand over Marianne's cheek. "How good to know that the man you chose is also the man who saved your father's grandson." She gave her an unladylike wink. "I shall remind him of that as often as I dare."

Chapter Twenty-Five

A week out of Southampton, the *Fair Winds* sailed into a storm that buffeted the ship for three days and nights. Once it abated, the vessel caught a rare northeasterly wind that swept it toward America at a good speed, as if the Almighty Himself hastened their journey. The gale had been appropriate weather for Jamie's unending tempest of emotions and a good immersion back into the sailing life. He'd expected his feelings to soften once he stood at the helm and felt the sun and wind on his face. But each time he thought the pain was all behind him, one or more of the brides ventured forth from below deck to catch some fresh air, and Jamie's anguish began all over again.

The only consolation he could claim was the information Thomas Moberly had bestowed on him, confident it would be safe with him. Yet even that was painful when Jamie contemplated his betrayal of people who had trusted him. He'd lived in the bosom of Bennington's family, given every benefit but adoption. And, of course, Marianne's hand. Still, his heart twisted within him. How could a man of honor be a spy? He prayed General Washington would find another use for him in the Revolution. Even turning the *Fair Winds* into a warship to meet the enemy face-to-face would be more honest than making friends only to betray them.

Becoming a battle-ready ship would not be the first change for this fine old vessel. For fifteen years she'd admirably performed her original purpose—whale ship. Then Captain Folger had refitted her as a merchant vessel, turning her over to Jamie as they made plans for serving the Revolution in East Florida. With her newly reinforced decks, she could carry more guns and many more sailors to fight for the Cause. The sloop even had three private cabins in addition to his captain's quarters to accommodate the officers a warship would require.

At the thought of the cabins, Jamie grunted. Quince, who wasn't a crew member, had paid for his cabin as a contribution to the Revolution. He and his Emma resided there. Naturally, first mate Saunders deserved one, and there he and his Molly slept. The other three wives were crowded into the third to protect their feminine privacy. They and their husbands would have to wait until they reached land to enjoy all the felicities of marriage.

Ten days out, Jamie sat in his cabin writing in his logbook. Other than the storm, the voyage had been uneventful. The previous day, a British man-of-war had sailed past, some two hundred yards off to starboard, but she'd merely saluted and gone on her way. No doubt her captain regarded the Union Jack flying on the *Fair Winds'* mainmast, and Bennington's banner beneath it, as sufficient to dispel any need for searching a merchant ship. Jamie duly noted the non-incident in his log.

A rap sounded on the cabin's door just as Jamie closed the book. "Come."

The door opened, and Demetrius, the ship's Greek

cook, peered around it. "'Morning, Cap'n Jamie. Sorry to disturb you, sir."

Jamie beckoned to him. "Not at all. Come sit down." He put the logbook on its shelf.

Demetrius shuffled into the cabin and placed his bulging form into a chair in front of Jamie's desk.

"Did you learn any new dishes in London?" Jamie asked.

"Naw, Cap'n, nothin' new. Them English just cook roast beef." Demetrius smirked. "It's a shame what they do with a good piece of lamb."

Jamie joined his laughter, but he could think of more than a few fine dishes he'd eaten at Bennington's table, including an excellent leg of lamb. "What can I do for you?" He noticed the concern in the middle-aged man's eyes. "Did you forget to pack enough flour or sugar? Are we out of fresh vegetables already?"

Demetrius's shrug was more like a wince. "Not yet, sir, though we're goin' through 'em faster than I thought we would." He clicked his tongue and gave his head a shake. "Thought I'd brought aboard plenty of stores. Even counted the wives as I planned, knowing you wouldn't have the heart to put 'em off the ship when you saw how happy the lads were. But with six ladies, two of 'em needing to eat for two, if you get my meaning, we'll be eating a bit slimmer 'till we reach Boston." He eyed Jamie. "Just thought I should let you know so you won't think I'm trying to starve anyone."

"Thanks." Jamie pulled a book from his shelf, planning to read for the rest of the afternoon. Then he started. "Wait. Did you say *six* ladies? You mean there's a wife I haven't met?" Whoever this female was, she'd better be a wife, or Jamie would thrash the man who'd brought her aboard. He'd never countenanced wenching among his men, and certainly not aboard his vessel.

Demetrius's eyes grew round. "Not that I know of, sir. I just know I been deliverin' breakfast and supper to four grateful ladies in their cabin."

"Thank you, Demetrius." Jamie gritted his teeth. "Was there anything else?"

The cook stood. "No, sir. Just wanted to warn you about the stores."

"Very well. Don't say anything to anyone about our talk." The charge wasn't necessary. Jamie's cook did not engage in gossip.

After Demetrius left the cabin, Jamie shelved his reading and considered the situation. This crew was comprised of good men, every one. They knew his rules and abided by them.

But who was this sixth woman? And how had she come aboard without his seeing her? He mentally went down the list of crewmen. Three had left wives at home in Massachusetts, several had vowed never to marry, and some admitted sheepishly that their English lady friends had refused their proposals. Jamie snorted. Once Saunders set the example, there must have been a rush among the men to find willing mates. And he'd learned one or two of these ladies had first met the others when they came aboard. They would think nothing of this sixth woman being a stranger among them.

A spy. The thought was so jolting Jamie jumped to his feet and strode across the cabin into the narrow hallway. The second cabin was at the far end of the vessel, and he quickly closed the distance. There he pounded on the heavy wooden door.

"Ladies, make yourselves presentable." He hoped the sternness in his voice would send them hopping, and from the muffled squeals and thumps within, he surmised he'd succeeded. After several minutes, he heard the latch click.

As the door swung open, Jamie felt some invisible object slam into his chest.

"Good afternoon, Captain Templeton." Marianne stood before him, an innocent, beatific smile on her flawless face.

"Marianne." The breathless rush of Jamie's voice, the arch of his eyebrows, the widening of his intense brown eyes, sent a surge of satisfaction through Marianne. Her surprise was complete. And long overdue. If she had to stay in this stifling room one more hour—

"Captain, would you be so kind as to escort me to the upper deck?" Marianne glanced over her shoulder at the women she had come to regard as sisters in romance, for they had all shared their love stories to keep up their courage while the ship pitched and rolled in the storm. She then looked back at Jamie, whose expression now bordered on horrified—not what she had hoped for. "I have not seen the sun for ten days. Or is it eleven? Down here, it is difficult to know."

Jamie scowled at her. "What are you doing here?"

His growling tone cut into her. She'd never imagined he would be cross with her.

"Wh-why, I thought—"

"Don't speak." Jamie gripped her arm. "Come with me." He pulled her down the hallway, or whatever these narrow passages were called.

"Ouch." She tugged against him. "Where are you taking me? Are you not pleased to see me? Jamie!" Her last words came out on a sob.

He opened a door and almost shoved her inside. The room—cabin, she corrected herself—was much larger than the other and nicely furnished with a desk, several chairs, and a bed, or berth, built into the wall.

Marianne settled into a chair, huffing with horrified indignation and trying desperately not to cry. "Well, Captain Templeton, it seems I have made a serious mistake. Obviously, all your gentle protestations of love for me were nothing short of a lie."

"Don't," he growled again. "Do not for one moment think that this is about my love for you." He ran a hand through his hair, loosening many strands from his queue, a gesture she had heretofore found charming. Now it seemed the gesture of a man enraged. Enraged at *her*. Papa had never treated Mama thus.

"Jamie." She spoke softly, as Mama did when trying to soothe Papa's ruffled feathers. But unlike her mother, Marianne could not stop her tears. "I love you. I—I thought you loved me. Why should we be separated by foolish social strictures?"

Jamie bent forward, his hands gripping the arms of her chair, his nose inches from hers. "You have no idea what you've done." He straightened and crossed his arms. "Yes, I love you." His tone did not confirm his words. "But you don't belong here, and I can't return you. We are ten days out, and I can't afford to lose time."

She laughed, but it sounded more like a squeak in her ears. "But I do not wish to return." A bitter thought occurred to her. "If you despise me for following you, then take me to my brother Frederick. How difficult can that be? You are sailing to East Florida anyway."

Jamie skewered her with a look. "We're not going directly to East Florida."

"But…wh-where are we going?" She stared down, clasping her hands as more thoughts collected, revealing a horrifying idea. Quince's disrespect. Emma's subtle remarks, disguised as humor, regarding His Majesty. The way the other women aboard the ship avoided certain topics. Marianne lifted her gaze to the man she loved. "Jamie, where are we going?" She was not certain she really wanted to know the answer.

"Boston." The word exploded from his lips.

"But Boston is occupied by the rebelling colonists and—"

As he lifted his chin and narrowed his eyes, she understood at last. Jamie was not the man he claimed to be. He was a rebel, one of those who hoped to drive the British from American shores. But why would he have befriended Papa? What had been his purpose?

Shattering reality struck her heart and mind. He was a spy. And no doubt he had been spying on Papa from the moment he walked into Bennington House last March. Or perhaps it began last year, at the very same time she was falling in love with him.

Indeed, by running away to be with Jamie Templeton, Marianne had made a horrible, irreparable mistake. The realization stole her breath, and she thought she might suffocate. The room became a swirling eddy, pulling her downward. She gasped for air, barely aware of the captain bending over her until he touched her arm.

"Marianne."

The concern in his voice cut through her struggle, and she pulled in air at last. "No. Do not touch me." Bitter anguish tore through her, and she burst out in sobs she could not control.

Chapter Twenty-Six

He was a beast. No other word would suit him. And Jamie cringed to see the fear in Marianne's face as, right before his eyes, she realized she had run from the safety of her father's house into the custody of her father's enemy. Yet, after she regained her breath, only to succumb to violent weeping, he clenched his jaw, tightened his arms across his chest and stared out through the porthole to keep from taking her into his arms. Why had she not accepted the fact that they couldn't be together? Foolish, wonderful girl. To think he'd once doubted the depth of her love.

He'd never before frightened a woman, and it grieved him deeply to cause this particular lady such pain. He was a Christian above all else, dedicated to serving his Lord even before the Patriot cause. That included treating women with respect and honor. He'd let no harm come to Marianne, but he must stay as far away from her as possible on this vessel.

He shouldn't have told her where they were going. That had revealed everything. Now, if they were accosted by a British vessel, she'd have the tools to give them away. And even if he kept her below deck where she could not alert them, his usefulness to the Glorious Cause had been destroyed forever. He could never return to England, for Bennington would doubtless have him drawn and quartered. Marianne's actions had put an end to his spying. If he were alone, he would laugh out loud. God had granted his wish not to spy anymore.

How had she come aboard? Who helped her? How had the man on watch at the time failed to see she was not like the other women, despite her plain clothing?

As her sobs subsided, he ventured to look in her direction, steeling himself against the temptation to comfort her. There she sat, dabbing her lovely face with a linen handkerchief, staring unfocused at the bulkhead. Her cheeks had grown puffy, and her eyes still leaked copious tears, but her lips formed a firm line. Before she fully gained her emotional footing, he must uncover her accomplice in her mad scheme.

"Whom did you bribe to help you come aboard? My watchman?" Jamie had been too full of grief his first night on board to recall who'd performed that duty, a sure sign he'd slipped in his ability to rule his own ship. "One of the other women?"

She glared at him with chin lifted. Too late. He saw in her sapphire eyes he was now her enemy, and a familiar raw ache settled in his chest. But he must ferret out the information. Who among his crew could be persuaded to betray him this way? Would they also reveal the store of muskets in the hold if a British naval officer came aboard? At least Marianne didn't know about that. Or did she?

"Jamie." Aaron pounded on the door. "Jamie, may I come in?" The urgency in his voice only mildly alarmed Jamie. Aaron was a passenger. If the ship were about to be accosted, Saunders or the second mate would alert him. But

Aaron's interruption might disarm Marianne into revealing her accomplice.

No. Aaron *was* her accomplice. There could be no other explanation.

Jamie yanked open the door. *"You."* Guilt wrote itself across Aaron's face, and only the grace of God restrained Jamie from slamming his fist into his friend's jaw. Emma peered around him, her pale blue eyes blinking. "What were you thinking, man?" He shoved past the two of them, suddenly needing to breathe some fresh air.

Ascending to the main deck, he first saw Brody, one of the newly married crewmen, standing at the gunwale. Brody grinned and touched his hat in an informal salute. A growl rumbled in Jamie's throat, and he strode across the deck and up the steps to the quarterdeck. There Crane, another new groom, stood at the helm. At Jamie's appearance, he also saluted. "How do, Cap'n?"

Not trusting himself to speak, Jamie ordered him away with a jerk of his thumb and gripped the wheel himself. Crane left, scratching his head, probably wondering over the captain's ill temper. But suspicion crept into Jamie's thoughts. Had they all known about Marianne? Clearly, Demetrius had discovered it, although he didn't seem to know her identity. But what of the others? Had their wives said nothing to them?

"Saunders," Jamie bellowed into the wind. In seconds, his first mate stood in front of him, calm curiosity in his eyes.

"Aye, sir." Saunders touched his hat, as Brody had, in an informal salute, which until today had shown sufficient respect to satisfy Jamie. "Is everything all right?"

"No, everything is not all right." Jamie stared at the distant horizon. "Did you know that we had an extra passenger, a woman, on board?"

Saunders drew back and scratched his bearded chin. "Why, no, sir. Just Mrs. Quince, my Molly, and the other three ladies, our wedded wives." He tilted his head. "Are ye sayin' we got a stowaway?"

Jamie narrowed his eyes and glared at him. He'd always trusted this man…until now. Now Jamie didn't know whom to trust. "So you didn't know about—" He stopped, realizing his near mistake. If the crew learned of Marianne's title, he couldn't predict what their responses might be. "Mr. Quince brought along one of his wife's friends, though I've yet to determine why." Indeed, Aaron had lumped Marianne's entire family into one basket, despising them all. Why would he help her run away?

"He did?" Saunders shook his head. "Sorry, Cap'n Jamie. I should've been payin' more attention when he and his bride come aboard that night. Too much confusion with that extra shipment of wool and all, but that's no excuse."

Jamie believed him. "Very well." If Saunders didn't know about Marianne, few other members of the crew would, either. But how had the other wives kept the secret of their extra companion from their husbands? A fresh wind swept over him, and he inhaled deeply. Then a picture of Marianne came unbidden to his mind. She'd been confined to the cabin below deck for the entire voyage. "The lady might appreciate—"

"Sail, ho," cried the watchman in the crow's nest high above the deck. "Flyin' the Union Jack, Cap'n."

Handing the wheel to Saunders, Jamie retrieved his telescope from his belt and extended it to view the oncoming vessel. A British forty-gun man-of-war was bearing down on them, flying over the waters like a pelican about to devour a fish.

Taking the helm again, Jamie frowned at Saunders. "Pass

the word among the crew. They know what to do. Mind what we've practiced."

"Aye, sir." Saunders started to leave, but turned back. "And don't ye be worryin' about the wives, Jamie. They all know what we're about."

His words jolted Jamie. The women knew their husbands were secret revolutionaries, yet they'd kept their own secret about Marianne. Now he truly had no idea of whom to trust.

This had been a bad plan from the beginning, leaving his crew to gad about London for these several months. How could he expect healthy, reputable men not to seek the company of decent ladies? And once they married, how could they keep from revealing their true loyalties to their wives? Yet the ship couldn't have sailed back to America without repairs, which had taken far too long, leaving plenty of time for mischief and mischance. He should be thankful God had protected them all from something far more dangerous than marriages.

Lord, help us. Keep these English sailors from finding our cargo. His instinctive prayer reminded him God had permitted the storm that damaged the mast, and the hull had been long overdue for a careening, something not available in East Florida. No good thing could have come from sailing without those repairs. A certain peace settled over and within him. God had let *all* of these things happen. He would see them through.

The only thing Jamie couldn't reconcile with the Lord was the presence of a certain little aristocrat aboard his ship. And as the man-of-war came alongside, he realized that he'd not sent anyone to imprison her so she couldn't give them away.

Finding her way back to the ladies' cabin, Marianne sensed Quince and Emma close behind her. Were they following to support her or to make certain she did nothing wrong? But what harm could she do to anyone aboard this ship? In the cabin, the other four women eyed her with more than a little interest.

"Well?" Molly, the matronly woman somewhere near Mama in age, gave her a merry smile. "Did you get your man settled down?" She threw back her head and laughed. "My, I thought I'd split a seam seein' the cap'n so put out with you. Tell us, dearie…why, what are these tears?" She raised her arms and Marianne flew into her embrace, weeping against her shoulder for several moments.

"Oh, bother." Marianne lifted her head and blew her nose on her wet handkerchief. "I thought I had finished crying."

"Here, now." Molly handed her a dry cloth. "What's the matter with the cap'n? Wasn't he glad to see you?" She propped her hands on her waist in indignation.

Shaking her head, Marianne continued to sniff. What could she say to these dear women? All they knew about her was her first name and that she had fled her disapproving father to follow Jamie. So far, Quince and Emma had kept her identity secret. In fact, Quince treated her far better as plain Marianne than he ever had when she was Lady Marianne. What a strange twist of events. Now these new friends loved her, while the man she loved turned his back on her. While the man she loved turned out to be a traitor to her father and his king.

A familiar crewman—Nancy's husband—bustled down the passage. "All right, ladies," Brody said. "This is it. This is what we told you about. Do you all remember what to do?"

"That we do, Mr. Brody." Molly, who by reason of her age and strong personality had become the ladies' resident matron, motioned them to come close. She gave Marianne a long look, then turned to Quince. "Sir, does Miss Moberly know what to do?"

Quince wiped a hand across his mouth. "*Miss* Moberly, may I speak with you for a moment?" He tilted his head toward the companionway.

Marianne's thoughts scrambled in a thousand different directions. "What's happened? Are we in danger?" She followed him and Emma to a quiet corner not far from the cabin.

Quince gripped her upper arms gently and seized her gaze with dark, earnest eyes. "Lady Marianne, Mr. Brody's alert means we've been accosted by a British naval vessel."

She gasped. Had Papa sent someone to save her?

As if reading her thoughts, Quince gripped her more tightly. "You must stay with the ladies in the cabin and not make a sound." A pinch of fear crossed his face. "You do realize, of course, that if you give us away, we'll all hang— Jamie included, this very day—and this ship will be commandeered."

Marianne swayed, but this time not from the ship's motion. The lives of these traitors were in her hands. *Dear Lord, what shall I do?*

"I am taking Emma to our cabin. As passengers, we do not expect to be troubled by the British." Quince shook her gently. "Must we bind and muffle you and lock you in our closet?"

"No." The word came out without a thought, but in truth, she had no idea what she would do if the British sailors came below and questioned her.

Chapter Twenty-Seven

Jamie had learned from Lamech Folger, his uncle, mentor and East Florida partner, that full and friendly cooperation was the only way to appease these officious British captains. As the uniformed, thirtyish man climbed over the gunwale, Jamie smiled and tipped his broad-brimmed hat. "Welcome aboard, Captain. Jamie Templeton, at your service."

Flanked by several armed officers and perhaps fifteen sailors, the red-haired man eyed Jamie up and down. "I am Captain Reading of the HMS *Pride*. I see you are flying the Union Jack and Lord Bennington's flag." He glanced toward the top of the mainmast. "However, in these uncertain times, such symbols might be a ploy. You will understand that it is my responsibility to make certain no arms or contraband are aboard your vessel."

"Yes, sir, I do." Jamie thought the man looked reasonable enough, but one officer behind him wore a sneer, and the sailors, armed with cudgels, glared around the ship. A twinge of nausea struck Jamie, and he prayed their captain would not decide to press members of the *Fair Winds'* crew into service. "You will find a large volume of goods in our hold, sir. We sail to East Florida, where my business partner, Lord Bennington, expects to make a tidy profit among the Loyalists who are fleeing all that nonsense in the northern colonies." Should he offer this man his choice of the goods as a bribe?

The captain's left eyebrow flickered briefly. "We will search your vessel, sir, with your permission."

Jamie covered his anger with a coughing chuckle. This treatment was one of the many reasons for the Revolution, this unreasonable searching of ships. "Of course. I would expect nothing less from His Majesty's navy." He gave a quick little nod to confirm his words. "This is how you keep us all safe. May I show you around?"

Reading's eyes narrowed. "No, thank you, sir. My men know what to do."

Despite his growing rage, Jamie managed another smile. "Very well, sir. I am your servant."

Reading motioned to his men, and his three officers took several sailors each to search various parts of the ship, including below deck. The captain then glanced around the main deck. "We have lost several of our crew to unfortunate accidents, and require replacements. You may ask for volunteers or select them yourself. If you choose not to cooperate, I will make my own selections."

Raw fear cut into Jamie's chest. He would die for any of his men, but who else would die if he resisted this demand? And what of the ladies' safety? "Sir, I have a letter from Lord Bennington, also signed by Captain Thomas Moberly, of the HMS *Dauntless*. These should exempt my crew from impressments." Now he would learn just how powerful his former patron was.

After a brief, startled blink, Reading snorted. "You have

notable protectors, Captain Templeton. How shall I know the signatures are not forgeries?"

Jamie faked a lighthearted shrug. "I don't know, sir. But if you'll permit my first mate to fetch my papers..." He beckoned to Saunders, who always kept his head during these boardings.

"Very well." Reading gave a curt nod.

Saunders scampered below deck and within minutes returned with a brown leather satchel. Striding close to the British captain, he gave him a gap-toothed grin. "Here ye go, sir."

Leaning away with lips curled, the captain took the satchel. "That will be all." He set it on a nearby crate and untied the strings, drawing out the life-saving documents. His eyebrows arched as he read through them. "Impressive, indeed. Yes, I recognize Lord Bennington's seal." He frowned as he kept reading. "So Bennington's son has been made a captain. A good man, Thomas Moberly. But I see nothing here exempting your crew from impressments."

His heart hammering almost out of his chest, Jamie considered his options. The men had practiced what to do in case of pirate attacks, but they would have little defense against a forty-gun ship with sailors who were trained for warfare. Yet every person on this sloop had been entrusted to his care, a fact that gave him no other choice. He leveled a solemn gaze upon the British captain. "Captain Reading, I am not prepared to part with any of my crew."

Marianne was pleased to see Molly come to the cabin and take charge. After covering the single porthole, the five ladies huddled silently together in the locked, darkened room. Above them and in the companionway beyond the door, heavy footsteps thumped against the decks, while an occasional clunk of wood against wood sounded through the walls. Marianne felt Nancy tremble beside her, and drew the slender young girl into her arms. "Shh. It will be all right." Despite Jamie's—Captain Templeton's—betrayal, she knew him to be a competent captain. And of course the British captain would be reasonable and no doubt send them on their way once he had seen Papa's letter.

For the briefest moment, Marianne considered whether she should break out of this cabin and confess everything to her countryman. But Quince's words weighed heavy upon her heart. While Captain Templeton and even Quince might deserve to hang, she could not reconcile seeing these ladies' husbands likewise punished. An image of their captain strung up on a gibbet flitted into her mind and cut deep into her. *Lord, forgive me, but I love him still.* Yet he was a traitor to all she held dear, and every word he had spoken to her had been a lie.

Sudden pounding on the door startled her, and beside her Nancy jumped. "Open up, or we'll break down the door."

More trembling and several quiet sobs shook the women around Marianne.

"Mind yourselves, ladies," Molly whispered. "Remember what we're to do."

Marianne could hear footsteps shuffle across the dark room. A click of the bolt, another click of the latch, and Molly swung the door open.

A snarling sailor stuck a lantern inside, and his shadowed face took on a grotesque sneer. "Well, well, what have we here?" Behind him, two other sailors stuck their heads around the doorjamb, leering into the dark and making crude comments.

Molly tried to hold her place and block them from entering, but they shoved her aside.

"I'll take this one." The first sailor grabbed for Nancy, yanking her up from the cot. The other men laughed.

A bolt of rage and protectiveness flashed through Marianne. "How dare you?" She stood and dug her fingernails into the man's bare hand. "Let her go."

He yelped and then drew back his hand to strike Marianne.

"Stop!" An officer holding another lantern entered the low doorway.

The first sailor cursed and stepped back. "Aye, sir." His wolflike growl sent a shudder down Marianne's spine.

"What is this?" The officer's face glowered in the shadowed cabin. "Who are you women?"

"Sir," Molly said, "we are Christian ladies accompanying our husbands to East Florida."

Like the first sailor, the officer sneered. "Ladies, indeed."

"Yes, ladies, indeed." Marianne pushed in front of Molly. "I am *Lady* Marianne Moberly, daughter of Lord Bennington, under whose flag this ship sails." She heard the gasps around her and knew these gentlewomen would never regard her in the same way again. Yet she would still be their friend. Whatever lie she must tell, Lord forgive her, she would save them from these sailors, even if it also meant saving that scoundrel, Jamie Templeton.

The officer raised a questioning eyebrow and his mouth hung open for an instant. Marianne lifted her chin and gave him an imperious glare. He lowered his lantern and bent forward in a deep bow. "My lady, may I have the privilege of escorting you to the upper deck?"

Air. The thought of it almost undid Marianne. But she managed to maintain her hauteur. "You may, my good sir, but only if these ladies are permitted to accompany me. I will not have my friends left to the *care* of your sailors."

The man had the grace to look abashed. "Yes, my lady."

He offered his arm, and she set her hand upon it, praying for wisdom to say the right thing to his superior. Praying for the strength not to look at her erstwhile love, now her nemesis. Was there some way she could alert the British captain that Templeton was a spy and might be carrying secrets to the rebelling colonists in Boston? Nothing came to mind, but she felt certain the Lord would show her exactly what to do.

Coming out into the daylight for the first time in over a week, Marianne winced and blinked, shading her eyes with both hands while the ocean breeze caressed her face and filled her lungs with salty air. She felt a tap on her shoulder and looked back to see Molly, her eyes filled with fear and hope, holding forth a much-mended black parasol.

"Thank you, Molly." Marianne accepted the gift, offered perhaps to gain her favor in protecting Molly's husband from being impressed. Marianne chided herself for such a suspicious thought. But the revelations of these past few hours had utterly destroyed her starry-eyed foolishness. She raised the parasol and found relief from the sun's glare.

Surveying the scene, she noticed the officer who had escorted her on deck had moved toward his captain, a man of medium height who looked familiar. Beyond them, she saw the *Fair Winds* crew standing in a straight line, while several British sailors perused them as if searching for the right horse to buy. Or the right slave. The anger and fear in the Americans' faces sent a troubled pang through her heart. *So this is the reality of impressments.* Marianne shuddered to think what it would be like to be torn from one's friends and forced into an enemy's service.

"Lady Marianne." The captain strode toward her, a wide smile on his freckled face. "What a surprise to find you sailing—"

"Under my father's flag?" She did not return his smile or offer her hand. "Good day, Captain Reading. It has been some time since my brother introduced us when you both received your commissions as lieutenants." She lifted her chin and sniffed. "I shall write to him and describe this meeting."

"Ah, yes, well." Reading stiffened. "We are simply doing our duty to king and country, my lady."

"Indeed. And when does that duty include stealing my father's servants right off of his business partner's ship?" The words came out unplanned, but now she could not give Templeton away without betraying the entire crew. "Do you not realize that this ship carries official mail to the governor of East Florida? Through an act of Parliament, that duty exempts its crew from impressments." If she had not overheard Thomas discussing it with Papa, she never would have known of the law.

Reading tilted his head in a patronizing nod. "My lady, although your esteemed father is this captain's patron, the ship is still an American vessel, not a British mail packet. The law does not apply in this case."

Marianne answered his look with a glare while she considered his words. She would not lose her battle with this intractable man.

The British sailors now dragged away two men, one of whom must be married to Sally, for Marianne heard the girl sobbing behind her. The violence of the sailors toward the hapless men, one of whom was a sweet-faced boy she had seen in the hallway outside the ladies' cabin, seemed entirely unwarranted in light of the two men's cooperation. Perhaps they sought to sacrifice themselves for their fellows. As a British sailor lifted his club to strike, Sally wailed.

"Stop, this instant!" Marianne marched across the deck.

"How dare you? Release these men immediately, or you will regret it all your days."

The sailors obeyed, but one had the audacity to leer at her before looking toward his captain. Marianne turned back to Captain Reading. "In the name of King George and Lord Bennington—" she modulated her voice into a lower register and used a cold, hard tone, as Papa did when giving orders *"—release them."*

The shock that swept across the men's faces, both British and American, amused her. While of course she possessed no authority over these men, they had no idea how much or little influence she might actually wield with their superiors. As for Captain Templeton, he puckered a smile and winked away the glint in his eyes. His slight nod, like many that had secretly conveyed his feelings for her these past months, sent a tingle through her traitorous body.

"Captain Reading." Marianne sauntered back toward him, thrown slightly off balance when a swell lifted the ship, but quickly regaining her footing. Another approving nod came from Captain Templeton, but she did not acknowledge it. "If you hope to advance any further in your naval career, I suggest you do not make me unhappy. It may take months, it may take years, but my father, the Admiralty and His Majesty's Privy Council will hear of your treatment of the men who have been assigned the duty to protect me."

Captain Reading clenched his jaw and glared at her for what seemed an eternity. At last, he shrugged and waved his men away from their captives, then swept off his bicorne and bent toward her in an exaggerated bow. "Your servant, my lady." He spun around and barked orders at his crew to leave.

The British sailors clambered into their small boats, but Marianne would not let herself breathe until the last man had returned to His Majesty's man-of-war.

Chapter Twenty-Eight

Marianne stood at the railing with the five other ladies and Mr. Quince to watch the HMS *Pride* tack away, leaving the entire crew of the *Fair Winds* unharmed. When the other vessel was some distance away, even as the crew members hoisted the sails to catch the wind and carry their ship in the opposite direction, everyone cheered. All Marianne felt was desolation.

The other women now eyed her with an odd mix of expressions. Nancy gazed at her as if she were a saint, no doubt because Marianne had stopped the sailor who'd tried to assault her. Sally kissed Marianne's hand and thanked her for saving her husband from impressment. Eleanor glared, her lips curling in disapproval, but Marianne could not guess why, for the woman had always been pleasant to her before. Molly's posture devolved into that of a servant. Only Emma treated her no differently.

How could Marianne continue to share that cramped cabin with women who either worshipped or despised her?

"Lady Marianne." The all too familiar voice spoke behind her. "May I have a word with you?"

She turned to see Captain Templeton standing tall and proud. No, not proud. Intense. His dark brown eyes held her gaze, and her insides began to flutter. She would not do this. She would never again succumb to his charming ways. Pushing past him, she walked toward the steps leading below, even though she dreaded returning to the airless cabin.

He gripped her arm. "May I speak with you?" It was more of a command than a question.

"Let me go."

"Jamie, let her go." Quince stood nearby with Emma, who sent Marianne a quivering smile.

"Stow it, Aaron." Templeton's handsome, well-tanned face creased with annoyance. "You have yet to answer to me for her being here. Don't try to interfere now."

Quince bit his lip and shrugged. "Don't do something you'll regret." He put an arm around Emma and moved away.

The intensity in Templeton's eyes increased. "I must thank you, my lady, for saving my crew from impressment. That, above all, makes your presence aboard my ship nothing short of a blessing." He loosened his grip and winced. "Forgive me. I would not hurt you for the world."

"But you would deceive me…deceive my father, my brothers—" She stopped, recalling the undeniable improvements in Robert's character, little Georgie being saved from drowning, the lightened moods in family gatherings because of this man's humor. Gulping down sudden tears, she leaned away from him, aware of the shuttered glances sent their way by the other women and the crew. "You are a liar and a brigand, a traitor and a spy."

He had the audacity to laugh. "I do believe you've put an end to that latter occupation."

She yanked her arm from his grasp…and felt the loss of his touch. Still, she would not look at him but stared off across the wide, desolate sea at the retreating HMS *Pride*. "Ha. If I could have told Captain Reading the truth about you without ruining these innocent women's lives, I gladly would have watched you hang from your own yardarm." No, that would have destroyed her…and Emma, too. For undoubtedly Quince was also a spy.

"But you did *not give me away*." The mirth in his voice drew her sharp look. "To show my gratitude, you may have my cabin, so you'll be more comfortable for the rest of the voyage. I'll sleep in the crew's quarters, and you'll have access to my library and other amenities."

She drew in a deep breath, grateful for the fresh sea air, and glanced beyond him, where the other ladies watched this little drama. No doubt they would be pleased to have a bit more space in their cabin, but it grated on her sensibilities to accept anything from this man. Yet her thoughts continued to contradict her sentiment. How could she deny that, traitor or not, he had done far more for her family than they had done for him?

"I thank you, Captain Templeton. I accept your offer. And you can be assured you will be paid for my passage when we reach my brother Frederick's home." She could not stop her voice from quavering. "Whenever that might be."

Jamie watched Marianne—*Lady* Marianne, for that was the way he must think of her now and forever—walk gracefully across the rolling deck toward the ladder, her proud carriage stirring a rush of emotions within him. When she'd accosted that pompous British captain, all of Jamie's anger toward her had dissolved, and he'd seen God's grace clearly enacted. Profound relief flooded him as he considered the miracle that had just unfolded. He wouldn't try to imagine how many good people aboard this ship might have died without her interference, for he knew not one of his crewmen would have suffered his fellows to be impressed. Jamie himself would have joined the fray without a second thought for the consequences.

And now he must also forgive Quince for his part in Lady Marianne's flight. Of course the romantic rascal had intended to secure Jamie's happiness by sneaking her aboard the ship. Instead, now that she realized he'd been spying on her father, she'd never forgive him, and the final obstacle to a future together for them had been set in place. Because of it, Jamie felt an aching loneliness he doubted would ever go away.

Shaking off the tendrils of gloom threatening to entwine around his heart, he thanked the Lord he still could manage to do something of value for the Glorious Cause. If they could catch the right winds to help them sail against the Gulf Stream, they might reach Boston in another six or seven weeks. There he would report his findings to General Washington and receive his orders for taking the Revolution to East Florida. In the meantime, he must treat Lady Marianne with utmost care. Should they encounter another British man-of-war, he would need her continued goodwill toward the other ladies to once again avert tragedy.

Until such time, he would give her the run of the ship, for she had endured many days of confinement below deck, a fact that stung him when he thought of all she'd given up for love of him, only to face a terrible reality. He would never throw it in her face that he'd warned her, that he'd refused to court her, and only in his weakest moments had surrendered to his longing to hold her in his arms and kiss her. One thing now was certain. Because she'd stowed away, he couldn't escape her presence, and the rest of this voyage would shred his already tattered soul.

He'd not felt the discomfort of a crewman's hammock for seven years, and over the next few nights, he discovered how much he'd grown since his eighteenth birthday. Either his feet or his head must hang out one end or the other, and his shoulders had grown much broader, so he felt folded in half by the canvas sling. Further, the snores of his sleeping crewmen kept him awake and cross. Never mind the smells of sweat and bilge water. He considered taking the helm at night, but a captain should be up and about in the daylight, so he must make do with whatever sleep he could get.

Over a week had passed since the incident with the *Pride,* and Jamie permitted himself some small pleasure in watching Lady Marianne walk about the deck each day. The ragged black parasol wasn't appropriate for a lady who'd always had the best of everything, yet she seemed to take no notice. Jamie offered to bring out one of the fashionable new parasols from the cargo hold. But she snubbed him outright, refusing to answer him or accept the gift, even when the sun's reflection on the sea colored her cheeks with a pink blush and scattered faint freckles across the bridge of her pretty porcelain nose. Surely now she must realize how much she would have sacrificed in becoming his wife. Even if he'd not been a spy and, in her eyes, a traitor, no doubt by now the foolishness of her undertaking would still have been impressed upon her.

Molly and the others ladies hovered around her. Except Eleanor, who kept her distance, though Jamie could not guess why. And his freedom-loving crew members seemed all too willing to give her the homage due to a queen. Even Quince fell under Lady Marianne's spell and permitted Emma to attend to her former mistress's needs. Jamie would have laughed, except that no one but he seemed to realize how their fawning over this lady aristocrat contradicted their dearly held belief in freedom. While this couldn't cause too much trouble as long as they were at sea, he began to wonder if she held the power to sway some of them away from the Revolution. But what nonsense that was, after all he and his crew had been through together. Too little sleep— and a broken heart—were distorting his thinking.

Marianne tried to read the books from Captain Templeton's library, but found her mind drifting like flotsam swaying hither and thither on the ocean waves. She could not imagine what drew men to the sea. If required to spend her days sailing back and forth across the ocean, she would die of boredom. But then, to be fair, the other women, none of whom had ever sailed before, seemed to enjoy themselves without reservation once their mal de mer ceased— thanks to her ginger tea. While Marianne could not comprehend what they saw in their uncultured American husbands, she could not help but feel a few pangs of jealousy over their marital happiness, something she would never enjoy.

And then there was the strange attraction these Englishwomen had for the rebellion in the colonies, a truly contradictory behavior. Once Marianne's identity was revealed, they showed her every courtesy her rank demanded, which placed upon her the task, indeed, the responsibility, of reclaiming their loyalty to His Majesty and England. Once the ladies were won, she would help them win over their husbands. But how to go about it? What would Mama do?

Why, she would give a ball.

During the day, Marianne heard the steady metered songs of the men as they went about their work. In the late evenings, the music of a fiddle, fife, flute and drum wafted from somewhere on the ship. While the unknown musicians did not possess exceptional talent, she felt certain they could manage some country dances, a hornpipe, perhaps even a minuet on the rolling deck of the ship. Of course, there must be a supper, too. She would consult with Demetrius about the extent of his food stores when he brought her dinner this very evening.

Despite the renewed sense of purpose these plans gave her, she continued to weep herself to sleep each night, for her heart ached at the realization she had never truly known Captain James Templeton. She had loved an ideal, a noble knight who did not exist, and found the real man, however charming, to be nothing but a deceitful scoundrel no better than Robert's disgusting former friend, Tobias Pincer.

But she was her father's daughter, and she would beat this scoundrel at his own game. She would spy on him and his crew and find out how to undercut his every move.

Chapter Twenty-Nine

"Demetrius says he will add some special spices to the salted beef and make oat cakes with raisins." Seated at the captain's desk, Marianne enjoyed the delight in Molly's eyes at this pronouncement. The woman held the esteem of the other ladies, and Marianne wanted to make her an ally in her plans. "We will have *four* removes, even a fish course." Mama would be shocked by fewer than seven removes, with twelve being her preference, but Marianne must make do with what was available. "With peas, pudding and cider, it should make a fine supper. Demetrius has some table linens, and I have given him permission to open the crate of Wedgwood china my mama shipped for my brother's wedding gift. Demetrius and his son will serve as footmen. He says they even will wear white gloves. Can you imagine that? We will set a fine board here in my cabin."

"Oh, my lady, how grand." Molly breathed out the words on a sigh. "The other ladies and I will dig out our finest dresses from the packing barrels and freshen them in the breeze." A frown flitted across her face. "I wish we could do something to help you."

Marianne expected this offer. "Why, you can decorate this cabin and the entire ship. Hmm." She glanced around the room with its stark furnishings. Other than a dozen or so books, two lanterns, and crossed swords mounted on the wall, not one decorative figurine or picture graced the chamber. Captain Templeton had removed his sea chest and other personal items, but his lingering woodsy scent stirred her senses.

She quickly changed the direction of her thoughts. "I would like to have flowers for the table. Do you suppose you could fashion some from bits of fabric? I understand there is a large shipment of lace, silk, cotton and other such material in the ship's hold, all bound for a mercantile shop in East Florida. We can sprinkle the artificial blossoms with perfume." When she reached the colony, she would pay the merchant for the fabric. "If there is any bunting to be had, we'll drape it around the deck."

"Aye, my lady." Molly nodded with enthusiasm. "We're all handy with a needle." Another frown touched her brow. "Do you think the unmarried men will be cross not being invited to our grand supper? My Mr. Saunders says it's not good to have a grumbling crew."

Another concern Marianne had prepared for. "To prevent that, we shall send portions to each of them. And perhaps, if your husbands agree to let you dance with those other gentlemen, they will anticipate the festivities with the same enthusiasm as the rest of us." Marianne tapped her chin thoughtfully "I shall dance with them myself. That should take care of everything."

"Indeed it should." Molly clasped her hands to her chest as if trying to contain her glee, a response that assured Marianne her efforts would not go unrewarded.

When she sent the older woman to apprise the captain of

her desire for a ball and supper, his positive response surprised her. But then, why would he deny his crew both the anticipation of a grand event and its fruition? His compliance, along with Marianne's new freedom to wander the ship at will, gave her all the means she required to begin winning back the crew's loyalty to the king. Each time a pleasant memory of the captain intruded into her thoughts, she forced herself to remember God's true purpose in permitting her ill-advised flight from her home.

"Jamie, you're missing all the fun." Aaron climbed the ladder and ambled across the quarterdeck. "I'd take the wheel, but we'd end up in Bermuda…or back in England."

"We'll head south soon enough, God willing." Jamie squinted into the afternoon sun as he watched the empty horizon. On the main deck, Flint and the other musicians played their lively tunes, while the rest of the crew took turns dancing with the six ladies. Jamie chuckled. He was having difficulty not tapping his feet in time with their music—or laughing at the dancers. His merrymaking men, who could keep their footing in a storm or climb the sheets without misstep, all had need of Mr. Pellam's services. But Jamie's former dance master would be appalled to see Lady Marianne smile so beguilingly and take the roughened hand of a sailor who that very afternoon had scrubbed the deck on which they now danced.

"Seriously, Jamie." Aaron clapped him on the shoulder. "Find someone else to take the wheel, and dance awhile. No doubt a certain young lady would be pleased to be your partner."

"Haven't you noticed?" Jamie gave him a wry grin. "Lady Marianne no longer speaks to me. Maybe it's my pride, but I'll not try again. The men shouldn't see their captain treated with disrespect." Yet he wondered how he could avoid talking to her. And, in fact, longed to do so.

"They seem a bit smitten with her, don't they?" Aaron leaned against a secured barrel and gripped a line above his head for balance. "All that will be over when we reach Boston."

Jamie sent him a sidelong glance. "What makes you think so?" He'd worried about leaving his crew loose in London, where their loyalties might be swayed, but no other plan had presented itself. And now even Saunders and his Molly had abandoned talk of the Revolution in their adoration of Lady Marianne.

"Oh, come now." Aaron punched Jamie's arm. "These are good fellows, true to the Cause."

Jamie grunted. "I've always thought so. But when you think of what we're facing, what we each must give up to win this revolution, maybe they'd prefer to settle down someplace with their brides until it's all finished. I doubt any one of them would turn down land on a Caribbean island." He gripped and turned the wheel as a large swell rolled beneath the ship.

On the main deck, the revelers laughed as they struggled to keep their balance, even Lady Marianne. His lost love continued to surprise Jamie. She'd found her sea legs all too well.

"Whoa!" Aaron's arms flailed about as he tried to stay upright. Jamie caught his shoulder and righted him. "Thank you, my friend. Can't wait to get back on land. Whose idea was it for me to come with you on this mission, anyway?" His hearty laugh rang out in contradiction to his complaint. "Say, I'm going to drag someone up here to take your place. My Emma would be pleased to dance with you." He staggered across the rolling deck and down the ladder before Jamie could stop him.

Not that he wanted to. By the time Simpson had joined him on the quarterdeck, Jamie felt the bite of mischief. If he could not have Lady Marianne for a wife, or even for a friend, he could put aside his pride and show her his goodwill, maybe reminding her of better times. In fact, he would first go below and don one of his new jackets bought on her brother's advice.

Marianne had no choice. She must place her hand in Captain Templeton's as they moved along the length of the dance line on the way to meet their own partners again. She did not look at him, even when he lightly squeezed her fingers. Nor even when he put his hand on her waist to swing back in the opposite direction—although a thrill shot up her spine at his touch.

"Did Mr. Pellam not tell you, Captain?" she asked above the music. "You are not to grab a lady's waist, but merely touch it."

His dark brown eyes twinkled with mischief, an expression she had grown to love and now must hate, as he bent close to her ear. "Forgive me. You seemed about to fall."

A pleasant chill swept down her neck, but she attributed it to the light wind blowing over the deck. "Have you not noticed, sir? I have very little trouble regaining my footing when adversity or disappointment strikes."

"I *have* noticed, my lady." His grip loosened, but his smirk remained. No doubt the rascal took pride in the strength of his arms and his impressive dancing skill, but she would not give him the satisfaction of her compliments on his grace. Or on his handsome blue silk jacket and tan breeches. Or his shaving balm, a heady bergamot fragrance that brought her some relief from the smells of his unwashed crew. He bent close again. "I've also noticed you've beguiled my men."

She shuddered away another chill and gave him a prim nod. "Indeed I have, and you would do well not to forget it."

His laugh grated on her nerves, and she longed to slap his handsome, self-assured face. Yes, she bore the blame for being here now, but he'd never loved her. Of that she was certain. Those two times he'd kissed her—*no,* she must not think of such things. Lost in a bittersweet memory, she missed a step, only to be rescued by Jamie's strong arms. *Captain Templeton's* strong arms. Goodness, who had invited him to this dance? They swung around the circle, and he returned her to her partner—a Mr. Samples, whose dancing left much to be desired—while reclaiming Emma as his own partner. Her maid, her *former* maid, had the nerve to give Marianne a teasing smile. Had the whole world gone mad? What a cruel joke had been played on her by this man.

As the dance ended, she now faced a worse dilemma. When she and Molly designed the seating for the married couples, Molly had presumed the captain would take the head of the table. Marianne dared not forbid it. And now she, as hostess, must take this odious man's arm as they proceeded to supper in his own cabin. No. She simply could not do it.

"Captain Templeton, sir." Molly looped her arm in the captain's, a gesture Marianne found a bit common, although she knew the warmhearted older woman meant nothing by it. "Will you and Lady Marianne lead us down to supper?"

The captain had the good grace to appear flustered when he looked at Marianne. Then a familiar teasing grin touched his lips as he patted Molly's hand and disengaged from her. "I would be delighted, Miss Molly." He bowed and offered Marianne his arm. "My lady."

Molly's hopeful smile forestalled any protest. Marianne did not curtsy, but touched the captain's arm, albeit lightly that she might not feel its muscular strength through the silk sleeve.

He guided her down the ladder, through the long companionway toward the ship's back—the stern, she reminded herself. In the cabin Demetrius and his son, Stavros, a boy of about ten years, waited beside the beautifully laid table, wearing the semblance of livery Marianne had suggested: brown breeches, white shirts with blue sashes angled across their chests, and white gloves. They had laid planks between the captain's desk and a small table, arranged benches and chairs to accommodate the twelve guests, and covered the boards with a heavy ivory tablecloth, clean but a bit worn in several spots. The Wedgwood china looked exquisite, and even the tin cutlery had a sheen to it. A large bouquet of hand-sewn flowers formed an exquisite, multicolored centerpiece. The lavender perfume Marianne had given Emma for a wedding gift had been splashed upon the artificial blooms and now filled the cabin with a scent to vie with the savory fish course. As crowded as the cabin was, Marianne felt gratified to sit at the foot of the table while Captain Templeton took his place at the head—for she was as far from him as possible.

At Marianne's nod, Demetrius and Stavros began serving, beginning with her and the captain, moving on to the first mate, and so on in descending rank. Not expecting this rough lot to exhibit proper manners, she had prepared the ladies to lead their husbands. To her surprise, Captain Templeton appeared to have done the same with his men, for they followed his example, spooning their soup without slurping and using their linen napkins often. Marianne stifled an urge to compliment the captain. After all, such good manners were not extraordinary. Everyone should eat properly. But when he explained to Simpson that he must not speak across the table, but rather to the persons seated on either side of him, Marianne could hardly contain a smile of approval. Captain Templeton might be a traitorous scoundrel, but he was also a gentleman.

Outside the porthole, an orange-and-red sunset streaked the sky, while inside the cabin lanterns swung on hooks and cast deepening shadows around the room. Demetrius carried away the salted beef and left the cabin to fetch the final remove.

In the companionway, the sudden thump of rapid footsteps neared the cabin. Marianne turned to see a sailor dash in the door, his eyes wide.

"Cap'n Jamie, sir, a British frigate is closing fast on us from the north."

Chapter Thirty

While the ladies gasped and the men groaned, the captain's cheerful countenance dissolved into caution. "You must forgive us, ladies." He stood and maneuvered around the table and out of the cabin, with his men in his wake.

"Lord, help us." Nancy wrung her napkin.

"Shh." Molly patted her hand. "It'll be all right."

"Blimey," Sally huffed. "I'm not staying down here just to have those ruffians threaten us again." She hurried out.

After quick apologies, Nancy and Molly followed her.

"We'll be in our cabin." Quince took Emma's hand to lead her out, and Marianne ached to see the concern in their faces.

Only Eleanor remained in her chair, lazily chewing on a biscuit.

Seated near the door, Marianne tried to stifle her rising panic. *Lord, is this the time? Show me the way to contact this captain and turn Jamie—Captain Templeton—over to him.* The prayer sat like lead on her heart, but she rose from her chair and gazed across the remnants of her fine feast. How inconvenient of this frigate to happen along just when everyone was having such a pleasant time.

Before she could move away from the table, Eleanor stood and, in two long steps, reached the door and barred it. "Where d'you think you're going?"

Marianne drew in a sharp breath. "What? Why, I am going with the others to—"

"No, you aren't going anywhere." Eleanor fisted her hands at her waist. "Just sit yourself down, missy."

Terror flooded Marianne as she regarded the shorter woman of perhaps four and twenty years, whose muscular arms were visible through her gauze sleeves. Never in her life had Marianne experienced such a threat. She had no idea what this woman might do.

"What do you mean, Eleanor?" She emitted a shaky laugh. "I merely want to be with the other ladies on deck. What if the British sailors come below, as they did before, and no one is here to protect us?"

"What if?" Eleanor snorted, a most unladylike sound. "Won't be no different from what the *Quality* men do to my sort when they get the notion."

Nausea rose up in Marianne's throat. "I cannot imagine what you mean." But she could. She had come upon Tobias Pincer kissing an unwilling scullery maid belowstairs in Bennington House. Without her intrusion, the girl might have suffered far more than an unwanted kiss. Her tearful gratitude had assured Marianne that the Lord had sent her downstairs to a hallway she rarely entered. Even rumors of her eldest brother…but she would not think of that.

Again Eleanor snorted. "Your sort never does imagine it." She leaned toward Marianne, eyes narrowed. "Because you *choose* not to see."

Marianne swallowed hard. What would this woman do to her? "But I can see you now, and I would like to see the other ship, and wouldn't you like to see your husband and

be reassured that all is well? In fact, I must go upstairs and
ensure that none of our crew are kidnapped…impressed, as
I did before." She felt so breathless, she thought she might
faint.

"Ha!" Eleanor did not smile. "Everybody else is all
gooey-eyed at your title, *Lady Marianne,* but I see what
you're about. You got caught unawares the first time, but I
don't believe for a minute you'll help the cap'n again." She
leaned back against the door and crossed her arms. "You
think nobody can see you hate him? You stowed away and
followed him, but he rejected you." Now she laughed, a
dreadful cackling sound for one so young. "You'd make us
all suffer to settle that score." She reached out and shoved
Marianne's shoulder. "Set down, girl, before I set you
down."

Marianne dropped back into her chair and gripped its
arms. If she braced herself, she could kick Eleanor away and
escape. But her legs felt limp, and no stroke of courage
coursed through her to strengthen them. She had never struck
another person and could not imagine doing so. *Lord, help
me. What shall I do?* What had Eleanor said? What had some
"Quality" man done to her to make every aristocrat her
enemy?

"Well, then, Eleanor, if we are not going up on deck,
come sit with me." Her voice shook, but she forced a smile.
"Let us talk to pass the time."

Eleanor laughed, again a mirthless, unpleasant sound.
"Right. We'll talk." She pulled a heavy chair in front of the
door and sat. "Tea parties and balls. Fashions and French
coiffures." She spat out her words, but her eyes filled with
sadness.

Only halfway mindful of the muted sounds of men
shouting above them, Marianne forced her attention to

Eleanor and nodded as if listening to one of her dear little orphans at St. Ann's. "If that is what you would like to discuss. But perhaps first you will help me."

"Help you? Ha. Not likely."

"No, I do not mean do something for me. I mean help me understand what you are saying. What is it that my *sort* chooses not to see?"

Eleanor's jaw dropped. Then her eyes narrowed. "What do you care?"

Marianne considered her question. "I suppose it is because you and I were becoming friends before you knew who I am. Do you remember during the storm how we all encouraged each other, sharing our ginger tea, singing hymns and telling funny stories? I think those many long hours of suffering together made me realize that women are all alike, no matter what our birth rank might be."

A cautious smile appeared, but sadness still filled Eleanor's eyes. "Aye, we did laugh."

"But now you must tell me…" Warmth spread through Marianne's chest, a sincere affection for this woman. Of all the ladies, including brave Molly, Eleanor seemed to possess the stoutest heart. Marianne could imagine her fighting off anyone who tried to snatch her husband from the ship. "Why have you come to hate me?"

Eleanor shook her head. "Not you by name, just by class, though to be fair, you never put on airs with us." She traced a finger along her chair arm. "Awright, then, I'll tell you." She inhaled a deep breath. "I was born in a village in Sussex outside Lord de Winter's manor." Her lips curled in distaste. "When I was fourteen, I went into service in his lordship's house. He had a son just two years older than me…."

With growing chagrin and nausea, Marianne listened to her story. Having met Lord de Winter's heir her first season in society and endured his unwanted notice, she had no doubt Eleanor's story was true.

"And then they cast me out." Eleanor gazed toward the porthole. "No money. No references. And my wee babe…" Her voice cracked, and she sniffed. "He lies buried outside the churchyard because his mother was not wed."

An icy chill swept up Marianne's arms, and a soft sob escaped her. She tried to recall if any housemaid had been dismissed from her parents' service when her brothers were of that age, but she had been too young to notice such things. Compassion filled her, and she reached out to grasp the other woman's hands. "Oh, Eleanor, I am so sorry. And so very sad for you…and your dear son. I do believe every word you said."

Eleanor gave her a crooked grin. "You're a good sort, after all, Lady Marianne." She grimaced. "I'm sorry for scaring you. If you want to go on deck—"

Marianne laughed softly. "No, there's no need. If someone comes for us, we shall see to it then." She could not fathom the change now occurring inside her, but knew as surely as she breathed that God had ordained for her to hear this woman's story. Never before had she fully comprehended the cruelty and hypocrisy of many people in the society in which she had been reared. Perhaps her parents and Grace Kendall were the only sincere Christians Marianne knew.

"Guess they never boarded us." Eleanor went to the porthole and glanced out. "I never heard a sound of 'em coming below, and I don't see the frigate."

Marianne gulped back a sob at this news, and a strange sense of reprieve filled her. She touched her cheek and found it damp. Were these tears of sympathy for Eleanor? Or of relief that she had not been required to speak to the naval captain? For as surely as Eleanor had kept her from leaving this cabin, Marianne knew the Lord had prevented her from exposing the *Fair Winds'* captain. Perhaps that made her a traitor, too. Perhaps she now must choose between betraying her country and betraying her heart. For despite his lies, despite the conviction that she would never marry such a scoundrel, she would love Jamie Templeton until the day she died.

The British frigate sailed within twenty-five yards of the *Fair Winds* and dropped its sails. On its quarterdeck, the captain lifted his bicorne hat and saluted Jamie. "Ahoy, Captain Templeton."

"Ahoy, Captain Boyd." Jamie returned the salute as he sent up a prayer of thanks. They had first encountered HMS *Margaret* last February on their way to England, and had earned the captain's trust because of their connection to Bennington *and* because of the crate of oranges Jamie had given him. Jamie prayed the captain would still be as well disposed toward them.

"What's your heading, sir?" Boyd cupped his hands to help his voice carry.

"East Florida. Will you come with us?" Jamie infused his voice with good humor. "There'll be another orange harvest in a few months." A reminder of his gift couldn't hurt.

"We'd do well to have 'em to stave off the scurvy, sir." Boyd turned to speak briefly with a sailor. "We spy ladies on your ship, Templeton."

"Aye, sir." Jamie must cut off any wayward thoughts in that regard. "Some of my crew married in London, and their wives are eager to help us colonize East Florida."

"Ah, very good. Building His Majesty's empire."

"May I send you a crate of claret, sir?" Although Jamie

didn't expect this captain to try to take any of the *Fair Winds* crew, a gift should ensure it.

"I say, that would be most kind." The dark-haired man gave him a slight bow. "We've done without for a long time."

At Jamie's order, Saunders and two other sailors brought up the wine and lowered a boat to carry it to the *Margaret*. During the interval, Boyd called out a warning to Jamie to steer wide of the northern colonies, adding that the conflict had already given rise to American pirates who would gladly seize the merchant vessel. That news was not unexpected, although Jamie regarded those pirates as privateers.

When Saunders returned, he handed Jamie an exquisitely carved tomahawk pipe.

"A very fine gift." Jamie held it high. "I thank you, Captain Boyd."

"Took it from an obstinate Indian fellow in Nova Scotia. That's where we've been since March, when those confounded rebels drove us out of Boston. Bad show, that. We're headed back to Plymouth for more weaponry and troops. Then we'll teach those rebels their place."

Jamie swallowed a retort, even as a familiar thought nagged at him. How could he go to war with good men like this one? "I'll heed your warning about the pirates, sir."

The ships hoisted sails once again and moved in opposite directions. While lifting a prayer of thanks for the uneventful encounter, Jamie also sought the Lord's wisdom about the privateers, who should be putting their efforts toward the war, not harassing American vessels. For now, Jamie must sail under the Union Jack and Lord Bennington's flag when encountering British ships. But hidden in a safe place under the floor of his cabin was the Grand Union flag, a design General Washington had approved early that year. Jamie had obtained one before sailing to England, but wondered if privateers would respect the Continental flag. Or would he at last have to fight his way past well-armed ships seeking to keep him from his destination?

Chapter Thirty-One

"A ship at sea is a very small world." Marianne walked arm in arm with Molly around the *Fair Winds'* deck. Above them, puffy white clouds reminded her of the pastries Papa's chef always made, a far better fare than the weevily hardtack she now ate. "How do these men manage to spend their lives at sea without going mad with boredom?"

Molly chuckled. "Why, 'tis a good thing they do manage it. How else would people and things get from shore to shore across the wide ocean?" She gave Marianne a worried glance. "Meaning no disrespect, my lady."

"Tut, tut, Molly. Are we not friends? You may say anything to me." In the past six weeks since Marianne's ball and supper, she had grown closer to all the women. Like Eleanor, each one had a story of hardship and heartbreak. And, just as she had done by foolishly stowing away aboard this ship, they had risked their lives for a future filled with hope beside the men they loved. At least in East Florida, none of them would face the dangers of the war. Marianne had no doubt her brother Frederick would help them all find occupations in St. Johns Towne, where he served as magistrate and managed Papa's plantation.

"You're a true Christian, Lady Marianne." Molly squeezed her arm, a familiar gesture Marianne no longer found inappropriate.

"And you, as well, Molly." She lifted her face to the breeze and inhaled a deep, refreshing breath. Then gasped. "Look. A seagull. Two, three." She released Molly and hurried to the ship's railing to study the horizon. "Does that mean we are nearing land?"

Molly came up beside her and gave her a teasing grin. "Why not ask the captain?"

Marianne wrinkled her nose. "I would rather..." No, she would not speak ill of a man everyone else on board respected. "...not."

Others on deck noticed the large white-winged birds, as well, pointing and smiling or laughing. That was proof enough to her that the gulls were harbingers of good things to come. She had no need to speak to Captain Templeton, whom she always managed to avoid despite the small world of the ship.

To be fair, he too had kept his distance, only occasionally retrieving charts or books from the cabin he had charitably surrendered to her. At his knock on the door, she would make herself presentable, then slip past him into the narrow companionway, returning only when he left, leaving his familiar manly scent behind...along with too many bittersweet memories.

The ritual of staying apart was tedious but necessary. For sometimes, when she watched him man the wheel or engage in friendly banter with his crew or ably lead the ship through a storm, her heart threatened to betray her as she recalled the merry times they had spent with Robert and Grace...or when she recalled his tender kisses. And sometimes, she would turn to find him staring at her across the deck, a sorrowful frown on his sun-browned face, an expression he quickly hid with an impudent grin and an overdone bow. She would avert her gaze even as her heart leapt. Clearly, traitor or not, he suffered as she did. Clearly, he did love her as she loved him. Yet they were and must always remain mortal enemies.

Several days later, long after sunset, Eleanor came to Marianne's cabin. "Come on deck, Lady Marianne. There's lights in the distance. Boston, my lady. *Boston.*" The happy glow on her face dimmed. "Forgive me, ma'am. I know this isn't what you want."

Seated at the captain's desk, where she had been reading by lantern light, Marianne bent her head to hide sudden tears. "No, it is not what I want, but we shall all be in East Florida soon enough after the captain concludes his business here." Whatever that might be.

"But…" A frown darted across Eleanor's face. "My lady, did you not know? We ladies aren't going to East Florida. We're staying here in Boston to help with the Cause."

Marianne opened her mouth, but no words would come. Indeed, what would she say? More treachery. Why had she ever thought she could sway these women or, even more impossible, their husbands? From the beginning, these Englishwomen planned to join the rebellion. And why would they not, after their tragedies and disappointments suffered in the land of their birth? Yet what hope did they have in these colonies, where the mad uprising would soon be crushed by His Majesty's navy and army?

"Go watch the lights, Eleanor. Go look to your new home." Marianne ached to touch land once again. But she would not set one foot in this disloyal colony. In that small way, she could demonstrate her own loyalty to her king and her country, no matter what the other women did.

After a fitful night of sleep, she came on deck to find them moored at the docks. Someone mentioned that these were the very wharves where the infamous Boston Tea Party had taken place back in '73. While the other women laughed, no doubt giddy because they would soon disembark, Marianne tried to swallow her growing grief. Now she would be alone, for she and Emma would be the only ladies left on board, and Emma spent all her time with Quince.

Someone pointed above to the mainmast, where the Union Jack and Papa's flag had been removed, replaced by a red-and-white-striped banner with a blue field in one corner behind red and white crosses.

"'Tis the Continental flag, ladies," Mr. Saunders gleefully announced. "The flag of the Grand Union of the thirteen colonies."

A cheer went up from the others, while Marianne released a weary sigh and returned to her cabin. Sorrow upon sorrow would overcome these good people soon enough. Let them enjoy their ill-founded moments of joy. All she wanted was to take refuge from the gaiety in sleep.

A light tap sounded on the door before she could lie down. She opened it to find Captain Templeton dressed in one of his finer coats, a gentle smile gracing his lips. Her heart jumped to her throat.

"I thought you might want to go ashore, my lady." Was that hope in his eyes?

"I thank you, but no." She looked away, unable to still her trembling brought on by his nearness.

He caught her chin and sought her gaze. "It would do you well, *Lady* Marianne."

She stepped back, breaking his touch…and wishing for

it again. "I care not for your concerns for my health. I will walk the deck for exercise, but I will not set foot on these traitorous shores." Her tone lacked conviction, but she could not change it.

Captain Templeton nodded, his gaze still kind. "I go to visit friends. The lady is my cousin and the sister of Frederick's wife. Would you like to meet her?"

Marianne's heart skipped. Soon she would meet Rachel. Soon she must face Frederick, who had urged her to renounce her feelings for Jamie. Now she understood why. Did this mean her brother also had chosen the rebel cause? Nausea threatened to overtake her. She swallowed hard.

"You may convey my…" If she said "good wishes," it would imply approval of their disloyalty. "…my kind sentiments our kinship warrants. Perhaps we shall meet one day under better circumstances."

Disappointment clouded his dark eyes. Young as he was, sun and wind had weathered his complexion, making him appear older than when they had sailed from Southampton just over two months ago. His dark blond hair was now bleached golden by the sun.

"Very well. As you wish." His expression now blank, like that of a footman, he backed out of the cabin, pulling the door closed behind him…depriving her of his strong presence.

Marianne rushed to grasp the latch, to chase after him. But her hand stilled on the curved brass. She crumpled to her knees on the hard wooden deck and wept. "Lord, help me. Oh, please help me to stop loving that man."

"Half of the muskets are to be unloaded here." Charles Weldon lounged back in an upholstered chair in his home above his mercantile shop. "The rest must be delivered to

Colonel William Moultrie in Savannah for the Georgia militia. He's made one foray into East Florida but was turned back at Sunbury. These muskets might be just what they need for the next attempt."

"Very good." Jamie took a drink of the first real coffee he'd had in over a month. "How goes the war?"

"Washington's in New York and expects to engage the British any day. In late June, our Patriots repulsed a British sea attack in Charleston Harbor. We're building our navy and have plenty of men willing to join, but we need ships faster than we can construct them."

"Too bad we can't use the Nantucket shipyards." Jamie's *Fair Winds* had been built there.

Charles grimaced. "The islanders' neutrality prevents it. When the British gave the whalers the choice between English service or being sunk, most chose to survive. With no whaling income, the island is pretty much closed down, and the people suffer. The Quaker leadership insists on remaining neutral, although some younger men want to fight."

Jamie sat up, his chest clutching. "And Dinah?" If his younger sister was in danger of starvation, he must sail to the island and rescue her.

Charles stared down at his hands. "I wish I could give you a good report."

Jamie's caution grew to alarm. "What's she doing?" In truth, he barely knew Dinah, for their parents' deaths had forced their separation in childhood. Yet their rare meetings had instilled in him a great love for her, and family loyalty demanded that he help her if he could.

"That's just it." Charles shrugged. "We have no idea. We do know she does not favor the Revolution…nor is she anywhere to be found on Nantucket Island."

"Dear Lord, protect her." Jamie put his head in his hands.

"It's no surprise that the Quaker elders influenced her attitude toward the war, but where on earth would the child be if not there?"

"She's not a child anymore, Jamie." Charles clasped his shoulder. "She's a strong, feisty and opinionated young woman. She'll be all right. You already have enough to do." He stood and walked across the room, retrieving a colorful cloth from a trunk to hand to Jamie. "Look. We have a new flag. Susanna and Eliza have made several, and I'll be happy to give you one."

His heart pounding, Jamie unfolded the flag, a white woolen-and-linen pennant with red stripes and a blue field sporting a circle of thirteen white stars. "I like this even more than the Continental flag. Thank you. I'll fly it with pride."

"Good man." Charles's broad smile eased into a frown. "We've lost many good men, Jamie. And the fighting has only begun." He sat down and stared at his hands. "Granny Brown's younger son died."

Jamie swallowed a groan. No more than sixteen years old, Wilton Brown had been eager to fight for independence. "We all knew many would die for the Cause. I remember hearing about Patrick Henry's declaration to the Virginia House of Burgesses, 'give me liberty, or give me death,' and how we all cheered in agreement. If we don't mean it, we should send up a white flag, beg forgiveness and let King George continue to grind us under his heels."

Charles chuckled. "That'll not happen. You haven't heard the outcome of the Continental Congress, have you?"

Jamie eyed his kinsman with an artificial glare. "No, I've not heard. Out with it, man, before I forget you're married to my cousin, and pound it out of you."

"Whoa, old boy." Laughing, Charles lifted his hands palms out in a gesture of surrender. "There's a reason some of us fund the Revolution while others fight it. John Hancock and I prefer to put our money behind our warriors." He rose again and retrieved a large folded paper from his desk. "Here, take a look at this. You'll see what we're willing to commit to the Cause. Nothing less than our lives, our fortunes and our sacred honor."

The power of his words sent a shiver down Jamie's spine. "So they did it." He unfolded the printed broadside and silently read the words. *When in the course of human events it becomes necessary for one people to dissolve the politi cal bands which have connected them with another...* He read the entire page until he came to the last line, reading aloud the words Charles had just spoken. "'...and our sacred honor.'" His throat closed, and he could see the fervor in Charles's face, too. "Praise be to God for what He has brought to pass." He studied the document again. "These names listed at the bottom—they all signed it?"

"Yes. The Virginian Thomas Jefferson composed the declaration, and by the end of July most of the delegates signed it in Philadelphia, others signing later. The *Pennsylvania Evening Post* printed it on July 6, followed by other newspapers. I have no doubt there's a copy in every Patriot home in every colony." He chuckled. "No, no longer colonies. We are now, as this document says, free and independent states. Some have suggested we call ourselves the United States of America."

"Ah, praise God," Jamie repeated. "For He will surely bless us with success." He gently refolded the paper. "Has Frederick Moberly seen this?"

Charles shook his head. "I doubt it. We don't have much communication with East Florida because of the British navy, and overland contacts are difficult. Will you take one to him?" He retrieved two folded newspapers from his desk.

"And I have one for you, as well. Eliza has memorized every word and is teaching them to her sister and brother."

Along with his satisfaction over receiving the document, an unexpected pang struck Jamie's chest. His cousin's children, Eliza, Abigail and Charles, reminded him of Lady Marianne's nieces and nephew, children whom he'd grown fond of during their brief acquaintance. Little Georgie's adoration after his rescue from the pond made Jamie think he'd had some good influence on the young aristocrat.

Charles reached over and nudged his shoulder. "I said, will you have some pie?"

He grunted. "Sorry. I was lost in my thoughts."

"Not happy ones, if that moping face tells me anything." Charles narrowed his eyes. "What happened to you over there?"

Jamie gazed around the cozy parlor, so simple in its furnishing compared to the grand homes where he'd whiled away his months in England. Instead of larger-than-life paintings in ornately carved and gilded frames, these walls held Susanna's small sketches in simple frames. Instead of heavy velvet drapes, these windows were bare. And the well-worn furniture had not been re-covered in some time, no doubt because Charles was putting his small profits into the war. But this cozy abode was not ruled by an autocratic father, just an honest Christian merchant who was risking it all that his children might be free from a king's tyranny. That made it a far better home than all the fine manor houses in the world. And yet...

"You may recall when I was here last year that I'd met a young lady in England." Jamie swallowed as an unexpected ache filled his chest.

"Don't you dare say another word." Susanna appeared in the doorway with a tray of apple pie and a silver coffee server. She set it on the low table in front of the settee and shoved a blond curl beneath her crisp white cap. "Not until I serve your pie and can sit down to hear your story." Her dark eyes sparkled. "Now that Rachel has married, I've wondered how long it would be until some female made a landlubber out of you." She handed Jamie a slice of pie on a pewter plate. "Now, tell me all about this lady."

Jamie eyed his cousin, as dear to him as a sister, for her father had raised him from childhood. "I wish I could give you a happy report." Instead, he told them of his decision to break off with Lady Marianne because of the Revolution, their subsequent sad yet idyllic summer of companionship, her foolishness in stowing away aboard his ship, and finally, her horror upon discovering his true loyalties.

"James Templeton." Susanna placed her fists at her waist. "Do you mean to tell me you left that poor lady someplace instead of bringing her to our home?" She glared at him, his "elder sister" once again, as in their childhood. "What have you done with her?"

Even Charles eyed him with concern.

"Done with her?" Indignation rose within him. "The woman ravages my very soul, and you want to know what I've done with her?" He crossed his arms against this outrage. "She refuses to come ashore. Says we're traitors and wants nothing to do with us." He returned Susanna's glare. "I gave her my cabin and the best food Demetrius could prepare." Susanna continued to stare, further raising his ire. He bent toward her and narrowed his eyes. "I slept in a moldy hammock in the crew's smelly quarters."

"Well, then." Susanna glanced at Charles. "There's nothing to be done but for me to visit Lady Marianne right away. Husband, will you come with me?"

Charles waved away the idea. "No, my dear, I will leave that to you. Jamie and I have more important things to attend to." At his lift of an eyebrow, Jamie knew he referred to the muskets.

Susanna marched from the room, but her crossness did not truly offend Jamie. Knowing his dear cousin, he felt certain she would extend some kindness to Lady Marianne, who no doubt needed more than a little benevolence right now. Yet even the assurance of Susanna's generosity stabbed at his heart. He should be the one to minister to the woman he loved more than life, but she refused his every attempt.

He poured thick cream on his apple pie and dug in. Despite Demetrius's best efforts, Jamie had not eaten anything this tasty in over two months. Perhaps as the war continued, he would have few such delicacies to enjoy.

"Susanna," he called, "be sure to take her some of this pie."

The loud clatter of pots and dishes gave a more informative response than words. Jamie and Charles chuckled. Then Jamie sobered as the pie turned to dust in his mouth.

"The unfortunate result of this complication is that I must now send a report to General Washington to explain why I can never return to Lord Bennington."

Chapter Thirty-Two

Marianne fanned herself in the stifling heat of the cabin. She knew a breeze swept over Boston Harbor, one that would cool her on this early September evening. But she would not go up to the main deck, would not put herself in the position of being leered at by sailors or workmen on the wharves. How strange it seemed, after her life in a great manor house, to prefer the misery of this tiny cabin, which sometimes served as a refuge and other times a prison. One small comfort came from the bottom of the single satchel she had brought from home, her forgotten leather-bound journal in whose pages she poured out her heart, using Captain Templeton's quill pens and ink. He had denied her nothing and surely would not mind her using them. But the many words she recorded became muddled on the page as her tears caused the ink to run, just as her thoughts were muddled over this whole affair.

To her great sorrow, just this morning Emma had come to say goodbye. Marianne's little lady's maid, rescued by Mama from the orphanage to a better life than she would have had in any other occupation in England, would now be the mistress of her own home. When Emma announced that Aaron Quince owned a farm in the hills of west Massachusetts, Marianne found herself filled with a curious joy on her former servant's behalf, even as she despaired over her loss. Yet she feared Emma's happiness would be destroyed if Mr. Quince joined the rebellion.

What was she thinking? Of course he had joined the rebellion. He had come as Jamie Templeton's valet to spy for their cause. Marianne could not imagine what useful information her father's servants could have told him. Or whether or not they would say anything if given the chance. But she had no doubt that Quince had searched the house in the family's absence—probably with Emma's help. Marianne felt wicked for thinking such a thing, but after Jamie's— Captain Templeton's—betrayal, whom in this world could she trust?

A soft scratch at the door startled her, and her quill slid across the page, leaving a jagged black line. She rolled her blotter over the ink, closed the journal and slid it into a drawer.

"Wh-who is it?" She cleared her throat, which was raspy from little use and many tears.

"Lady Marianne." A woman's voice, but not familiar. "May I come in?"

Caution accompanied her across the wooden floor. She hesitated, then slid the bolt and pulled open the door. The unmistakable aroma of roast beef and apple pie nearly knocked her over. Her mouth began to water, and her knees grew weak. She gulped. "Yes?"

"Good day, my lady." The dark-eyed woman of about thirty years wore a broad-brimmed straw hat over a white cap, and a plain blue muslin gown. "I brought you something to eat." She lifted a large brown basket covered with a white cloth embroidered with tiny blue flowers.

"Please, come in." Jamie had sent food. Oh, how his tender care shattered her heart. Marianne had not even realized her own hunger. Stepping aside, she waved the diminutive woman in.

Her plain countenance, made pretty by her merry smile, was like Molly's, the sort to inspire goodwill. "Thank you, my lady." As if Marianne were doing *her* a favor.

"And I thank you, Mrs....?"

"Mrs. Charles Weldon. But you must call me Susanna."

"Ah." Frederick's sister-in-law. "And you may call me—"

"Why, Lady Marianne, of course." Susanna bustled about, laying a large linen cloth over the flat desk, then placing on it an exquisite white, bone china plate with a delicate blue pattern to match the basket cloth. She brought out several small, covered tureens and proceeded to ladle out roast beef, gravy, carrots, peas, yams, preserves, apple pie, cream and fresh buttered bread—and not a weevil to be seen.

Marianne almost fell into her chair. "Susanna, I am grateful." She could barely compose herself enough to maintain her manners as she cut into the tender beef. Without the linen napkin Susanna had draped across her lap, she feared she might have drooled like a baby. "This is the very best roast beef I have ever eaten."

Susanna smiled. "Thank you, my lady." She remained standing, just as the maids, butlers and footmen did at home. But this was no servant. She was Marianne's relative by marriage.

"Please call me Marianne." She took a sip of the delicious coffee Susanna had poured. "And please sit down." She indicated the chair across the cabin.

"Thank you." Susanna dragged the heavy chair across the

wooden floor and sat with folded hands. "My, you've had quite an adventure, haven't you?"

At her gentle, maternal tone, Marianne gulped down her bite, took another sip of coffee…and burst into tears.

"Don't you want to take her to Nova Scotia, Cap'n?" Saunders stood beside Jamie at the helm while the crew shoved off from the Boston wharf and hoisted the sails. "Them British'll make sure she gets back home safe and sound."

Jamie turned the wheel to catch the wind. "That was my first thought. But our mission to Charleston is urgent, and she'll be better off with her brother in East Florida."

"I s'pose you're right." Saunders stepped to the railing and shouted to the men on the main deck. "Make ready for the change of flags as soon as we reach the mouth of the harbor." When he came back, he wore a worried frown. "D'you think she'll give us any trouble if we're stopped again?"

That was a question Jamie had yet to resolve. Susanna had refused to discuss her visit with Lady Marianne, saying it was women's talk, nothing to do with loyalties or the Revolution. "We can trust your Molly to make sure Lady Marianne stays below deck. Once we deliver her to Frederick Moberly, she will be his responsibility." The idea sat heavy on Jamie's heart.

In one way, he treasured her presence on the ship, for it would be the last time he spent in her company—if one could call it company, the way they avoided each other. Still, just watching her amble around the main deck gave him an odd sort of joy. She took to sailing well, and he knew she'd helped the other women on the passage from Southampton. Her beauty had not diminished in spite of the rugged voyage, nor had her spirits flagged. True, he'd seen traces of tears on her porcelain face from time to time, but she always spoke words of cheer to the crew, and he often saw her laugh with Molly for some unknown reason. More women's talk, he supposed.

As they sailed south, his only attempt to communicate with her beyond polite greetings was to leave on his desk one of the newspapers Charles had given him. With little hope of a response, he prayed the Lord would move her to read it and to understand the Cause he was willing to die for.

Smitten with curiosity, Marianne nudged the folded, yellowed newspaper with one finger. Had it been a sealed document, she would have opened it straightaway, assuming Captain Templeton had left it by mistake. But here it sat, so he must want her to read it. She would not, of course. Papa had frowned upon her reading newspapers, saying they contained only gossip not fit for a young lady to know. She must assume American newspapers would be even worse.

Wearied by being back at sea, she cheered herself with thoughts of seeing Frederick, even though she dreaded learning the truth about his loyalties. If Rachel was as pleasant, well-spoken and kind as her sister, Marianne would love her. In addition to feeding her, Susanna had insisted upon washing and mending Marianne's small wardrobe, and even had aired her bedding.

Of course Marianne would love her new niece or nephew, who had been expected this past July. An ironic laugh escaped her. She would have to write to Mama and Papa about their new grandchild, Mama's first. But perhaps the missive would not be delivered if the colonists' war continued and covered the seas.

An unnerving suspicion occurred to her. Now that Jamie could no longer spy on Papa, would he use his ship for the rebellion? The thought terrified her. Why, any British warship could easily sink this lightly armed vessel. But then, from what Thomas had said last June, no place was safe for anyone during a war.

Irritation swept through her. Why must there be a war? Why must these colonists speak against the king? Why could they not pay their taxes, as Papa did on the sale of produce from his plantation? She would demand an answer from Frederick.

As white-capped waves swept past the porthole, she paced the small, hot cabin. Her much-used fan had broken at last, so she snatched up the folded newspaper to cool herself. Its limp pages fell open and drifted down to the floor to reveal in large letters at the top Declaration of Independence.

Intrigued, she picked it up and began to read. After the first few lines, she felt the need to sit. As her eyes swept down the page, her mind began to comprehend. Her heart began to believe. This was not the work of common ruffians, but of well-spoken and thoughtful souls who had been brought to the end of their reasoning powers and now must take decisive action, just as she had done over two months ago. Like these colonists, she had sought a peaceful means of obtaining what she believed to be God's will—a tragic error on her part. But the authors of this paper listed honest complaints, many of which she knew to be valid.

Had she not seen her countrymen try to steal sailors from this very ship? Had she not heard from Susanna a tale of misuse by British soldiers, who had quartered in her home, ate her children's food and harassed Susanna and Rachel? How could such things be endured? Even at home, news of the Stamp Act and other taxes had generated sympathy for the colonists. And some members of Parliament, such as her father's former friend Lord Highbury, advocated exactly what this paper now demanded: that the united colonies should be permitted to become their own nation. Indeed, not permitted, for they had gone beyond seeking approval for their actions. They declared before all the governments of the world that they were henceforth free and independent states, and absolved themselves of all allegiance to the Crown—a staggering pronouncement.

At the last line of the document, Marianne felt a tremor sweep through her, for in it she read the character of Captain James Templeton. Like the men who wrote this, he had pledged his all to support their revolution, even at the risk of his life and fortune. And his honor? Could a spy claim that his honor was sacred? Before she could complete the thought, the biblical story of the Hebrew men sent to spy on Jericho came to mind. If God could bless their efforts and not call it sin, how could she condemn Jamie for doing whatever was required to help his country? In fact, was she any better than a spy, to have sneaked around her father all her life to manipulate him?

Marianne brushed away the tears and perspiration covering her cheeks and forehead. She must go to him now and tell him that at last she understood, at last she believed his cause was just. She entertained no delusions his revolution would succeed, for His Majesty's armies would easily defeat the colonists. But win or lose, rise or fall, she would stay by his side—if he would have her.

She folded the newspaper with care and held it close, like a precious treasure. Sliding the bolt and opening the door, she pulled a blast of heat into the cabin, along with the dreadful but familiar smells of bilge water and rancid air. A handkerchief held to her nose and mouth, she hurried along the companionway to the ladder, eager to breathe the fresh sea air. Eager to see Jamie and declare her understanding of his motives.

As she climbed the steps, angry shouts met her ears. Once on deck, she saw a frigate bobbing alongside not twenty yards away. In the center of the *Fair Winds'* main deck stood a uniformed officer and a group of armed British sailors. Two of the men aimed their muskets directly at Jamie's chest.

Chapter Thirty-Three

Our lives, our fortunes and our sacred honor. So be it, Lord. Jamie stared back at the British captain, whose sneer had almost earned him a fist planted on his equine nose.

"I have need of all my men, sir." Jamie scrambled for calm—not an easy task with two muskets pointed at his chest—and sent up another prayer that this man would listen to reason. "We are bound for Loyalist East Florida, and the unruly seas around the Carolina shoals require every sailor."

"I care nothing for your problems, Captain. We are at war, and my needs exceed any that a merchant vessel might have, even a *Loyalist* merchant vessel." His tone shouted his suspicions. "We will search every corner of this vessel and—"

"Really, Captain, this is entirely too much."

Lady Marianne's unmistakable voice almost felled Jamie. Now everything truly was lost. Would his crew remember what to do? Would they be the brave lads he expected them to be? One thing he knew. If God granted him life, he would do all in his power to save Lady Marianne during the coming melee.

She marched toward them in her inimitable way, and he saw the incriminating newspaper clutched in one hand. The sailors who aimed their muskets at him eyed her. At this diversion, he should try to seize their guns. But one man remembered his duty and looked back at Jamie.

"Here now, don't you move." The youth pasted on a fierce look, enough to show he meant business.

"And who might you be, miss?" The captain stared at Lady Marianne, running his eyes up and down, and Jamie vowed to make him pay for the disrespect he showed her.

"I am Lady Marianne Moberly." She lifted her chin and glared at him. "This ship sails under the British flag and my father's banner, and I am more than sick of you nautical ninnies who continually delay my arrival in St. Augustine."

Jamie thought he might fall over from relief, but quickly pulled in a bracing breath.

The captain narrowed his eyes. "How do I know—"

"How dare you?" Marianne's lovely cheeks grew bright pink, and her eyes blazed. "I will report you. What is your name, Captain? Do you have any idea who my father is? Lord Bennington, a member of His Majesty's Privy Council, that's who. I will not suffer one man to be removed from this ship." She moved close to the British officer, putting her face near his and jutting out her jaw. Jamie had been on the receiving end of that scowl and had felt it sharply, but would the captain be equally intimidated? Whether yea or nay, Jamie cheered her courage. Once again his ladylove showed her mettle, although he could not guess why.

"I…well, madam…" The captain looked at his men, at Jamie—who gave him a lopsided grin—and finally at the paper clutched to Lady Marianne's chest. "May I ask, madam, what you are reading?" A sly smile touched his lips.

She looked down as if she'd never seen the paper before. "This?" Her blue eyes blinked, and Jamie could see her mind spin. "Why, an American newspaper, of course. I am taking it to my brother in East Florida. He is Mr. Frederick Moberly, son of Lord Bennington, *and* His Majesty's magistrate."

That's my girl. The bold truth. That should confound him. Jamie winked away a fond look. He had no idea why she was helping him yet again, but prayed she would not back down.

"I see," said the captain. "And why not a London newspaper?"

"How *dare* you question me, you officious idiot." Now real rage covered her face. "My father will hear of this. The Admiralty will hear of your insults to a British lady."

The man stepped back, palms out as if to ward off her attack. "Madam, please. Have you no idea that we are at war?"

She followed him, and he nearly tripped in his retreat. "*If* you would like to continue fighting in this war and not spend it on a prison hulk, I suggest you be on your way." Placing one fist at her waist, she shook the newspaper toward Jamie. "Captain Templeton, why did you not show this man my father's letter?"

Suddenly pale around the edges of his tanned skin, the captain also looked at Jamie. "You have a letter from Lord Bennington? Why did you not say so?"

Jamie could not get the *Fair Winds* away from the frigate fast enough. He grabbed the sheets himself, along with his crew, to hoist sails. He'd heard a man could die of apoplexy and thought he might have come close to it within the past two hours since the other ship had accosted them.

Lady Marianne stood at the bow, her long raven curls blowing loose in the brisk breeze. Once the ship had caught the wind and he'd set their southerly heading, Jamie approached her, but with caution. Just because she had confronted the British captain to prevent an impressment, Jamie could not assume she had changed her loyalties.

"My lady." He leaned one elbow against the gunwale at a respectful distance from her, trying to appear indifferent, yet guarding his heart against another rebuff.

The shy smile she gave him shattered his defenses. "Have you finished all your captain duties?"

He puckered away a foolish grin. "W-well, um, there are always duties for the captain…." He waved one hand aimlessly toward the deck, the mast, the sails.

"I meant do you have time for a chat?" She glanced at the newspaper she clutched against her.

"Oh. You wish to talk with me?" Now, after all these countless weeks of snubbing him?

She looked upward and shook her head. "Yes, Jamie, I wish to talk with you." Her voice sounded like a soothing song. Her azure eyes caught the sky and sparkled like sapphires.

A flood of love and joy surged through him, and he turned away to gather his emotions, gripping the gunwale and bowing his head. For the first time in well over a year, hope for a future with Marianne exploded in his chest.

She touched his arm, and he jumped. And she jumped. And they both laughed.

She glanced away briefly, then settled her gaze on him. "I do not know what the future holds, Jamie. I do not even know if you will have me. But I love you with all my heart, and I want to spend the rest of my life, whether it be long or short, with you."

Her sweet, shy smile infused him with strength. He touched her cheek, and she pressed it into his palm. He slid his other arm around her and pulled her close, bending to brush a tender kiss across her lips. "Marianne."

In response, she melted against him. Somewhere in the distance, he heard men cheering, though he could not imagine why. For his happiness sang like music on the ocean winds, a symphony to his soul.

"I can understand why you wish to renounce your English loyalties." Marianne sat across the desk from Jamie as they ate their supper. "It is not just the matters discussed so convincingly in the Declaration. When I think of all the times we had to pretend when we were in Papa's presence, it makes me very sad. He claimed to want me happy, but would have denied me my only true source of joy simply because of an accident of birth. Yet for my countrymen…and my father, there can be no other way to structure society."

Jamie reached out to squeeze her hand. "You cannot know how close I came to asking for your hand after…" He shrugged and took a bite of meat.

"After you saved Georgie." Marianne adored his modesty. "I was so angry you did not."

"Will you forgive me…for everything?" His dark eyes shone with love.

Marianne gave him a smug smile. "I am endeavoring to do so." She looked beyond him to Molly, who stood ready to serve their next course. "You know, Molly, we could all eat together, you and Mr. Saunders, the captain and I."

"You're very kind, Lady Marianne. Perhaps next time."

"We shall do that." Marianne sipped her coffee, a tasty brew. "But, dear, you must not call me *Lady* Marianne any longer. Soon I shall be Mrs. Templeton, and just plain Marianne to my friends."

Molly's eyes twinkled. "Aye, my lady, but being English, 'twill be a hard habit for me to break."

"But you are American now, are you not?"

"Aye, my lady." Molly chuckled, then tilted her head toward Jamie and wiggled an eyebrow, as if to say Marianne should be talking with him.

Marianne did as the older woman suggested. She gave Jamie a quivering smile. "I suppose I shall be an American, too."

He gazed at her, concern creasing his forehead. "Will it be that difficult?"

She set down her fork and smoothed her napkin in her lap. "A lifetime of loving one's country cannot be undone in a few days…or by reading a single document, no matter how well reasoned and written. Please understand that I cannot truly renounce my homeland, at least not yet. The war will not last forever, and then…" She could not speak of her doubts about the Revolution's success.

"You think we'll fail."

Tears sprung to her eyes. "I fear it."

He again reached out to her, and the warm touch of his hand on hers sent a pleasant chill up her arm. "Well, then, if it does…" His voice held a startling merriment. "We'll just have to sail to Mexico or California or China to escape the Crown's retribution."

Molly's eyes widened, and Marianne gaped. They both laughed.

"You have thought this through, have you?" Marianne gazed at the man she loved beyond reason.

"I've counted the cost as best I could, but I'll leave the future to the Almighty. And my deepest instinct says that

He'll bless our newborn country. Our…*my* duty is to do my part to ensure it." He gently squeezed her fingers.

Marianne returned an affirming grip on his hand. "And my duty is to stand by you. Wherever you may go, I ask only that you let me go with you."

His eyes twinkling, Jamie glanced over his shoulder. "Molly, would you give us one minute?"

Molly beamed. "Just one minute, Captain." She curtsied and left the cabin, closing the door behind her.

Jamie tugged Marianne up from her chair and held her in a gentle embrace. "Dear one, are you sure you can do this? Are you sure you can leave everything behind for me?"

Her heart ached that he needed to ask, but after their difficulties, she understood why. "Yes, I can do this."

"Because—" he went on as if she had not spoken "—when you choose to do that, you are choosing the Revolution, too."

She sighed her agreement. "Yes, I understand."

"And it means we are at war with your family, including Robert. Including Thomas."

Marianne looked at Jamie's cravat, a white silk neckpiece of Robert's choosing, and sorrow touched the edges of her soul. "I know."

"You've counted the cost?"

Her eyes blurred, but she nodded. "I have counted the cost."

He brushed away her tears and bent to kiss her, and she stood on tiptoes to give as much as she received. Kissing Jamie Templeton was a very fine diversion, indeed, one she could—and *would*—engage in as often as possible.

"Captain. Lady Marianne." Molly knocked on the door, then opened it. "Your minute has passed."

They moved back from each other just a few inches and laughed.

"Molly…" Jamie set a quick kiss on Marianne's nose. "You're an excellent chaperone."

"Yes, she is." Marianne leaned against his broad chest, feeling his strength. And wishing, just a bit wickedly, that Molly were not quite so diligent in her duties.

Chapter Thirty-Four

"Kezia Marie." Marianne held her three-month-old niece and cooed softly. "Your mama's blond hair and your papa's blue eyes. And all the sweetness of your grandmamma." She swayed back and forth, gazing at the tiny, perfect round face. "Rachel, how did you choose her name?"

Rachel watched from her chair, a maternal glow on her own face. While she resembled her pleasant-featured sister Susanna, this little lady was a true beauty, and motherhood seemed to enhance her loveliness. "My mother's name was Kezia, a Bible name. Many girls in Nantucket are named for the daughters of Job. And of course, Marie is for your own mother. Frederick said it would sound silly to call her Kezia Maria, so we change the final *a* to an *e*." Her fair forehead crinkled into a frown of concern. "I pray Lady Bennington won't mind."

Marianne laughed. "She will not mind in the least, but oh, how I wish Mama could be here to hold her first grandchild. She was quite thrilled to learn you were expecting."

"Yes." Rachel's smooth forehead crinkled again. "Frederick does not often speak of it, but I know it breaks his heart to live so far from his parents. Well, his mother, at least." Her face grew scarlet. "Oh, dear. Forgive me. I know your father has always doted on you…I mean, well, my goodness, I do not seem able to say this right at all."

Marianne kissed her precious niece. "Never mind. I know how Papa has always favored me over my brothers." Her voice caught. "All that has ended now."

"Will you write to him?" Rachel lifted her arms to receive her baby, then opened her dressing gown to feed the fussing infant.

Marianne's own arms suddenly felt empty, and she hugged herself. "Oh, yes. I must tell Papa that I stowed away, that Jamie did not kidnap me." She walked to the second-story window and gazed toward the indigo fields, where numerous black slaves tilled the green plants. One day soon, she must question Frederick about keeping slaves. "But Jamie says he will not dare to go back."

"No, I suppose it wouldn't be wise." Rachel smiled down at her daughter, humming softly. She had a sweet alto voice, and Marianne looked forward to singing duets with her. "Nor can Frederick return. While he has not told your father—or anyone here in St. Johns Towne—of his decision to support the American Revolution, he knows it would be too difficult to hide from Lord Bennington."

"Yes, our father always finds a way of disconcerting his sons. My brothers are all good men, but Papa has never made it easy on any of them. I am surprised but grateful that Frederick has found the courage to go this far on his own, something I pray for our three brothers." Pulling up the fan on her wrist, Marianne waved it before her face. The scrimshaw fan was a gift, carved by Rachel's father, dear Mr. Folger. Marianne had instantly fallen in love with the old whaler who had raised Jamie so well. "My, did it take you long to grow accustomed to this heat?"

"I can't really say I have." Rachel lifted Kezia to her shoulder and patted her back. "I grew up in Massachusetts, and we can have very warm summers there, but the heat is nothing like East Florida's. However, our many trees provide relief, and cool water comes from deep within the earth to fill our cisterns and revive us." She gave Marianne a sympathetic smile. "I'm sorry we can't make you more comfortable."

"I do not mean to complain." Marianne chided herself for revealing her discomfort. "I would endure far worse to be with Jamie."

"Yes, I understand." Rachel kissed Kezia's forehead. "Betty," she called toward the bedroom door.

The maid soon appeared. "Yes, Mrs. Moberly."

"Please change Kezia and see that she naps." Rachel gently lifted her baby, and the maid cradled her in her arms. "We'll be back in a few hours."

"Yes, ma'am." Betty took the infant away.

"Now." Rachel rose and walked to her wardrobe. "If you'll help me into my gown, we can join the men."

Marianne's pulse raced. She had patiently waited for Rachel to complete her maternal duties. Now their attention could be focused on the wedding. Her soon-to-be sister quickly dressed, and they held hands and descended the staircase.

The rest of the family awaited them in the drawing room. Mr. and Mrs. Folger, handsome *older* newlyweds, who were Rachel's father and Marianne's cousin Lydia, sat hand in hand on the settee. Mr. Saunders and his Molly, along with their friend Mr. Patch, stood nearby. By the hearth, Jamie and Frederick laughed over some private joke, but both broke off abruptly at the appearance of Marianne and Rachel. Jamie was first across the room, with Frederick right behind, and they each claimed their respective ladies.

"Lady Marianne." Jamie took both of her hands in his, and his dark eyes sparkled with tender affection. "Are you ready to become plain Mrs. Templeton?"

Before she could answer, Frederick nudged his shoulder. "Now, Templeton, remember what I said. She requires much pampering and many compliments, or you will be very sorry. Oh, and do not forget the diversions. She requires parties and balls—"

"Tut, tut." Marianne tapped her brother's arm with her new fan. "You are speaking of the child I used to be. In case you have not noticed…"

"She is a wise and beautiful woman," Jamie finished. "Now, if we can proceed to the church…" The eagerness in his voice sent a thrill through Marianne's heart, fanning her own excitement.

Amid much chatter and gaiety, the company exited the house, with the ladies taking their places in the carriage and the men riding horseback. Marianne laughed to hear Frederick teasing Jamie about having to ride, and she looked forward to seeing Jamie surprising her brother with his newfound ability to manage a horse more than adequately. Just as she herself planned to manage her home, wherever Jamie decided to settle. For within the hour, Lady Marianne Moberly would cease to exist, and the American housewife with the plain title of Mrs. James Templeton had every intention of taking very good care of her tall, brave, handsome husband.

Jamie thought his heart would burst for joy as he stood hand in hand with his bride before gray-haired Reverend

Johnson, vicar of St. Johns Towne. In her new rosy-pink gown, hastily sewn by Rachel's capable hands, Marianne was more than beautiful…she was exquisite. As the minister led them in their marriage vows, Jamie looked down into Marianne's fathomless blue eyes and drew in a long breath to steady himself. He was humbled to think that he, an orphan, a former whaler, a merchant of no great wealth, could secure the love of this extraordinary woman. For his sake, she had given up a life of ease and plenty, and he would do all in his power to make it up to her.

And yet along with this priceless treasure God had bestowed upon him came another responsibility. If they were to live their lives in freedom, he must do his part to help the Revolution succeed. Perhaps his connection to Lord Bennington's family would somehow provide the way. Perhaps that connection would be a hindrance. Only time would reveal how things would turn out. But this time, instead of making any assumptions about wealth or class or rank, Jamie would more diligently seek God's will in the matter. And this time he and Marianne would pray together and wait for His answer, just as they must do in regard to his sister. Jamie's appreciation for his bride's tenacity grew when she declared they must not rest until they learned of Dinah's whereabouts.

Mrs. Jamie Templeton. How good that sounded. As Marianne and her newly wedded husband left the quaint little church, she felt as if she were walking on a cloud on the way to their wedding supper.

The vicar's young wife, who Marianne learned had once snubbed Rachel, had almost fallen into a swoon when introduced to *Lady* Marianne. Mrs. Johnson insisted upon preparing the wedding supper on the lawn behind the vicarage. For the sake of peace, Marianne had accepted with the condition that the entire community *and* Jamie's crew would be invited.

While village children scampered about, musicians played and revelers ate from the lavish buffet, Jamie took Marianne's hand and sought the quiet of the sanctuary to be alone with her.

"My dear, beautiful bride." His eyes had not ceased to shine this entire day. "Now that we're wed, we must plan for our future." His intense gaze softened. "You know of course that I must find a way to serve the Cause."

She gazed at him through sudden tears. "Yes, I know."

"And you're not afraid?"

She laughed softly. "I did not say that." She drew his strong, callused hands up to her lips. "We do not know how the war will end. I pray His Majesty will see reason and let the colonies be free to establish their...*our* own country." She brushed a hand across his tanned, well-formed cheek. "This I do know. God has brought us together, and while we both shall live, I ask only this—that anywhere you go, wherever it is in this world, you'll let me go with you."

A frown flitted across his noble brow, but he nodded. "To be apart from you is not to live at all."

She returned a rueful smile. He had not promised what she asked. But somehow she understood. And even if he denied her request, she would never stop loving him. So much lay ahead of them, but owning Jamie Templeton's heart was worth any sacrifice she must make.

What was she thinking? This was her wedding day! Casting off her gloom, she gave him a quick peck on one cheek, then tugged him toward the door. "Come, my darling husband. Our guests are waiting."

He pulled her back into a firm embrace and kissed her until her knees grew weak. "Come, my darling wife. Our *life* is waiting."

* * * * *

Dear Reader,

Ever since I was an adolescent girl watching Richard Greene in the television series *Robin Hood,* I've had a great love for all things English. Not until I was much older did I learn that one of my direct ancestors was an Englishman who sailed to Lord Baltimore's colony of Maryland in 1665. Despite these treasured connections to England, I am so thankful for the courage and wisdom of those Patriots who rebelled against the Crown and established the United States of America—much as grown children sometimes must break ties with parents who hold on too long.

Still, we Americans have much for which to thank our mother country: English Common Law, on which our legal system is based; the writings of John Locke that influenced our founders to establish a democratic government; and best of all, a godly faith that established a Christian tradition in America and made true justice and democracy possible.

Thank you for choosing *The Captain's Lady,* the second book in my Revolutionary War series. In these stories, I hope to inspire my readers always to seek God's guidance, especially when making the decision about whom they will marry.

I love to hear from readers, so if you have a comment about *The Captain's Lady,* please contact me through my Web site, www.Louisemgouge.com.

Blessings,

Louise M. Gouge

QUESTIONS FOR DISCUSSION

1. As the story begins, we learn that Marianne and Jamie have a history: they fell in love when Jamie was in England the previous year. Marianne strongly believes that her love for Jamie is God-given, so she can hardly wait to see him alone to reaffirm her devotion. But even though Jamie still loves Marianne, he has decided their love can never be because he plans to spy on her father. How does that affect his behavior toward her? How do you think you would behave in similar circumstances if you were a man of honor like Jamie?

2. As a self-made man, Jamie possesses a strong yet modest sense of his own worth. But as a guest of the earl of Bennington, he must pretend to accept the rules of a society where people are valued more for birth rank than good character. Have you ever been in a situation where wealth was the criteria for the amount of respect you received? Where did you fit in the hierarchy? How did you feel about your place? How did you view others?

3. When she falls in love with Jamie, Marianne clearly sees beyond social rank to the real man. What makes her look beyond surface and material qualities to the man inside? How does her mother affect her views? Why do you think the countess ultimately gave her blessing on Marianne's love for Jamie?

4. Marianne has always had her parents' approval and love, yet her father is clearly disappointed in his four

sons. Why is the earl so demanding of his sons but not his daughter? How would you feel in Marianne's place?

5. At the time of our story, England was a "Christian" nation, yet the king and ruling class felt they had a right to force the American colonists to remain a part of their growing world empire. How do you suppose they reconciled a biblical Christian faith with their drive for world dominance?

6. Jamie is a sincere and spiritual Christian, yet he has come to London to spy on Lord Bennington. How can he reconcile his faith with the lies he must tell to succeed in helping the Revolution? Is there ever a time when it is acceptable for a Christian to lie? To spy? What examples can we find in Scripture to help us decide what to do?

7. In the midst of his spying, Jamie realizes he has a spiritual responsibility to help Robert Moberly comprehend the love and salvation of God. Even then, Jamie worries that Robert's new faith might be weakened if he discovers Jamie's covert activities. What unusual circumstances prompt you to share God's love with others? Do you feel responsible to live your faith so others won't stumble?

8. Although Marianne is twenty years old and knows her own mind, her society expects her to be obedient to her father. Jamie somehow manages to stick to his duty and leave her, even as his heart is breaking. Is Marianne right or wrong to take matters into her own hands? Why? Why not?

9. Marianne's biggest internal conflict is not about running away from home but about knowing what to do once she discovers Jamie is her country's enemy. Why does she finally choose to intervene to prevent the impressments of Jamie's crew? What does this say about her character? What would you do in similar circumstances?

10. Marianne has been "delicately" raised by loving parents, who gave her both material possessions and a spiritual heritage. How do you think she will manage in her new home in the East Florida wilderness without a lady's maid and other trappings of wealth? How will she manage spiritually?

11. Even though Marianne and Jamie marry, they never reconcile their differences about the war. Marianne assumes the colonists will fail, and Jamie knows he must continue to do his part for the "Glorious Cause." What kind of future do you foresee for them?

12. Which character changes the most in the story? Marianne? Jamie? In what ways did each one mature and become stronger? In what ways did they stay the same?

When his niece unexpectedly arrives at his Montana ranch, Jules Parrish has no idea what to do with her—or with Olivia Rose, the pretty teacher who brought her. Will they be able to build a life— and family—together?

Here's a sneak peek of "Montana Rose" by Cheryl St.John, one of the touching stories in the new collection, TO BE A MOTHER, available April 2010 from Love Inspired Historical.

Jules Parrish squinted from beneath his hat brim, certain the waves of heat were playing with his eyes. Two females—one a woman, the other a child—stood as he approached.

The woman walked toward him. Jules dismounted and approached her. "What are you doing here?"

The woman stopped several feet away. "Mr. Parrish?"

"Yeah, who are you?"

"I'm Olivia Rose. I was an instructor at the Hedward Girls Academy." She glanced back over her shoulder at the girl who watched them. "My young charge is Emily Sadler, the daughter of Meriel Sadler."

She had his attention now. He hadn't heard his sister's name in years. *Meriel.*

"The academy was forced to close. I thought Emily should

be with family. You're the only family she has, so I brought her to you."

He took off his hat and raked his fingers through dark, wavy hair. "Lady, I spend every waking hour working horses and cows. I sleep in a one-room cabin. I don't know anything about kids—and especially not girls."

"What do you suggest?"

"I don't know. All I know is, she can't stay here."

Will Olivia be able to change Jules's mind and find a home for Emily—and herself?

Find out in
TO BE A MOTHER,
the heartwarming anthology from
Cheryl St.John and Ruth Axtell Morren,
available April 2010
only from Love Inspired Historical.